In the Valley of the Shadows, Tom Began to Play

If pure crystals of sound could ever be imagined then such, most surely, were what the Star Born quarried from within himself. Nor did they fade and die. Each cluster of notes seemed to hang suspended, trembling in the velvet blackness, till the next one floated out to join it. Fragile as snowflakes, each one perfect of its kind yet each a fragment of a sublime harmony incomparably more intricate and marvellous than itself, they drifted, singing, far away out upon the trackless tideways of empty space beyond all human knowing.

And so he played on, lost in his own miraculous dream of perfection, until out of the ringing darkness a faint and nebulous light began to filter back. Dim shapes condensed out of the shadows—a stone archway opening upon a flight of steps which rose beyond until they were lost behind a shifting curtain of shade.

He knew that she was there, listening; knew that if he could only find the key to unlock those doors of shadow he could draw her back to him . . .

Books by Richard Cowper

A Dream of Kinship
The Road to Corlay
A Tapestry of Time

Published by POCKET BOOKS

Richard Cowper
A TAPESTRY OF TIME

PUBLISHED BY POCKET BOOKS NEW YORK

This novel is a work of fiction. Names, characters, places and
incidents are either the product of the author's imagination or are
used fictitiously. Any resemblance to actual events or locales or
persons, living or dead, is entirely coincidental.

POCKET BOOKS, a division of Simon & Schuster, Inc.
1230 Avenue of the Americas, New York, N.Y. 10020

ISBN: 0-671-62500-4

First Pocket Books printing October, 1986

10 9 8 7 6 5 4 3 2 1

POCKET and colophon are registered trademarks
of Simon & Schuster, Inc.

Printed in the U.S.A.

For Jenny

CONTENTS

AUTHOR'S NOTE

This is the final story in that sequence of tales and novels to which I have given the generic title *The White Bird of Kinship*. It sprang to life eight years ago in the novella *Piper at the Gates of Dawn*, flowed on into *The Road to Corlay*, broadened out into *A Dream of Kinship* and has at last reached the sea in which 'we may our ends by our beginnings know'. But sooner or later in any sequence of novels a point is arrived at when the author becames painfully aware that there is a limit to the amount of background information which he can hope to incorporate in each successive book without grievously restricting the flow of his narrative. Throughout *A Tapestry of Time* I have been grappling with this problem and the result can perhaps best be described as an honourable draw. Which is really only to say that *The White Bird of Kinship* begins with the very first words of *Piper at the Gates of Dawn* and ends with the very last words of *The Cartwright Papers*.

R.C.

PART OF FIRST
KINGDOM

BRITTANY   NORMANDY

CORLAY

ALENCON

EUROPE
CIRCA A.D. 3000

FRANCE
LYON

TORINO

NEW
MARSEILLES
DRAGUINAN   NICE

SPAIN

ITALY

PART I

The Singer and the Song

THE LOCAL WIND which the Romans had once called 'magistralis'—the masterful one—and which the tribes who then lived in those regions had abbreviated to 'mistral' was blowing relentlessly from the north-west under a noonday sky of the palest steel blue. Ranked along the terraced slopes of the seaward-facing hills the tormented olive trees hissed and groaned, while away to the south the bruise-black surface of the sea was scored again and again as though by invisible claws.

Between two of the olive trees a rope had been stretched taut. Fixed to it in such a way that it served both as a wind-break and an awning was a sheet of multi-coloured canvas, its lower edge anchored to the ground by the half dozen large stones which had been placed on the leeward side. Such was the force of the buffeting wind that every now and again these anchor weights rocked restlessly beneath the bellying sail.

In the shade afforded by the awning a young man was stretched out full length upon the ground. His arms were bent and his head was resting upon a pillow contrived from his laced fingers. He was watching with absorbed interest the shadow of a small lizard which had scuttled up the outside of the wind-shield and then had paused like a marauding dragon upon the painted battlements of an upside-down castle. From there it darted off sideways on to a

stylized cloud and, this proving unsatisfactory, finally settled for two inverted peaks of a distant mountain range.

The wind-shield had been improvised out of a painted
backcloth extracted from the property cart of the Theatre
Foscari (Proprietor Maestro Andrea Xavier Foscari) which
in this month of June A.D. 3039 was engaged in its annual
summer tour through the towns and villages of the Alpes
Maritimes of Southern France. The company consisted of
Andrea, his wife Angelina, their two sons Roberto and
Francesco and their daughter Maria. The young lizard-
watcher had been invited to join them when, some three
weeks earlier, Signor Foscari had chanced to hear him and
his sister performing in the market-place at Rocquevaire.
Their act was simple enough—the young man played upon
a twin-barrelled set of pipes while his sister sang—but such
was the enchantment of the piping and so sweet was the
girl's voice that even the notoriously tight-fisted Rocque-
varians had been moved to dip into their pockets when she
passed among them to take up the collection.

Foscari had contrived to strike up a conversation with
the two of them and over a glass of wine learned that they
hailed from the First Kingdom in the Land of Mists. Having passed the winter in Spain they were now making their
way across France into Italy. It subsequently emerged that
the young man's name was Tom and the girl's was Marie
though her brother never addressed her as anything other than 'Witch'—a word he translated for Foscari's benefit
as *ensorceleuse*.

Andrea complimented the piper upon his mastery of the
French tongue and thus discovered that the young man had
spent eight years at Corlay in the Isle of Brittany. 'Corlay!'
cried the Maestro. 'Then you must surely be acquainted
with Kinsman Marwys?'

Tom laughed. 'Indeed I am. I studied under him for
many years.'

'Oh, a remarkable man is Kinsman Marwys,' Andrea enthused. 'And a great traveller.'

'We call him "The Wanderer",' said Tom. 'In the last six months we must have spoken to at least a dozen people who know him. How did you come to meet him?'

'It was four or five years ago when we were touring the towns around Torino. For a week they hold an Easter fête in Piossasco. Marwys played two evenings for the dancing when the regular piper hurt his hand. A most remarkable musician is Kinsman Marwys and a fine wood-carver too. It is a privilege to know such a man.'

'You are Kin, Mr. Foscari?'

Andrea smiled broadly and tilted his hand from side to side. *'Fa lo stesso*—it's all the same,' he said. 'You know how it is.' His warm brown eyes dwelt thoughtfully upon the girl. 'You stay in Rocquevaire tonight, Alouette?'

'I don't know,' she said. 'Do we, Tom?'

'There is a room going begging in the Hotel Post,' said Andrea. 'The food there is excellent. Tell them Signor Foscari has sent you. And come and see the show this evening. You will meet Angelina and our children. So. It is arranged. And we will all dine together after the performance.' He swigged off his wine, rose to his feet, grasped them both warmly by the hand, smiled down upon them, and with a flamboyant salute strode away across the market-place bawling at the top of his lungs: 'Tonight at eight o'clock the World Renowned *Teatro Foscari* will be performing here in your *piazza!* No one can afford to miss the theatrical experience of a lifetime!'

Witch (her full nickname was 'Witchet') was not in fact Tom's sister though they allowed people to think so because of the modicum of protection it afforded her. They had shared childhood together until Tom had left their village home on the Island of Quantock in the First Kingdom and had gone off to be trained for the priesthood at Corlay. When at the age of nineteen he had decided to renounce

13

his calling he had invited Witchet to accompany him and the two of them had set off to see the world, supporting themselves along the way by the supreme skill of his piping and her singing.

At the port of New Barnstaple they had boarded a ship bound for Bilbao on the northern coast of Spain and from there had made their way southwards to Granada where they had found shelter for the winter in the household of a prosperous landowner who had recently been converted to Kinship. Señor Fernandez had seen in Tom a potential tutor in English and music for his three beautiful daughters. Unfortunately, before the second month was out, he had also perceived in the person of young Witchet a golden peach formed exactly to his taste and much too close and too tempting to be resisted. Señora Fernandez, perpetually alert to such dangers, had hardened her heart to the tearful pleadings of Dolores, Lucia and Margharita and had sent the luckless young couple off into the cold rains of February with a gold crown apiece by way of token compensation.

Spring had found them in Perello on the eastern shore of the Gulf of Ebro, both now speaking fluent if ungrammatical Spanish, their scant worldly possessions increased by the sum of one guitar which Witchet was struggling to master, and their repertoire by many new songs, several of them composed by Tom. It was at Perello that they had settled upon a vague plan of travelling across the south of France into Italy then heading up through Switzerland and eventually striking Alençon in the Isle of Normandy where Tom's closest friend, David Ronceval, was studying medicine at the Kinsmen's Hospital. With this object in mind they had crossed the border into France in April and had descended upon the great trading port of Toulouse. Having sought out a vessel bound for the Seven Kingdoms they entrusted to its captain a long and affectionate letter home describing their adventures and concluding with a promise to be back in Tallon in time for the New Year festivities.

In Castres they purchased an elderly donkey with an obstinate temperament and a woebegone expression and they towed him along behind them through the mountains (he lay down in the road if ever they attempted to ride him). In a village near Lodéve the small daughter of the local schoolmaster took a great fancy to their donkey and he to her. Realizing he had at last reached the land of his heart's desire he refused to budge another step and they finally parted with him to the schoolmaster in exchange for a melon, a cheese, and two litres of harsh red wine.

From Lodéve they hiked down to the Gulf of Languedoc and were ferried in a fishing boat over the graves of long-drowned Nîmes and Arles to the Island of St. Rémy at the mouth of the Durance. Three weeks later they found themselves at Rocquevaire, both by now as brown as desert sand and with Witchet's fair hair bleached almost to silver by long days of wind and sun. And thus it came about that shortly before eight o'clock in the evening they clambered up on to the rim of the waterless bowl of the marble memorial fountain in the town square and gazed out over the heads of the crowd who had gathered to watch the entertainment.

The Foscaris' stage was the porticoed dais in front of the *mairie* which had been converted into a makeshift theatre by the simple expedient of draping a pair of blue curtains from a pole and erecting two ornate folding screens on either side to serve as wings. A wide banner suspended from the balcony above did dual service as proscenium and advertisement, announcing in letters of gold to those few who were still ignorant that this was indeed the universally renowned TEATRO FOSCARI.

As the last chime of the church clock faded on the warm still air there came the brisk roll of a drum backstage, then a stirring trumpet call. This was followed by a few seconds

15

of pregnant pause before the curtains were suddenly thrust aside and Signor Foscari, resplendent in a superb costume of red velvet and lace and brandishing a silver-headed cane stepped forward, swept off his plumed hat and bowed in acknowledgment of the generous applause. Having replaced his hat he spread his arms as if he would embrace the whole square and proceeded to promise them all a feast of unparalleled delights the like of which they had been denied since his last visit to their own town twelve long months ago. 'Tonight there will be . . . (the cane swept up: the drum rolled) *Magic!* (the cane swept down: again the drum rolled) *Drama!* (up with the cane once more) *Acrobatics!* (down for the second time) *Jonglerie!* AND . . . (the cane was hovering on high: the drum having a fit of hysterics: Foscari's eyes seeking inspiration in heaven. The fingers of his left hand gathered at his pursed lips, leapt upwards, exploded like a bursting rose) Beauty beyond compare! Damsels to feast your eyes upon and feed your wildest dreams! (a storm of applause: cheers: whistles) All this, I, Andrea Foscari, have here in store for you in the one . . . the only . . . the inimitable . . . *Te-at-ro Fos-cari!!'*

Despite the impressive introduction the entertainment was neither better nor worse than a dozen similar spectacles which Tom and Witchet had observed in the previous six months. The one remarkable exception was a second sight act performed by the Maestro himself and a young girl whom they guessed must be his daughter. It formed the climax to the first half of the show and would no doubt have proved little more than a baffling diversion had not Tom happened to become involved in it himself.

Foscari introduced the girl to the audience as 'Maria the Miracle Child' who, when placed in a state of profound and mysterious trance by virtue of his own potent magical influence, would pass among them and by simply being permitted to handle personal articles possessed by members

16

of the audience would tell the owners things about that object and about themselves which it was impossible for her to know. There followed a minute of elaborate hocus-pocus accompanied by the inevitable drum roll from backstage and then Foscari announced that Maria had now entered the realm of omniscience and was ready to perform.

Taking her by the hand he led her down the steps into the crowd. After some moments of banter a woman in the audience was persuaded to part with a silver bangle which Foscari proceeded to describe, holding it up for all to see before passing it over to the girl.

By craning his neck Tom was able to catch a glimpse of the child with her eyes shut tight and the bracelet pressed to her forehead. She held it thus for some ten or fifteen seconds and then began to speak in a sing-song Italian which Foscari translated. She saw the sea, he announced. She saw a ship with three tall masts. A great storm. Waves breaking over rocks. (Someone in the crowd cried out and there was a patter of clapping.) A fisherman. A net. People dancing. A wedding. That was all.

'It is magic! Wonderful!' cried the woman whose property it was. 'My boy, Henri, fished it up out of the deep sea at la Ciotat two years ago. Who would have believed it?' The crowd applauded and cries of: 'Here! Try this! I have something!' were heard from all sides.

Foscari and the girl moved through the throng selecting objects at random—a comb, a clasp knife, a pair of spectacles—and for each the child described the scenes which the articles evoked in her mind. Without exception each owner confirmed the uncanny accuracy of her insights. Finally they approached the fountain where Tom and Witchet were perched. Foscari, recognizing them but not betraying the fact that they were already acquainted called out to Tom: 'Come, sir, surely you must have some article to test Maria's remarkable powers?'

For a flickering instant Tom was aware that this had all

happened before, that it was a part of some already woven pattern. He reached inside his jacket, drew out his pipes and held them out.

Foscari took them from him and held them aloft for all to see. *'Les flageolets jumeaux,'* he announced. *'Merci, monsieur,'* and he presented them to Maria.

It seemed to Tom as if it were all taking place in some slow and inevitable dream. He watched as Maria raised the pipes and pressed them to the pale olive skin of her forehead. She held them there for no more than a moment then gave a violent shiver and thrust them back at him. Gazing up at him wide-eyed she whispered the single word: *'Morte'*, then turned upon her heel and darted back through the crowd to vanish into the shelter of the wings.

Foscari, momentarily at a loss, shrugged apologetically, spread his hands, and then, ever the showman, cried: 'The strain has told upon her. It sometimes happens so. She is but the helpless slave of her mysterious gift! Bravo, Maria!' and led the willing applause while his wife and his sons emerged from behind the stage rattling wooden bowls of small coins and passed among the audience.

By half past nine the show was over and the crowd had begun to disperse. Fifteen minutes later the stage had been dismantled and loaded into a covered wagon. With Witchet at his side Tom approached Signor Foscari and congratulated him.

'Ah, but they are such skinflints, these ones,' grumbled Andrea. 'At Draguinan we will hire the arena for three nights and charge for entrance. It is the only way. No matter. We will soon rinse away the taste of their stinginess. Roberto! Francesco! Come and meet the two young *inglesi* I spoke of.'

There were handshakes all round and Tom said: 'And where is Maria?'

'Her mother has taken her off to bed,' Andrea informed

him. 'She has a—how do you say? *emicrania?* headsickness? Not serious. She will be better in the morning.'

'I thought she was brilliant,' said Tom. 'Really extraordinary.'

'Oh, she can do better than that,' said Andrea. 'But yes, she is something special, hey?'

'It's real then? Not just a clever trick?'

Andrea winked at him. 'The first one we must nudge a little—to get things moving. The rest she does all on her own.' He brushed his hand first to the left and then to the right across his luxuriant grizzled moustache. *'Morte,'* he murmured, eyeing Tom curiously. 'You know what that means?' He whipped his thumb across his throat in a slicing gesture. 'Was she right?'

'I don't know,' said Tom. 'Perhaps. I would have to ask her what she saw.'

'Oh, she will not remember. The curtain has come down.'

'You mean she really does go into a trance?'

'Sì. Like so!' Andrea snapped his fingers and laughed. 'We make a fine show of it, naturally. But come. After all that shouting I have a throat on me like a lime kiln. *Avanti!'*

A table and chairs had been set out in the vine-trellised inner courtyard of the Hotel Post and an oil-lamp was shedding a soft glow beneath the deepening purple of the night sky. While Francesco, the elder of Foscari's two sons, went off to fetch his mother, Andrea sat himself down at the head of the table and gestured to Tom and Witchet to take places on either side of him. Roberto chose the seat on Witchet's right and smiled at her shyly. The patron appeared with two bottles of wine which he uncorked and set down before Signor Foscari. 'How was the house?' he asked. 'Any good?'

'Good for Rocquevaire,' said Andrea. 'That is to say lousy. Draguinan will be better. Grasse better still.'

The patron laughed and poured out red wine into three

tumblers. 'They have spent all their money on the lottery. The new tickets went on sale this morning. How many are we tonight?'

'Six. Maria is indisposed.' Andrea raised his glass, drank off the wine and held the glass out to be refilled. 'What have you got for us, my friend?'

'A fine cassoulet. Do you wish your soup now, or will you wait for the others?'

'Go ahead. Bring it. They'll be here presently and I'm famished.'

The patron padded off in the direction of the kitchen. In the town a *carillon* began sprinkling out the chimes of the tenth hour like drops of holy water. A foolhardy moth blundered against the lamp glass and spiralled downwards into the shadows. Andrea sighed hugely and stretched his arms. 'Vitchet?' he said. 'What sort of a name is that?'

'A *sobriquet*,' said Tom. 'In English it means "little Witch".'

'Alouette suits her better, for she sings like a bird sings.'

'Did you get that, Witch? "Alouette's" French for skylark.'

Witchet nodded, and at that moment Madame Foscari and Francesco entered the courtyard followed closely by the patron who was carrying a large tureen and a stack of pewter soup plates. More handshaking followed and Tom enquired how Maria was.

'She is asleep, thank God,' said Angelina. 'She had like a sword—here.' She drew a line with her fingertip down the centre of her forehead. 'One feels so helpless.'

'Does she get it often?' asked Witchet.

'Not often so bad, but quite often, yes.'

'I used to get them too,' said Witchet. 'I have some medicine a Kinsman made for me. It is very good. It is made from—what's the word for herbs, Tom?'

'*Sì—sì, erba,*' said Angelina. 'You are Kinsfolk, are you?'

Witchet nodded.

'Ah, those pipes!' exclaimed Andrea, turning to Tom. 'But of course! I am stupid. You are *serpenti*, hey?' He thrust his tongue out between his teeth and touched it with his fingertip. 'Like Marwys?'

The patron's wife appeared with a basket of bread which she handed around. Madame Foscari ladled out soup and passed the plate down the table to her husband. 'Guests first,' he said, handing it on to Witchet. 'Roberto. The wine.'

When everyone had been served Andrea dunked his spoon and slurped up a noisy mouthful. 'Excellent,' he said. 'You won't find a better table than this in Rocquevaire. It's good, eh, Alouette?'

'Very good,' said Witchet.

'Esecrabile!' squeaked a little voice from the wine bottle. *'E assolutamente esecrabile!'*

Witchet gaped down at the bottle in open-mouthed astonishment.

'That is a very coarse wine,' observed Andrea solemnly, pointing with his spoon at the bottle. 'It has no taste.' And he slapped the wooden table top and roared with laughter in appreciation of his own joke.

Roberto nudged Witchet with his elbow and whispered to her in French: 'It is Papa who does it.'

Tom asked Andrea how long he had been a showman.

'All my life,' was the reply. 'We Foscaris have been in the business for generations. For twenty years my grandfather owned a half share of the *Maestoso* in Bolzano. Then he quarrelled with his partner over a woman. There was some legal swindle or other. Grandpapa kept the signora and Giuseppi kept the *Maestoso*. A year later Giuseppi had the signora too and all Grandpapa had was his memories. Since then the Foscaris have steered clear of bricks and mortar. Life is harder on the road but the worries don't last so long. Isn't that right, Angelina, my love?'

'Finish up your soup, old man. You talk too much.'

''Women!' groaned Andrea. 'They never appreciate priorities.' He laughed tolerantly and returned his attention to his plate.

Francesco asked Tom if it were true that he was a Kinsman.

'I was,' said Tom. 'For about a month.'

'What happened?'

Tom shrugged. 'I changed my mind.'

'You broke your vows?'

'You are thinking of the Old Faith,' said Tom. 'It's not like that in Kinship. No one binds us to it. We are not damned if we change our minds.'

'There are many Kinsfolk in Italy now,' said Angelina. 'The Kinsmen shame our priests.'

'How do you mean, *signora?*'

'They do good things and do not make a meal out of it. Two years ago when plague came to Vittorio the priests locked up the churches and fled. The Kinsmen stayed behind to nurse the sick and comfort the dying. When the black shepherds returned they found their flocks had moved on to greener pastures. One hears many such stories.'

'It's true,' said Andrea. 'Strip off a cassock and ten to one all you'll find under it is a moneybag. And as for the *Falconi* . . .' He rolled his eyes. 'Wolves would be more appropriate. *Briganti* to a man. The winter before last, in Mondovi, they offered us five crowns to put on a private show in the barracks. We struck hands on it. Next day when I went round for my money the Capitano first thanked me for my generous contribution to the noble cause and then kicked me down the stairs. It's true. I couldn't move my right arm for a week. That's the *Falconi* for you. I suppose I should count myself lucky not to have ended up in the cells.'

'Didn't you complain to the Civil Guard?' asked Tom.

'You're joking.'

'I am?'

'To the *guardia* all actors are *zingari*—thieves—vaga-bonds—rubbish.'

'I didn't know that.'

'You really surprise me. Take my advice. When you are in Italy always keep a silver quarter in your shoe to bribe the *sergente.* He won't expect more from a *zingaro.'*

'You mean we'll need permission to perform?'

'Of course. *La patente di recita.* But don't worry. I will give you one. I have dozens of them. Or, better still, come in with us. We shall be in Torino by the first of September. And we could do with some real music in the show. How about it, Alouette?'

Witchet smiled and looked across at Tom.

'Well, Toma, what do you say?' demanded Andrea.

'You really mean it?' asked Tom.

'Indeed I do. After supper you will show us what you can do. Not for *me,* you understand. I already know what you can do. But for the rest of us. Do you agree?'

'All right,' said Tom. 'If I'm not too drunk by then.'

'Eccellente!' laughed Andrea, reaching out for the bottle and refilling the glasses. 'Let us drink to that.'

When the dishes had been cleared away Witchet fetched her guitar and for half an hour she and Tom played and sang in the inn courtyard. By the time they brought their recital to a close the audience had grown to something over a score as passers-by, wandering out for an evening stroll, found themselves drawn in and held captive like moths entangled in an enchanted web. As the last note drifted away into silence there came what sounded like a long, regretful sigh, then, in a spontaneous flickering, a dozen small coins were tossed through the lamplit air to fall clink-ing upon the stones at the performers' feet. Whilst Tom and Witchet smilingly acknowledged the applause the pa-tron produced another bottle of wine and presented it to Witchet with his compliments.

'Did I lie to you?' whispered Andrea to his wife. 'They are magic and that bottle is the proof of it. Those two can charm silver out of stones. Have you ever heard better in your life?'

'Not even in my dreams,' she replied, 'and that is the truth, old man. They have the skill of angels.' And bending down she retrieved a coin which had rolled beneath her chair and slipped it into her pocket.

Early next morning the two wagons of the theatre rolled out of Rocquevaire and headed towards the coast. Driving the first was Signor Foscari and perched up on either side of him were Tom and Witchet. They were barely out of sight of the town before they had come to an amicable arrangement whereby the two young *inglesi* were to have a quarter share of all profits after deduction of basic expenses. The rest of the morning was spent discussing how the show might best be adapted to accommodate their talents.

That evening the troupe gave the first of the new style performances on the waterfront of the little fishing port of St.-Colombe. There was no time for the company to do more by way of advertisement than to blow a trumpet and beat a drum and shout their presence from the wagons as they rolled down towards the harbour basin. Half an hour later, peering out disconsolately from the wings at the meagre audience which had assembled, Andrea gave as his opinion that they would be fortunate if they collected enough to pay for their supper. Then, ten minutes before the show was due to start, and without saying a word to anyone, Tom disappeared.

Witchet, who was appealed to as soon as his absence was noticed, could only say that she was sure he would be back in time for the opening. With just two minutes to go she was proved right. There was an excited squeal from Maria: *'Guarda! Toma!'* and through the wide stone archway that led into the centre of the town they saw Tom marching towards them playing on his pipes and followed by a troop of chattering townsfolk. He led them up to the front of the stage, gestured to them to spread themselves out and then waved his hand cheerfully towards the wings.

With a muttered: *'Dio guardi!'* Andrea crossed himself, growled hoarsely: *'Francesco! la tromba!'* and then, as the first trumpet note sounded, stepped out through the curtains.

The arrangement had been that Tom and Witchet were to perform three songs to close the first half of the show, during the last of which the collection would be taken up. In the event so insistent was the clamour for an encore that they performed no fewer than five and, just before the final curtain, they were sent out again by Andrea for a second turn during which Francesco, Roberto and Maria filtered among the audience to glean the stubble.

At supper that night Andrea seemed unable to make up his mind whether it was *'un miracolo'* or just an extraordinary fluke. 'Once in Perugia we took two collections from one show,' he mused, 'but that was during the wine carnival and everyone was blind drunk. If they were drunk tonight it was on your music and that is something I have never witnessed before in my life. How do you explain it, Toma?'

Tom laughed. 'Obviously they enjoyed the show. What else?'

'No, no,' said Andrea. 'You brought them to us. How did you do it?'

'I simply told them they couldn't afford to miss the Theatre Foscari. They must have believed me.'

Maria who had been following this exchange while glancing from one to the other now said: 'It is in the pipes, Papa. And in his tongue.'

Tom smiled at her. 'What is?'

'The magic, Toma.'

'And what magic is that, Maria?'

'Something I feel,' she said. 'She knows it too,' and she nodded her head towards Witchet.

Tom took out his pipes, looked at them and then handed them to her across the table, but the girl shook her head and would not take them from him.

'Permesso?' said Andrea.

Tom passed them over.

Andrea turned the instrument over curiously between his fingers then, raising his head, said: 'Who made these? Do you know?'

'An old man who once lived in the Fifth Kingdom,' said Tom. 'They called him Morfedd the Wizard.'

Andrea's eyebrows twitched. 'Is that so? *Un stregone?* And how did you come by them?'

'They once belonged to my father.'

'So? He too was a piper?'

Tom nodded.

'A Kinsman?'

'Yes.'

'Those things which fathers bequeath to their sons are doubly precious,' said Andrea handing back the pipes. 'Guard them well.'

Tom restored the instrument to its place in the specially fashioned inner pocket of his leather jacket and turned to Maria. 'One day you must tell me about that magic you feel. Will you do that?'

She gazed at him sombrely with her huge dark eyes. *'Sì,'* she said. 'One day I will tell you.'

From St.-Colombe they proceeded on a leisurely tour along the coast, Andrea having formulated a convenient theory that fishermen were by nature more generous than farmers. 'They live by the grace of fortune,' he explained, 'so with them it is easy come, easy go. And besides, the grapes grown within sight of the sea make a better wine.'

The weather remained fine; they played to appreciative audiences; food and wine were plentiful and cheap; and eventually even Angelina had to admit that they had never known a better summer season. The two young *inglesi* found themselves becoming an integral part of the *'famiglia Foscari'*. By the end of the second week the sixteen years old Roberto (who as 'The Divine Roberta' played the female lead in various stirring melodramas) had fallen deeply in love with Witchet, somewhat to the detriment of his ancillary skills as a juggler. All too often when he should have been working out routines with Francesco he was to be found giving 'Alouette' an Italian lesson or simply lying with his chin pillowed on his bent arms gazing at her dreamily while she practised her guitar. Her way of coping with the situation was to treat him as if he were a younger brother. Since her heart belonged wholly to Tom the method worked well enough.

Early in June as the little caravan turned inland and began heading in the direction of Draguinan, one of the wagons fractured a shaft. They had no option other than to unload it beside the road, effect a temporary repair and haul it off to the nearest village blacksmith. Tom, Angelina and Maria stayed behind in the olive grove to keep an eye on things. They rigged up a makeshift shelter against the mistral and then Maria and her mother set off in search of milk and eggs, leaving Tom stretched out in the shade with only his own thoughts for company.

For several minutes he watched the shadow of a little lizard which was exploring the sun-freckled backcloth above his head and he toyed idly with the notion that it was a marauding dragon which was growing larger and larger as it moved ever further into the deeper recesses of the perspective. Then, without warning of any kind, he was no longer gazing at the shadow of the lizard but through the portal of a strange and phantom archway beyond which he glimpsed a flight of stone steps rising upwards to vanish in cloudy darkness. For a timeless moment he was aware of a sense of desperate yearning so profound it was an anguish to him. His very soul seemed to grow small and faint within his breast. In his ears there was a sound like the far-off beating of great feathered wings. Then the vision faded and was gone and he was back in the real world once more.

He closed his eyes and shivered violently. A cold dew of sweat broke out all over his body. He sat up, thrust his head down between his bent knees and waited until the trembling had subsided. After a while he rose to his feet and walked out into the open grove. Having selected a tree he sat down with his back against its trunk and gazed out across the waters of the distant bay which held the long-drowned city of Toulon.

His experience (he himself would have called it a *huesh*) had left him deeply troubled. For one thing it was the first he had had since leaving the Kingdoms all of nine months ago; for another it was quite unlike any he had ever had in his life. Always the *huesh* had brought him a glimpse of something which lay in wait in the future, as when he had his recurrent vision of Lady Alice drowning in the Lanvaux Channel and had been able to be there on hand with David Ronceval to drag her out. The whole of his childhood and adolescence had been coloured and shaped by this extraordinary gift which he had inherited from his mother. The *huesh* came without warning, sometimes as the merest fleeting glimpse, sometimes so starkly vivid that it seemed more real than the reality itself, but always it came true eventually and when it did he recognized it for what it was.

And suddenly he found himself recalling the moment when he had handed his pipes to Maria in Rocquevaire market-place and he realized how that moment too must have lain somewhere in some all but forgotten *huesh* far back in his past. But this latest vision belonged to a different order of experience altogether. If it had links with anything in his past then it shared lineage with that blinding moment of revelation when he had first played the Boy's pipes to Alice in New Exeter castle or when he had been drawn back to Tallon to seek for Witchet in the land of eternal shadow. Yet neither of those two moments had ever been presaged by the *huesh*. Above him the silver-grey leaves of the olive tree rattled and hissed in the hot, dry wind. He tilted back his head until the flickering needles of the sun pricked his eyeballs and, for no particular reason, found himself thinking about Witchet.

He was still sitting there with his knees drawn up to his chin when Angelina and Maria returned. As well as milk and eggs they had found cheese, salad and dried figs. Maria scooped a handful of the fruit out of the basket and brought them across to him. 'These are good, Toma,' she said. 'Try them.'

He took one of the figs from her and bit into it. The pips crunched grittily between his teeth. *'Delizioso'*, he said. *'E veramente delizioso.'*

She sat down beside him, arranged the fruit in her lap and then turned her head and contemplated him thoughtfully. 'What have you been doing?' she asked in French.

'Nothing.'

'No one can do *nothing*, Toma.'

'Well, thinking.'

'What about?'

'Many things.'

'Tell me one.'

Tom glanced at her out of the corner of his eye and smiled. 'You,' he said. 'I have been thinking about you.'

'Truly? What about me?'

'About something you said the other day.'

'Ah,' she said, nodding her head. 'I remember that. About the magic, yes?'

'Are you going to tell me?' he asked.

'But you *know*, Toma.'

'Do I?'

'Of course you do. You have'—she lifted a small,

golden-brown hand and clenched it into a fist—'*la potenza.*
Am I not right?'

'And the pipes?' he asked curiously. 'Is that where it
lies, this power?'

She selected another fig from her lap and handed it to
him. 'Yes, in the pipes too,' she agreed. 'But most in you,
Toma. Why do you ask me what you already know?'

'Because the first time you saw me you said something
to me which I did not understand.'

'Really? What was that?'

'Back in Rocquevaire, during your act with your father,
I gave you my pipes to hold and you ran away. Do you
remember that?'

She shook her head. 'What did I say to you?'

'*Morte.*'

'*Morte?*' she whispered. 'Oh, Toma, did I really say
that?'

Tom glanced into her sweetly troubled face. 'I'm not
sure,' he said. 'Perhaps it was something else. You only
whispered it. Do you never remember what you tell people
during your act?'

'Only the bits I arrange beforehand with Papa.'

Tom flipped away the stalk of his fig and licked the
stickiness from his fingers with his strange, forked tongue.
Then he dipped his hand inside his jacket and drew out the
pipes. He turned them over and over and the dappling sunlight striking against some concealed facet within one of
the twin barrels, glittered like a diamond.

'Play me something, Toma.'

Tom raised the pipes and rubbed the twin mouthpieces
softly against the tip of his freckled nose. 'I will if you'll
look at me,' he said.

Her dark brown eyes rose wonderingly till they met the
mysterious green and gold of his own. He lowered the
pipes to his lips, smiled at her, and began to play.

He had played scarcely a dozen notes before he lowered

the pipes and, still with his eyes holding hers, said quietly:
'Maria?'

'*Sì.*'

'Tell me what you saw when you held these pipes in
Rocquevaire.'

She murmured something in Italian which he could not
follow.

'Tell me in French,' he said.

'There was a dead boy and a dead man and a girl weeping.'

'You saw them killed?' he asked curiously.

Already tears were beginning to glint along the fine dark
lashes of her own eyes. 'Arrows,' she whispered. 'I saw
black arrows and red blood like berries.'

'And that is all you saw?'

A single tear brimmed over and coursed down her cheek.
'In the window with the boy there was snow too.'

'Those things are all in the past, Maria,' he said. 'They
happened long, long ago,' and setting the pipes back to his
lips he launched into a lilting improvised tune which sparkled like a sunny morning in May. When he had trilled it
to a birdsong finish he leant over and helped himself to the
last of the figs. 'Payment for the piper,' he said with a
grin. 'We share it between us.' And he held the fruit up
against her mouth.

She laughed and bit the fig neatly in two with her small
white teeth.

Tom stood up, pulled her up to her feet, and hand in
hand they wandered off to seek Angelina.

By the third week in June the Theatre Foscari had crossed
the river Argens and had climbed up into the hills as far as
Pareuse. While they were packing up the wagons after the
evening show Andrea slipped away. He returned half an
hour later looking thoughtful. 'What is it, old man?' said
Angelina. 'A bad quarter in your change?'

Andrea shrugged. 'Rumours. You know how it is.'

'How do I know how it is unless you tell me?' she retorted. 'What rumours?'

'There is some talk of trouble on the road to Draguinan.'

'What sort of trouble?'

'Briganti.'

'Mother of God! When?'

'Last week they say.'

'What are you going to do?'

Andrea stroked his moustache and contrived to look both uneasy and a trifle sly. 'Charleois is expecting us in Draguinan on Wednesday.'

'And what use will we be to Charleois with our throats cut?'

'Now you are being ridiculous, woman! Always you exaggerate! There is a guarded post coach leaving at first light tomorrow. It is arranged that we shall travel with them.'

'Arranged? How arranged?'

'We pay one crown before we leave. Another when we reach Draguinan.'

'Two crowns! But that is robbery! Who needs *briganti* with you to strike such bargains for us?'

'Then go and do better if you can,' said Andrea sulkily. 'I shall not be offended,' and he strode off and relieved his feelings by swearing at one of the horses.

During the night the weather changed. Warm, moist air came wafting up over the hills from the Gulf of Genoa, tangled with the expiring mistral and by the morning had piled itself up into monstrous thunderheads above the pine forests which lined most of the high road between Pareuse and Draguinan. Having done its worst the south wind then died away leaving behind an atmosphere like tepid soup through which the wan disc of the rising sun glimmered like the tarnished lid of a copper pan.

The motley little convoy rolled out of the east gate of Pareuse shortly after six. The armed escort consisted of three bowmen, two on horseback and the third seated alongside the coachman on the driving bench of the coach. Another man, a State Messenger of some kind, rode inside. One of the two outriders took up a station at the head of the caravan and the other trailed along behind Francesco's wagon at the rear.

For the first two hours they made steady progress. On the upward slopes they all got down into the road and helped to push. Dust rose in a fine white powder and stuck to their sweating faces. In the gloomy light it made them look like masked figures from a *Commedia dell'Arte*. 'Soon the worst will be over,' panted Andrea. 'From the brow of this hill it runs flat for five kilometres, then it starts to drop.'

The words had scarcely left his lips when the brooding sky immediately to their left was ripped apart by a jagged blade of lightning so bright it left them all momentarily dazzled. The two horses pulling the post coach reared up squealing in terror; there was an explosion like the crack of a giant whip followed by an eerie, ominous sighing. The coach driver yelled and heaved back on his reins; the traces rattled and the horses plunged forward into a lumbering gallop up the hill with the coach crashing and swaying behind them. In next to no time a gap of two hundred metres had opened up between it and the Foscari wagons. The bowman at the rear swore horribly, dug his spurs into his horse's flanks and galloped off in pursuit leaving the Foscaris to follow as best they might.

By the time they were under way again the coach and its escort had vanished over the brow of the hill. 'They will wait for us at the top,' cried the perspiring Andrea. 'Come on, move, you lazy brute! Hup! Hup! Hup!'

As they toiled up the final slope another lightning flash splintered the sky above the forest. Some warm raindrops the size of penny pieces flopped on to the roadway and scored long grey streaks in the layer of dust upon the canvas hoods of the wagons. But when they struggled over the brow of the hill there was no sign of the coach anywhere. 'The bastards!' groaned Andrea. 'The miserable piss pots! May their poxy foreskins rot! That ever I should have trusted such ordure!'

Tom laughed. 'It wasn't really their fault. The horses bolted. We're sure to find them down the road somewhere.'

'In Draguinan, that's where we'll find them, Toma,' said Andrea morosely. 'And when I do I promise you you'll truly hear something to remember.' He hauled himself up into his seat and urged the horse forward. The noise of the iron-shod wheels was all but drowned in the weltering rumble of the thunder.

They had advanced less than a mile when, without warning, the bottom dropped out of the sky. For five bewildering minutes it was as if they were trapped beneath a waterfall. It was not like rain at all. It pounded down upon the hoods of the wagons like demented fists hammering on a drum. The din inside was almost unbelievable, and such was the power of the onslaught that a mist of minute droplets was forced through the stoutly woven canvas. It hung suspended in the air like a faint grey smoke and gathered in tiny beads along their eyebrows and their eyelashes.

'Papa!' shouted Francesco. 'We are crazy to go on in this! The road is becoming a river!'

'There is a barn ahead,' bawled Andrea. 'Follow me.'

By the time they gained the shelter they could scarcely have been any wetter if they had swum to it. For the final two hundred metres they were obliged to wade knee-deep through swirling muddy water and coax the unwilling horses along behind them. Tom and Roberto dragged open the huge wooden doors. As they drove the wagons into the barn they all felt as relieved as if they had struggled ashore from a shipwreck.

Angelina produced a bottle of cognac and they passed it

from hand to hand. At her insistence they stripped off their drenched outer garments and hung them up to drip. Then they gathered at the doorway and peered out. The rain streaming off the shingle overspill hung like a curtain of glass beads before their faces, but already the initial force of the downpour had slackened and shapes of individual trees were becoming dimly visible on the hillside opposite. Andrea was beginning to reminisce about some other storm he had encountered on his travels when Roberto touched his arm and whispered: 'Papa, we have company.'

They all turned their heads and saw two caped and hooded figures emerging from the trees about a hundred metres up the slope to their right. Between them they were carrying a pole and suspended from it by the legs was what appeared to be a dead sheep. The newcomers sloshed on through the teeming rain until they were within some fifty paces of the barn, then they paused, peering ahead, and seemed to be having a muttered conference. After a minute they advanced again and approached the open doorway.

'Fine weather for frogs!' called Andrea cheerfully.

The leader of the two gave a small upward jerk of his head by way of greeting and Tom saw his eyes gleam white as peeled eggs in the shadow of his leather scuttle as he glanced this way and that counting the company.

'A new Drowning,' observed his companion lowering his end of the pole to the ground. 'Caught out on the road, were you?'

'Road? River you mean,' said Andrea. 'We could have used a boat.'

As the leader stooped to let down his end of the burden Tom glimpsed the tell-tale shape of a crossbow outlined beneath his knee-length leather cape. He wondered if they were poachers.

'Out of Draguinan or Pareuse?' enquired the talkative one.

'Pareuse,' said Andrea. 'We've got a show booked in the Ring at Draguinan for tomorrow night.'

'A show, eh? What are you then? Players?'

Andrea improvised an ornate bow. *'Il Teatro Foscari. At your service, Monseigneur.'*

The man grinned and pushed back his hood to expose a skull as round as a cheese, covered in a short, wiry stubble of reddish hair. An old scar had twisted up his left eyebrow into a sort of permanent query. His cheeks and chin were unshaven; his teeth yellow and mis-shapen; his eyes a pale, washed-out blue. He employed them to survey the company and allowed them to linger upon Maria. 'Actors, eh?' he said. 'I don't know as I've met any actors before.'

'And what is your trade, *m'sieur?*' asked Tom.

'Eh? Oh, me? I'm a woodsman.'

'Not a shepherd?'

'Shepherd?' The man blinked. 'Oh, *that.* Just lending M'sieur Montfort a hand. He's the shepherd. Right, Nikko?'

The taller man muttered something inaudible then stepped back out into the rain, screwed up his eyes and squinted down the road in the direction of Draguinan.

He did this twice more within the space of the next ten minutes. On the third occasion he put two fingers to his lips and blew a piercing double whistle. Within seconds they all heard, like a faint and distant echo, an answering call.

Tom glanced round and caught Andrea's eye with an unspoken question.

Scar-brow intercepted it and laughed. 'Our shepherd's whistling up his dogs,' he said. For some reason this observation seemed to amuse him enormously.

He was still chuckling when his companion came back into the barn and looked round at the assembled company. His eye settled on Angelina. 'You can cook, lady?'

'Certainly I can cook, *m'sieur.'*

He turned and prodded the dead sheep with his toe. 'There is meat,' he said.

Angelina looked down at the carcass and then up at him. 'But who is to butcher it?'

The man called Montfort indicated his companion. 'He will.'

'And the fire?'

Montfort tilted his chin first at Roberto and then at Tom. 'Make her a fire,' he said. 'There is wood back there.' He pointed a finger towards the far end of the barn and then stepped outside again.

Tom and Roberto glanced round at the others then made their way up to the far end of the barn where they discovered a corner hearth of rough, blackened stone. Rain had entered down the chimney and turned the dead ash beneath the rusty iron grid into a soggy grey pudding. But there was still plenty of dry wood. Roberto collected up an armful of straw and brought it across to Tom. 'Are they *briganti*, Toma?' he whispered.

'What do you think?' murmured Tom.

'I think so. He scares me—that Montfort.'

'Then the sooner we get this done the better,' said Tom. 'Go and fetch the fire-box.'

By the time the fire was well alight Scar-brow had skinned and gutted the sheep and divided it in two by hacking it open with a hatchet all down the length of its spine. Angelina scored the carcass, rubbed in garlic and salt, and then between them they arranged the meat across the hot grid. Meanwhile Witchet and Maria had gathered up the wet garments and hung them close to the hearth.

Scar-brow wiped the blood from his hatchet with a handful of straw and restored it to the thong on his belt. As Maria moved past him he twitched her skirt. 'And where have you flown from, sparrow?'

'From Italy, *m'sieur.*'

'A macaroni, hey? How old are we?'

'Fourteen, *m'sieur.*'

''Twixt sour and sweet.' He exposed his yellow teeth in a wet-lipped grin and winked at her.

Maria nibbled her bottom lip and went and stood close beside her father near the door of the barn.

Thunder was still growling over the high hills to the north and rain was still falling steadily but the southern sky was growing lighter by the minute and the level of water in the pool between the barn and the road was dropping visibly. By and by they heard the clip-clop of horse hoofs. Montfort splashed his way across to the road, cupped his hands to his mouth and shouted: '*Ça va?*'

There was an answering shout, but too far off for those in the barn to make out what it was.

Francesco who had been rubbing down their horses came over to Andrea and asked him in a whisper what he made of it.

Andrea pulled a doubtful face and rocked his hand back and forth.

'Should we not leave now, Papa?'

'It is best we play the innocents,' murmured Andrea. 'Besides, I am not so sure they would let us go.'

The clop of hoofs drew steadily nearer. A puff of blue woodsmoke curled down from the chimney, hovered above the rain-pocked surface of the pool and slowly dispersed.

'Where's Gorjo?' yelled Montfort.

'The *merdes* got him,' came an answering shout.

Between the trees that partially screened the barn from the road Foscari and his son and daughter now saw a group of five men advancing down the highway. Three were leading heavily laden horses and all had crossbows slung over their shoulders. Two of them were carrying two weapons apiece. As they came up to him Montfort greeted each one with a light blow of his right fist on the chest or arm and directed him in at the gateway.

They splashed up to the barn doorway where they gaped with undisguised astonishment at the onlookers.

'They're actors,' explained Montfort, with the merest flicker of a grin. 'The Foscatis or some such.'

'Fosca*ri*,' corrected Andrea. 'Andrea Foscari. At your service, gentlemen.'

'And what do you actors do for drink?' demanded one of the newcomers.

'We have some wine,' said Andrea. 'And a little cognac.'

'That'll do nicely,' said the man, unslinging his two bows and a bolt harness and leaning them up against the open door. 'Obliged, I'm sure.'

Andrea climbed up into one of the wagons and handed down three bottles to Francesco who in turn passed them across to the men.

Scar-brow left his station beside the fire, came forward and drew one of the newcomers aside. 'What happened to Gorjo?'

'He bought the joker.'

Scar-brow sucked in his breath. 'Go on.'

'They had a *merde* boxed up inside. Gorjo stuck his head through the window and—*zuc!*' The man speared a thumb towards his own left eyeball. 'He couldn't have felt a thing.'

Scar-brow winced and sipped a painful '*aieee!*' between his clenched teeth. 'And the others?'

'Not a scratch among us. One of the *merdes* scarpered. Legged it up into the woods and we lost him.'

'But it was a good hit?'

'The best yet. Over five c's in shiners we reckon.'

'Five *hundred!* And Gorjo's missed it.'

'His luck ran out. So what's with this bunch of pretties?'

'Christ knows. They were here when we got here.'

'How many of them are there?'

''Bout half a dozen. Ah, they're nothing. Just the old fart and his missus and a bunch of kids.'

'They can talk, can't they?'

'Who to, for Christ's sake? Shit, man, we'll be half way home before they'll find an ear to listen.' He plucked his companion by the sleeve and drew him close. 'Some juicy tail though. Go see for yourself.'

A mouth-watering aroma of roast mutton wafted through the barn and the men began to drift down towards the fire. Angelina carved off a thick slice and held it up on the point of the knife. 'Shall you be first to try it, *m'sieur?*' she said to Montfort.

Montfort nodded one of the others forward. With a mumbled *'Merci, m'dame,'* the man took the meat from the knife point and bit into it. 'It's good that,' he said with unfeigned relish. 'Really good.'

One by one the others shuffled forward and took theirs. Montfort was the last. Unlike the rest he produced his own knife and speared his portion upon it. Then he walked away and took up a position by the door which afforded him a clear view of the road.

Angelina handed round generous second helpings to the men and then served her own people. The bottles were passed round from hand to hand. Everybody sat about relishing the wine and the good meat and the warmth of the fire. But for all that the atmosphere quivered with a sort of electric tension and Tom was not the only one who was uneasily aware that nothing more substantial than the common interest of the fire and the shared meal prevented it from disintegrating into fragments.

When the break came it was with the same sort of explosive suddenness as the other storm had broken. One of the men had called out for more wine and Maria was taking a bottle across to him when Scar-brow thrust his hand up underneath her skirt, caught hold of her leg and dragged her down on to his lap. Astonishingly she kept hold of the

40

bottle and even contrived to proffer it to the man who had called for it as though somehow this might stave off the catastrophe. For a long moment everything seemed to freeze as starkly as in the interval between the lightning flash and its inevitable roar, then Scar-brow laughed, wrapped his other arm around her and held her pinioned fast. The man who had called for the wine reached out, seized the bottle from Maria's hand and said to Scar-brow with a grin: 'After you with her, mate.'

Then many things happened all at once. Andrea started forward, was tripped by an outthrust leg and crashed full length to the floor: Francesco, springing to his father's aid was felled by a forearm like an iron bar across the back of his neck: Tom's arms were seized from behind, a knife point jabbed into the soft flesh beneath his chin and a voice growled in his ear. 'Easy, pretty boy, or you join the *merdes.*' There was a sudden, high, thin, birdscream of pain and terror from Maria which was abruptly choked off, and then only noises like animals jostling for food, and gasps and curses and muffled groans.

Tom felt the man who was gripping him growing hard and stiff with lust and out of the tail of his eye he caught a nightmare glimpse of Witchet stripped bare from the waist down, sprawled out face downwards, on all fours. One man had her head gripped tight between his knees, her snared wrists had been forced up between her shoulder-blades, and another man was crouched down behind her thrusting himself into her like a butting ram. Tom cried out and wrenched his head aside. Instantly the knife point jerked upwards, twisted agonizingly, and goaded him back to watch as with one final brutish lunge Witchet's first as-sailant spent himself, drew clear gasping, then shuffled round to change places with the other and the grisly ritual recommenced. The second was completing his turn when the knife was suddenly withdrawn from Tom's throat and he was thrust violently forwards. As he staggered towards

Witchet he was struck a savage blow on the side of the head and collapsed into merciful oblivion.

Montfort alone stood aloof from it all, watching impassively from the barn doorway with a cocked crossbow cradled in his left arm. When he judged that his dogs had had their fill he called out to them to take the Foscaris' horses and to distribute their spoil equally between the five animals. When this had been done he walked over to the still-glowing hearth and gazed pensively down at Angelina. With the toe of his boot he nudged her skirt down over her splayed and ravaged nakedness. His parting words were a sardonic permission for her to keep what was left of the roast meat.

They listened to the sound of the men's voices growing fainter and fainter in the distance till at last they could hear them no more. Only then did they dare to stir. Slowly Angelina rose to her feet, drew Maria up beside her and guided her outside like a sleepwalker. She dipped a corner of her petticoat in rain-water and began gently to sponge away the mess of blood and slime from her daughter's thighs. 'You are still alive, my little one,' she whispered, and then, overcome with grief and pity she drew the girl's head down against her breast and wept most bitterly.

Within the barn Witchet crawled across to where Tom lay and, finding he was still breathing, lay down beside him and cradled his unconscious head in her arms.

Andrea heaved himself up into one of the wagons and flung out a blanket. Then he climbed down, shook out the cover and spread it over them both. 'Come with me, son,' he said to Roberto. 'We two must leg it back to Pareuse and find some more horses. You stay here, Francesco. The *briganti* will not be back. Take care of your sister.'

He went out of the barn, found Angelina and Maria, and looked down at them with lustreless eyes. Then he kissed and embraced them both and told them what he was about.

'Let us thank God we are all still alive,' he said. 'That is the first thing.'

After they had gone Angelina took Maria back into the barn and dressed her in clean clothes. Then she raked up the embers of the fire and threw on some dry sticks. When they were burning brightly she flung into the heart of the flames the blood-smeared skirt her daughter had been wearing. That done she set about ministering to Witchet and Tom.

Tom returned to consciousness as though he were inching his way up a black and icy rock face, slipping, sliding backwards, and clinging on by his fingernails while great boulders hurtled past his head and thundered away to be lost in some unimaginable abyss far, far below. High above him someone was calling his name. It came drifting down to him and then away again like a voice carried on the back of the wind—'Toma, toma, toma . . .' He clung on desperately and, summoning up the last dregs of his strength, dragged himself up and over the lip.

'Toma?'

He opened his eyes.

'Ah, thank God. Thank God.'

A cold wet cloth was plastered across his forehead. He lifted a hand and pushed it aside. Above him Angelina's anxious face seemed to ripple like a reflection in a pool. 'Witch?' he groaned. 'Where's Witch?'

'She is safe, Toma.'

He caught hold of Angelina by the arm and pulled himself up into a sitting position. Around him the barn and the wagons rocked and swirled. Bright sunlight was streaming in through the open doors. 'They've gone?'

'An hour ago.'

'An hour?' he echoed incredulously. 'What happened?'

'No one was killed. They stole our horses.'

Tom raised his left hand and explored the flesh beneath his chin with his fingertips.

Angelina pushed his hand aside. 'Leave it,' she said. 'I have stitched up the wound.'

'But what happened?' he repeated. 'Tell me what happened.'

'They did what such ones do. But it is done, Toma. It cannot be undone.'

He stared at her. 'All of you?'

'*Sì*. What did you expect?'

She put her arm around his shoulders and helped him to rise unsteadily to his feet. As he did so Witchet appeared from outside and stood framed in the open doorway, silhouetted dark against the sunspill.

'Tom?'

He took a pace towards her, reeled, and would surely have fallen had not Angelina clutched him.

Witchet ran forward and flung her arms about him. 'Oh, Tom,' she whispered, burying her head in his chest. 'Oh, Tom.'

He held her to him and stroked her hair while renewed waves of giddiness broke over him and slowly subsided. 'I know,' he murmured. 'I know. I saw.'

'I thought they'd killed you,' she whispered. 'When I saw you lying there so still, I thought you were dead.' She held herself pressed tight against him and drew in a long sobbing breath of pure relief.

They went outside and sat down side by side on a pile of logs. Where the water had been there was now only an expanse of greyish mud. Above it wisps of steamy vapour were rising in the hot bright sun. 'Where are the others?' he said.

'Andrea and Roberto have gone to find more horses. Maria is lying in one of the wagons. I don't know where Francesco is.'

'How is Maria?'

Witchet glanced at him then looked away. 'They hurt her a lot,' she murmured. 'Tore her inside, Angelina says.

Now she's like she is when she's doing her act with Andrea, except that she doesn't say anything.'

Tom shuddered. 'And you . . . ? Are you . . . ?'

'I ache,' she said. 'That's all.'

'I should have killed them,' he muttered. 'I could have done it, Witch. I know I could. But it all happened so suddenly. And my pipes were in my jacket.'

'What are you talking about? How could you have killed them?'

'I did it once to save Alice,' he said. 'I could have done it to them too.'

'I don't know what you mean, Tom. What could you have done?'

He placed the thumb of his right hand in the open palm of his left and screwed it down, slowly and deliberately, as though he were squashing an invisible bug. 'That's what I should have done,' he said. 'And that's just what I will do if I ever catch up with them.'

Witchet looked into his face and saw it was set like a pale grey stone. She took his hands in hers and held them tight. 'But we're *alive,* Tom,' she whispered. 'Isn't that enough?'

'No,' he said. 'Not for me.'

'Well, it is for me,' she said. 'Just for now it is,' and she reached up and pulled his face down to hers and kissed him on the mouth.

In the second hour of the afternoon Andrea and Roberto returned on horseback. Accompanying them was a Sergeant of the Civil Guard and three mounted troopers. They saw the two Foscaris in at the gateway then cantered off down the road in the direction of Draguinan.

Andrea swung himself out of the saddle and came over to where Tom and Witchet were sitting. 'You are feeling better, hey, Toma?'

Tom nodded.

'You *inglesi* must all have skulls as thick as millstones, eh, Alouette?'

Witchet smiled wanly.

'So. How are the others?'

'Maria is still shocked.'

Andrea turned his head aside and spat. *'Bruti!'* he growled. *'Carnivori!* Such are not men but wild beasts. They have no human feelings, no shame.' He led the horse into the barn and Roberto followed him. As he passed in front of Witchet the boy glanced up at her and flushed darkly.

The wagons were just pulling out into the roadway when the troopers came cantering back and signalled them to stop. Andrea reined up his horse and waited for them to approach. 'Well?' he called. 'How is it?'

'You'll see for yourselves soon enough,' said the Sergeant. 'How many of them did you say there were?'

'Seven,' said Andrea. 'The leader was the one they called Montfort. And one of them had a scar here.' He touched his eyebrow.

'That's the same lot, right enough,' said the Sergeant. 'That Montfort's a renegade Falcon from Grenoble. There were two of them running the pack. The other's lying back there with a bolt through his skull. I'd say you people can count yourselves lucky to be alive.'

'Do you know where they've gone?' asked Tom.

'Up into the mountains around Castellane most like. They'll not be back this way in a hurry. They've made it too hot for themselves.'

'Then you're not going after them?'

'It's not up to me,' said the Sergeant. 'I'll report this to Grasse and they'll handle it from there. We're off now to fetch a cart for the dead.' He raised his right hand, nodded to them, and led his men clattering away back down the road towards Pareuse.

As Andrea shook the horse into motion, Tom turned his

46

head and watched the troopers go. 'They won't do anything, will they?' he said.

'Perhaps they will,' said Andrea. 'It will depend on who feels the pinch most.'

'The money they stole, you mean?'

'That's right. The money.'

'And what about what they did to us?'

'Us? Who are we, Toma? Are we princes? Great merchants? We are nothing, I tell you. Indeed we are not so very different from those accursed *briganti* when you come to think about it. Maybe it is to that we owe our lives.'

'But you would have killed them if you could.'

'Certainly I would have killed them. Like I would kill rats. Without compunction.'

Tom fingered the tender contours of the bruise on the side of his head. 'Have you ever killed anyone, Andrea?'

'No. Not yet. But there is always a first time. And that charmer with the scar would make a fine place to start.'

'You could do it now? In cold blood?'

Andrea glanced at him out of the corner of his eye. 'A father's blood does not cool so quickly, Toma. That I can assure you.'

The road curved round sharply to the right and then, almost immediately, to the left, skirting an outcrop of limestone. As they cautiously negotiated the second bend a flock of crows clattered up above the trees and swirled around cawing indignantly. A minute later they came within sight of the post coach.

A pine tree had been felled and allowed to drop three parts of the way across the road. In swerving to avoid it the coach had crashed into the ditch. It lay, tilted over on its side with two wheels off the ground. One of the horses which had pulled it was lying across the splintered pole shaft. The animal's foreleg had broken and a spike of red bone was poking through the skin. Someone, acting perhaps out of pity, had put a bolt through the creature's head.

Where the blood had run down into its eye a swarm of golden-blue flies was feeding busily.

Andrea reined up the wagon and with Tom at his side walked over to investigate. Sprawled in the ditch, in the area of shadow directly beneath the coach, they discovered two bodies. The head of one had been split right down to the teeth by a tremendous blow from a bill-hook or an axe. Brains were spattered in a sort of pinky-grey gruel all across the woodwork of the coach. The other corpse still had the last inch of a feathered bolt protruding from the blood blackened hole where his left eye should have been. *'Gesù Cristo!'* muttered Andrea, crossing himself. 'To think that might have been us, Toma.'

They made their way round to the other side and there they found two more bodies. One, whom they recognized as the driver of the coach, appeared to have broken his neck when he was flung from the box; the other was lying face downwards among the trees with three fledged shafts sticking out of his back. Of the third guard there was no sign.

They climbed back on to the road where they were joined by Francesco and Roberto and the four of them began dragging the tree aside. As they were struggling with it a hoarse voice called out from among the trees beyond the coach: 'Foscari! Hey, Foscari!'

They all glanced at one another with a sudden unspoken question in their eyes. Then Andrea murmured: 'Impossible. The *briganti* are gone for sure,' and tilting back his head he shouted: 'Yes, this is Foscari! Who calls him?'

There was a faint crackling of dead twigs being crushed underfoot then a figure emerged from among the trees some fifty metres from where they were standing. He came limping down the road towards them.

'That's the one who rode behind us, Papa,' whispered Francesco. 'How did he manage to get away?'

As the man approached they saw that his face and hands

were deeply scratched with briers and his leather tunic ripped in a dozen places. 'Well met, soldier,' said Andrea. 'You must bear a charmed life.'

'You too,' replied the other. 'What happened to you?'

'When you didn't wait for us, you mean?'

The man shrugged. 'We guessed you'd catch up. And now you have. What happened?'

'We took shelter from the storm in a barn. Then your *briganti* came and found us. That's what happened, soldier.'

The man looked at them then turned his head and glanced across questioningly at the wagons. He moistened his lips with his tongue. 'And the women?' he asked.

Andrea stared at him then, very slowly and deliberately he dredged up a mouthful of mucus and spat it out at the man's feet. 'You rubbish!' he growled. 'You call yourself a guard, you poxy rubbish! Why aren't you lying there with the rest of them, you brave hero you? I hired you to protect us, filth. Or have you forgotten? Out of my sight, ordure! Get away home and screw your miserable whore of a wife and lie to her about how brave you were today! But don't hang around us whining for sympathy. We've none to spare for mighty heroes like you!'

The man opened his mouth but no words came out. And suddenly, with a kind of sick shame, Tom realized that the fellow was weeping. Bright, bitter teardrops were glistening on his lacerated cheeks. He felt a sharp and terrible stab of impotent pity for the man, but he could do nothing. It was as though some sentient part of him had become frozen. He looked down at the branch he was still holding and he began jerking at it fretfully. A moment later Roberto and Francesco also began to heave at the tree. Then Andrea joined in. They attacked it like a hated enemy, wrestling and wrenching at it, heaving and straining, till at last they succeeded in lugging it clear. When Tom looked up again

49

the man had limped away past the wagons and vanished round the corner out of their sight.

That night after the others had retired to bed in their lodgings in Draguinan Tom went out alone and climbed up on to the ramparts above the town. The air was calm and milk-sweet, faintly perfumed with the scent of jasmine and wild lavender. All trace of the storm had gone. So clear was the sky that the quivering stars seemed to press down upon him with an almost palpable weight.

He stretched himself out full length upon the flag-stones which were still warm from the heat of the sun, and gazing upwards he tried to let his memories drain away into that unfathomable immensity. But ever and again, as though by a phantom knife point beneath his chin, he was forced back to some remembered instant of pain and horror, and a tide of rage rose up in him like a cloud of dark blood and dimmed the stars. Then he groaned aloud and closed his eyes and gripping hand within hand, strained with all his might as if he were still struggling to shift the enormous burden of the fallen tree all on his own.

As he lay there anguished and panting he heard footsteps approaching and the faint tapping of a stick upon the stones. The sounds drew closer and closer and finally stopped. He opened his eyes, looked up, and saw, dimly outlined against the starry heaven, an old man gazing down at him.

For as long as it takes to draw five deep breaths they looked at each other without speaking and then Tom heard the old man say: *The road is proving hard, eh, Thomas? It will be harder yet before it is done.*

Tom stared upwards and felt each separate hair upon his arms and legs rise and stir. 'Who are you?' he whispered. 'How do you know my name?'

Did I not witness your begetting. Star Born? Was I not present at your birth? Who was it walked by your side through the Valley of Shadows? You remember me.

'Yes, I remember you, old man. Why have you come?'
Because you summoned me.
'Then help me now. Give my heart ease.'
Look deep into my eyes. Thomas. Tell me what you see.
'I see only stars.'
Look again.
'That man weeping by the fallen tree.'
Again.
'No. No more.'
Look, Thomas. Look and tell me what you see.
'I cannot.'
You can. You must.
A barely audible whisper. 'I see Witch.'
Know yourself, Thomas. Be free.
And thus it was that out of the black horror, out of the
terrible flower of her appalling degradation sprang the mo-
ment of his own release. His tears and his own seed spurted
hot in the darkness, and he knew himself. 'Why?' he whis-
pered. 'Why? Why?'
*Without dark, no light: without black, no white: without
wrong, no right.*
'Morfedd?'
I am still here, Star Born.
'What must I do?'
Already the stars are pricking through the shadowy out-
line. The old man is melting away like mist, like a dream.
'Tell me, Morfedd. Tell me.'
A whisper, frail as a moonbeam, scarcely to be heard:
*You must seek for your own truth, Star Born. For you there
can be no other way.*
Silence. Peace. The stars leant down over him and
rocked him in their arms like the sea.

In the days which followed it became increasingly apparent that their experience had scarred them far more profoundly than most of them were prepared to admit even to

themselves. The knowledge of what had happened lay across them like a long sunset shadow and by its morbid light they saw each other differently. No longer was Roberto to be found sitting at Witchet's feet when she practised her guitar and there were no more Italian lessons. Instead he took to spying upon her, hiding himself in the bushes and peeking out at her when she went to bathe. Finally she became so exasperated that half in jest, half in earnest she complained about it to Andrea in the boy's presence. Without a word Andrea swung round upon his son and gave him such an almightly clout across the side of his head that he was knocked flying. Whereupon Witchet, overcome by remorse, burst into tears and begged forgiveness of them both.

But if Witchet's inner resources enabled her to come to some sort of terms with what had been done to her, Maria had no such defence. As the days passed she seemed to shrink ever more deeply into herself, withdrawing further and further from all human contact, wrapping herself up in her arms like some threatened animal if any man approached her. At last, one morning about a fortnight after they quit Draguinan, she refused to relinquish the sanctuary of the wagon. She lay there in her cot folded in upon herself like a flower bud that is destined never to open. In despair Angelina called Witchet in and asked what she should do.

Witchet looked down at the sad, despoiled little body which seemed asleep and yet was not asleep. 'Perhaps Tom can help her,' she said.

'Toma? What could he do that we have not done?'

'He has a gift,' said Witchet. 'He does not talk about it. But once when I was ill he came and made me well again. My father told me so.'

'What did he do?'

Witchet shook her head. 'I do not know, Angelina. But his friend David—the one who's a doctor—once told me

Tom had been gifted with a power over life and death. Do you want me to speak to him?'

Angelina looked down at her daughter and her eyes swam dark with distress. 'Whatever you will,' she sighed. 'I can do nothing more.'

Witchet climbed down from the wagon and went in search of Tom. She found him sitting on a rock beside the river writing something in a notebook and she called out to him. He glanced up, acknowledged her briefly, and returned to his work. She picked her way down to him, crouched beside him, and when he looked up again told him what she had come for.

'But you know what Maria's like with me, Witch,' he said. 'To her I'm just another *brigante*. And besides . . .'

'What, Tom?'

He looked past her, down at the rippling water, and shook his head.

'What were you going to say?' she insisted.

He sighed. 'I've changed, Witch. Changed in myself. I can't explain it to you. All I know is something happened to me back in that barn—something too awful to talk about. I just can't trust myself any more. It's all shifting sand. There's nothing firm left anywhere. Except maybe this'— he held up his notebook—'and even that I'm not sure about.'

Her eyes scanned his face as though she were struggling to decipher some curious inscription in an unknown tongue. 'I don't understand,' she said. 'Why can't you trust yourself?'

When he did not reply she repeated her question.

'Yes, I heard you,' he said, 'but I really don't know what to say. You see, Witch, the fact is I'm not at all sure that Maria isn't right. Maybe, deep down underneath, all men are *briganti,* all cruel, all barbaric. Only some of us hide it from ourselves—pretend we're not like that. Don't you see what I mean?'

'I know you're not like that,' she said.

Tom smiled wryly. 'You only make it harder for me, Witch. The more faith you have in me, the less I have in myself.'

'But I love you,' she said. 'If I didn't I think I should be like Maria is now.'

Tom stared at her as though he could not believe what he heard. 'What on earth are you talking about?' he demanded.

Witchet swallowed. 'If I tell you, will you promise me you'll try and help her?'

He nodded his head slowly. 'All right. If I can I will. I promise.'

She drew in a deep breath, lowered her head so that he could not see her face and then let the words tumble out like beads from a bag. 'When those two men grabbed hold of me I knew what they were going to do to me and so I stopped being myself. I flew away back to Tallon and looked for you. I flew all round Lydeard Hill calling for you and I flew low down over the Somersea and out over Taunton Reach calling "Tom! Tom! Tom!" all the time. I wasn't in my body at all and yet it *was* my body, my *real* body which was in the dream. The true me was miles and miles away looking for you. I wasn't ever going to tell you that because I thought . . . But it's true, Tom. It really is.'

Looking down upon her, listening to her, seeing her half-cringed almost as though she were expecting him to strike her, Tom felt his heart turn right over in his breast. *Know yourself, Thomas. Be free.* 'White Bird,' he whispered, 'Holy White Bird,' and dropping to his knees beside her he gathered her into his arms and buried his shame in her hair. 'You found me,' he whispered. 'Oh my own sweet witch, you found me but you didn't know it. I was back there in the barn with you. *I was those two briganti.*'

Angelina was standing beside the wagon when she saw Tom and Witchet walking hand in hand up the path from the stream. She sensed intuitively that something was subtly different between them but she was too preoccupied with her own anxieties to do more than barely acknowledge it. She did not really believe that the young *inglesi* could help her daughter for surely he would have done so long before this if he possessed the means, but she knew the Kinsfolk were credited with strange skills in the arts of healing and so she permitted herself the luxury of a faint hope. 'So, Toma,' she said. 'Alouette has told you?'

'She's told me. I'm truly sorry, Angelina.'

'And you can do nothing to help her?'

'We shall see. I think perhaps I can.'

'Truly, Toma?'

'Truly I think so.'

She gazed into his face and suddenly she was convinced that he was speaking the truth, that he really did have the power to make her child well and that he would do it. Overcome with emotion she seized his hands in her own and pressed them to her lips. 'I pray for you, Toma,' she whispered. 'What must I do?'

'Leave me alone with her,' he said. 'I will call you if I need you. Stay with her, Witch.'

He nodded to them both, drew in a deep breath and clambered up into the wagon where he released the canvas curtain and let it fall to behind him. When his eyes had become accustomed to the subdued light he made his way quietly along to the cot where Maria lay.

She was lying on her side with her knees drawn up and her slender arms tightly crossed over her scarcely budded breasts. Her back was towards him and she was wearing only a petticoat of thin white cotton through which he could clearly distinguish the serried knuckles of her spine. Her eyes were wide open and seemed enormous as they stared fixedly at the wooden panels of the cot a bare handsbreadth before her face.

'Maria?' he whispered. 'Maria, can you hear me?'

Her only response was to fold herself up even more tightly in her arms until she looked like some strange little golden shell cast up and abandoned on the shore by the ebbing tide.

Tom removed the pipes from his pocket, stripped off his jacket and laid it at the foot of the cot. Then he sat down on the vacant bed opposite and covered his face with his hands. After a minute he picked up the pipes again, murmured, 'Use me now as you will,' and began to play.

Out of the dark and swirling mists a soundless voice.

—*Is that you, Toma?*

—*Maria?*

—*Oh, Toma! Why has it taken you so long?*

—*I was afraid.*

—*But there is nothing to be frightened of. No one can hurt us here.*

—*You are alone?*

—*Yes. The old man has gone now. Come with me, Toma.*

—*Where to?*

—*To the Eye-Stone of course.*

He had been here before. He recognized the spectral outlines of this shadowy landscape. It was to this place that he had come in search of Witchet when she too was lost to the living world.

The track wound upwards, the mist thinned, and he found himself confronting a grey, humped rock which was pitted all over with dark holes like the skull of some titanic Argus. Pale lichens scabbed the bony contours and a chill wind honed mournfully among the empty sockets.

—*You must look now, Toma.*

The wind seemed to blow right through his own bones as he stepped close and peering into the nearest cavity saw deep within it, as though in some dim and tarnished mirror, the body of a naked man wallowing sluggishly in the waters of a rocky bay. Sightless eyes twinkled in the moonlight as the head lolled back and forth in a cradle of sea-wrack; the silver-lipped mouth gaped slackly as though locked for ever in the rictus of a scream; from between the gaunt rack of the ribs jutted the splintered stump of a crossbow bolt. Then a racing cloud masked the invisible moon and extinguished the lights in the drowned eyes. Sick at heart he turned away.

—*It is done. Toma. You have seen what you had to see.*
—*Why that, Maria?*
—*I do not know such things.*
—*And now I've seen it?*
—*We can go back.*
—*You will come with me?*
—*Yes.*

They retraced their steps down the stony track. The small phantom hand lay warm and trusting in his own. Then it was gone and there was only the mist swirling around him and the sound of his own piping beckoning him forward out of the shadows into the land of the living.

Tom laid the pipes aside, drew in a deep and shuddering breath and felt sweat running all down his back and chest in icy rivulets.

'Maria?'

'*Toma!* What are *you* doing here?'

Relief all but froze his tongue. 'I've been sent to fetch you.'

'But I am not dressed! Oh, you must not look at me! What has become of my frock? Have you hidden it?'

He smiled at her and gathered up his jacket. 'I'll call Mama,' he said. 'I expect she knows where it is.'

Witchet looked up as he appeared at the entrance to the wagon. His face, drawn and ghost pale, blinked down at her in the bright sunlight. 'Is she all right, Tom?'

'She's lost her frock,' he said. 'That's all that's bothering her.'

'Mother of God!' wailed Angelina, clasping her head in her hands. 'Is it true? Is it true?'

'Mama? Where is my frock?'

Signora Foscari crossed herself and burst into tears.

After supper that evening Tom and Witchet climbed up on to the summit of the hill behind their camping place. Far to the south, over the blue tops of the pines, they could just discern the line of the distant sea like a faint silver thread stretched out taut across the rim of the world. Around them the hillside murmured with late foraging bees; the golden air vibrated with the trilling of a million cicadas. They settled themselves down in a little saucer-shaped dip and then with one accord they turned and gazed deep into each other's eyes as though they were children again, determined to stare each other out.

At last, still holding his eyes with hers, Witchet raised her right hand and quietly un-hooked the cord that laced together the bodice of her dress. Then with her fingertips she coaxed the panels apart and taking his right hand in her own she raised it gently to her naked breast and began to stroke it softly back and forth. The tumultuous pulse of her blood flowed throbbing into his fingertips until it seemed to him as if they shared but one heart between them and that all life, all ease for pain, all meaning in an otherwise incomprehensible universe lay like the golden fruit of the tree of knowledge cupped there in his marvelling palm. He felt the soft bud of her nipple grow firm and sturdy as her quickening breath pressed it ever more eagerly against his hand; he saw her lips part, saw the tip of her tongue emerge, coral pink, between the neat white teeth, and then he saw her eyelids droop like the wings of a weary butterfly and she was sinking backwards, drawing him down to share in the feast of her love for him.

The sun set in a commonplace miracle of blood and amethyst and molten gold; the planet named for lovers emerged and hung like a perfect pearl low down in the western sky; and the last of the laggard bees droned off to its nest, all unperceived by the two who lay naked upon the enchanted slope stealing their own precious fragments from eternity.

When the sky above them was crowded with stars they dressed themselves and then lay back and gazed upwards. After a while Tom turned his head and looked at Witchet. 'Nine months,' he murmured. 'To think I've wasted nine whole months of my life, and all because I didn't know what I was looking for. Does that make sense to you?'

She smiled. 'But there have been times when you wanted to make love with me. Like when we went swimming by moonlight at Perello. You thought I didn't see but I did.'

'What did you see?'

'I saw you looking at me as if you hadn't really seen me before. I so wanted to take you in my arms, all silver-wet and salty from the sea, and to hold you right down deep inside me. But you ran away along the beach as if you were scared of something. Later you went off and sat out on the rocks by yourself and played your pipes. Do you remember that?'

'Of course I remember,' he said. 'That was when I first heard the song I call "Sea Witch".'

'And why did you run away?'

Tom laughed. 'A naked man can't hide his feelings in the same way that a girl can.'

'Is that the only reason?'

'No, of course not. You were right when you said I'd seen you as someone different from the Witch I'd known all my life. There were too many memories for me to handle—too many other Witchets stretching back over the years. Those were what I was running away from. I couldn't see *you* through *them*.'

'But they're still there somewhere.'

'What do you mean?'

'I'm sure there's somewhere where we're still the people we once were, and there's somewhere else where we're already the people we're going to be. Where we are now is just the bit in between.'

'You've never told me that before.'

'You've never asked me.'

'And is that how you explain the *huesh?*'

'Yes, I suppose so. I don't really know.'

Tom considered this in silence for a minute then he said: 'You're right about one thing, Witch. This isn't the only world. There's another one as well. I know because I've been there.'

'What do you mean?'

'You don't remember, but it's where I went to look for you last Bartholomew's Day. Magpie thought you were dead but you weren't. You were lost in what I call the Land of Shadows. That's where I went today to find Maria. She doesn't remember it either. But it's there all right. It's as real as we are now.'

Witchet reached across, slipped her hand inside his shirt and felt the steady thumping of his heart. 'Tell me about it,' she said. 'How do you get there?'

'Through someone else,' he said. 'It's the only way. It's as though they hold the lock and I hold the key. It's partly in me and partly there in the Boy's pipes. But it's not something I can *think* about—it's just something I know I can do when I have to. I have to sort of *feel* my way through to the other side—like feeling my way across a dark room and then opening a door and stepping out through a sort of mist into that other place. Once I'm there I know it—I recognize it. It's familiar but in a strange sort of way, like a dream I've dreamt lots of times before but which I can only really *remember* when I'm dreaming it. But when I'm in the Land of Shadows I know that really I'm someone else and there's some task I have to do but I'm not sure what it is.' He lapsed into silence as though the stream of his thought had meandered off and left his tongue behind.

'What do you mean "someone else"?' Witchet prompted gently.

'Someone called the Star Born,' he said. 'Someone out of The Testament.'

'You don't really believe that, do you?'

Tom sighed. 'I don't know, Witch. I've never *wanted* to believe it. But I can't seem to escape it. I've never told you this before, but last year, after Dave left Tallon, I got Mother to read to me. It's something she used to do in the old days before I was born. I really had to force her to do it because she was scared of what she thought she might find. Anyway in the end she did and then she told me that Marwys was right and that I was the Child of the Bride of Time—Old Morfedd's Star Born—so I suppose I must be.'

'But what does that *mean*, Tom?'

'Well, according to Marwys, the Star Born is destined to finish what the Boy started. I can't see it though. To me the Testament is just a whole lot of rhyming riddles which are supposed to be prophetic. The story is that old Morfedd wrote them and gave them to the Boy. From him they passed to Old Peter the Tale Spinner and from him to Gyre. Just before *he* died he gave them to my father and . . .' Again his voice faltered to a stop.

'And what, Tom?'

'I saw him today.'

'Saw who?'

'My father.'

'*Your father!* Oh, Tom, you *couldn't* have.'

But Tom's voice had taken on a new urgency. 'Yes, I did, Witch,' he insisted. 'It was when I was with Maria.

She led me to a place—a rock she called the Eye-Stone. I looked into it and I saw *him.*'

Beneath her hand she could feel him trembling. She pulled herself closer. 'What is it?' she whispered. 'What happened?'

'Without dark, no light: without black, no white: without wrong, no right.'

'What? What are you saying, Tom?'

He sat up suddenly. 'Morfedd,' he whispered. 'Morfedd was the old man. He must have been.'

'Tom? Tom, are you all right?'

'Know yourself. Be free.'

'Oh, Tom! Stop it!'

'What?'

'You're frightening me,' she said. 'And I'm cold.'

He put his arms around her. 'Hey, you're shivering,' he said. 'Here. Have my jacket.'

'Just hold me,' she said. 'Hold me tight.'

He unfastened the toggles on his leather jerkin, opened it up, then drew her close and folded the garment around her like a pair of wings. Her lips mumbled against his neck and he kissed the starlit silver of her hair. 'We ought to be going back now,' he murmured.

She shook her head and he felt her fingers fumbling with the buttons on his shirt. Next moment her bare breasts were nuzzling soft and warm against his naked chest, her mouth seeking for his. He needed no one to tell him then that no more precious gift existed either in this world or in any other.

In the third week of July the Theatre Foscari entered Nice, the great free city which controlled all the southern trade routes into Italy. It was the carnival season, the streets were decked with flowers and bunting, and dancing and revelry continued with scarcely a pause from early morning until late into the night. Never had the little company

worked harder or more profitably. Each day they gave three
performances and in a week had taken more than they had
in the whole of the previous month. In her wagon each
evening Angelina counted up the day's takings and handed
over his share to Tom. 'At this rate you will soon have
enough for the trousseau, Toma,' she said. 'So when is
this wedding to be?'

'As soon as we get back to Tallon,' said Tom. 'But first
we have a rendezvous with Dave in Alençon. After that
I'm taking Witch to see Corlay.'

'I have never been to Brittany,' Angelina mused, 'but I
remember Kinsman Marwys saying that it was very beautiful.'

'Tallon is even more beautiful,' said Tom, 'and it's pulling us harder every day. We've been thinking, Angelina.
Perhaps after all it will be better if we don't come with
you into Italy. We hear there's a merchants' caravan going
north on the day after tomorrow and a party of Kinsfolk
with it. They've invited us to travel with them as far as
Lyon. If we do we can be in Normandy by the end of
August and at Corlay in September. It seems too good a
chance to miss.'

Angelina gazed at him sadly. 'Ah, Toma *mio*,' she
sighed. 'Those are black words indeed. No sooner does the
sun begin to shine than another great cloud rolls up to cover
it. What shall we all do without you? For me it will be like
losing a son and a daughter. Have you spoken of this to
Andrea?'

'Not yet,' he said. 'We only heard about the caravan
from the Kinsfolk this morning. But I think we would be
wise to join them, Angelina. If we go on to Torino with
you it will mean the winter will be on us before we even
get to Normandy.'

'*Sì, sì*, Toma, I understand, though truly my heart feels
as heavy as a stone.'

'But we'll come to see you all again,' he said. 'How

could we bear to waste all that beautiful Italian you've taught us?'

She smiled and put out her hand and touched his cheek. 'I hope it will be so, Toma,' she said. 'Truly, with all my soul I hope it. But I feel a cold wind blowing about my heart.' She took his left hand in hers, turned it palm uppermost, and held it so that the lamplight slanted across it. She looked down at it and then murmured something in Italian of which he caught only the word *'strada'*.

'Tell me in French,' he said.

'I said you have a hard road ahead of you, Toma.'

He glanced up into her face and frowned. 'Someone else said that to me once, or maybe I only dreamt it. Not fame and fortune then?'

'It is a strange hand,' she said. 'I have never seen another like it. Has no one ever told you that before?'

'No. I don't think I've ever had my fortune told.'

She drew her fingertip over his palm in the sign of the cross, then folded up his hand and, leaning forward, kissed him on the forehead. 'Your fortune is what you will make of it, Toma,' she said. 'Come, let us go and join the others in the taverna while there is still some good wine left for us to drink.'

Later that evening they broke the news to Andrea and the others. Andrea accepted it philosophically as he accepted most things. 'Ah, but we shall miss you,' he said. 'We have shared some good times as well as some not so good, hey? But I think you are right to go north while the roads are still dry, so I am not going to try to dissuade you. And when we meet again we will have much to talk about. Then Toma and I will embrace as two proud fathers, as men of great standing in the world, eh, Alouette?'

Witchet flushed a delicate rose pink to the tips of her ears and buried her nose in a slice of melon.

Andrea laughed. 'If I had met you thirty years ago, Alouette, your piper would not have had it all his own way.

I would have swept you off your feet like a hurricane! And what sweet music we would have made together! All night long like a pair of nightingales!'

'Wind music,' scoffed Angelina. 'Like always.'

'And will you come back to us again, Toma?' Maria asked.

'Of course,' said Tom. 'Hand on my heart.'

'Next summer?'

'It's possible. What do you say, Witch?'

'I'd love to, Maria,' said Witchet. 'I think of you all as my second family.'

'Eccellente!' cried Andrea. 'So, next year, God willing, we will all be re-united in Rocquevaire. Let us drink to that! Next May in Rocquevaire!'

'In Rocquevaire!' they chorused. 'Next May in Rocquevaire!'

The caravan made up of fourteen great wagons and over fifty outriders was to leave Nice at dawn on the first day of August. The Foscaris came to the north gate of the city to wish them God speed and a safe journey. The sadness of parting was only slightly eased by the mutual reassurances that they would all meet again next year. They embraced and exchanged tokens of remembrance. 'We *will* meet again, Toma,' whispered Maria, choking back tears and hugging him to her with all her might. 'I know it. I know it.'

A post horn sounded the last call. *'Allez! Allez!'* shouted the wagon drivers. *'On roule! On roule!'*

One last kiss all round then Tom and Witchet scrambled aboard. Friendly hands made the bolts fast behind them.

'Addio, Alouette! *Addio,* Toma! God bless you! Safe journey!'

'Addio! Addio! Next year in Rocquevaire!'

'Sì! Sì! Next year!'

Massive iron-shod wheels grated on the cobblestones;

iron-shod hoofs clashed and clattered; iron chains jangled; wooden axles shrieked and squealed; all was din, shouting, apparent chaos, but they were moving.

Maria trotted along after them and flung a small paper packet into the wagon. 'Some figs, Toma,' she called. 'Remember me when you eat them.'

Tom took out his pipes and fingered a tune. Although it was almost drowned in the racket it somehow contrived to reach her ears. Her sad face lit up, her tear-bright eyes sparkled with sudden happiness, and with both hands she flung kisses after the retreating wagon as the first rays of the rising sun gilded the dome of the church high up on the Isle of St. Roch.

They passed the first hour of their journey becoming acquainted with their seven travelling companions. The senior member of the party was a balding, middle-aged lawyer, Doctor Puybareau, who had the odd, disarming habit of concluding almost every other statement he made with the words 'of course I may possibly be mistaken.' To which his plump little chicken of a wife would invariably append a verbal codicil in the form of 'you probably are, my dear.' The Puybareaus had been on a visit to their eldest daughter and were now returning with their two younger children to their home in Digne.

Next in seniority was Monsieur Brocaire who owned a textile business in Chabeuil on the eastern shore of the great inland seaway which had once been the Rhône valley. During his absence in Nice the factory had been left in charge of a younger brother in whom, it emerged, Monsieur Brocaire had but scant confidence. 'He takes his Kinship too literally,' he confided gloomily to Madame Puybareau, 'and consequently everybody takes advantage of him. If Philippe had his way we would be giving our cloth away, not selling it! Fortunately for me his wife comes from sound business stock—she's one of the Focarts from Grenoble—you've heard of them, I daresay?—Just as well, too, or I'd be a pauper by now.'

The two final places were occupied by two brothers, Simon and Peter Arache, who were travelling to Vienne to take possession of a new trading barque which they would then sail on her maiden voyage down the seaway to the port of New Marseilles.

The great North Highway, carved out of the rocks a thousand years ago, followed the course of the river Var and gave Monsieur Brocaire many an opportunity to lament how much they had still to learn from the engineers of the past. 'See there!' he exclaimed, pointing downwards to some inscrutable ruin far below. 'Who knows what that once was? Some great *barrage,* perhaps, constructed to harness the forces of Nature. What a waste! What a terrible waste!'

Doctor Puybareau adjusted his spectacles and peered down into the gulf. 'Yes, yes,' he said. 'I should say that was one of the points where they collected the power they called "electric"—but possibly I am mistaken.'

Overcome by a combination of the afternoon warmth, a substantial lunch and half a bottle of good wine, Madame Puybareau had dozed off, otherwise she would certainly have agreed.

'And this "electric", what was it precisely?' demanded Brocaire.

'A force,' said Doctor Puybareau vaguely. 'Simply a force, M'sieur. A power.' He stirred the air vaguely with his fingers. 'I know no more than that.'

'Like the water, you mean? That's a force all right. We harness it to drive the looms in the mill.'

'I think not,' said the lawyer. 'I seem to recall hearing someone say that it was invisible. An invisible electric force. Yes, yes. But possibly I am mistaken.'

'That doesn't make sense to me,' said Brocaire. 'What

use would it be if you couldn't see it? How could you manage it?'

'Ah, there you have the advantage of me, M'sieur. I am not, you understand, a practical man. But it is pleasant, is it not, to be able to speculate a little? When I was a young man it would have been as much as my life was worth to engage in a conversation like this. It could well have meant my professional ruin.' He glanced around at the others and nodded. 'We have much to thank the Bird for, my friends.'

'It's safe enough talking here among Kin,' said Brocaire, 'but there are still plenty of places where a man's well advised to keep his lips buttoned. The times haven't changed as much as all that, you know.'

'True, true. An open window can easily be closed again.'

'Or bricked up.'

'That also, alas.'

They both reflected a while in silence upon this unpleasant possibility then Monsieur Brocaire said: 'Is it true that they've got a whole library full of the old wisdom locked away in the Vatican?'

'I have heard it said so,' admitted Doctor Puybareau. 'Indeed I believe it is known as "the faucet", but I could be mistaken.'

'The faucet? Why's that?'

The lawyer removed his spectacles and returned them to their case. 'I should imagine it is because they fear to precipitate a second Drowning should they ever release it.'

Monsieur Brocaire's eyes widened visibly as the implication dawned upon him. 'The faucet,' he repeated. 'I take your point. Perhaps it's just as well if it stays there, hey?'

Doctor Puybareau nodded.

'After all, give or take a thing or two, we've managed well enough without it up to now.'

'I would not be the one to dispute it.'

'The faucet, eh? You know I've never considered that side of it before. Do you really think that's the way it was?'

'That is what we were taught when I was at college,' said the lawyer. 'A thousand years ago the poles were covered with a vast layer of ice many kilometres thick. Then the Old ones—our own forefathers, M'sieur—those same ones who constructed this very highway upon which we are travelling—the Old ones, I say, contrived to unlock the sovereign powers that held the atmosphere in equilibrium. Once the process was started they could not stop it. The ice melted, the rains fell, the seas rose, the land heaved, and a thousand great cities sank beneath the waves never to surface again. Paris, Bordeaux, Old Marseilles, Toulon—what are they to us today but names? Yet once they must have been great centres of commerce, humming with their populations of industrious citizens like hives of honeybees in the Alpilles. It is that we must never forget, Monsieur Brocaire. What has happened once could happen again.'

'But how could it happen again? There is no more ice left to melt.'

'Who talks of melting? Next time perhaps all the oceans of the world may *become* ice and we shall all *freeze* to death. Of course I could be mistaken.'

'You probably are, my dear,' muttered Madame Puybareau in her dreams.

Early in the evening on the fourth day out from Nice the convoy entered a town which stood at the confluence of two rivers half way between Digne and Castellane. As this was to be the Puybareaus' last night they graciously invited the others to be their guests at supper in the staging inn. The sudden influx of scores of hungry travellers all clamouring to be fed induced the landlord to set out extra tables in the courtyard and there the Puybareau party were accommodated. They were served with wine and olives and informed that it would be half an hour before they could expect to dine.

'If they say that it means an hour at least,' signed Madame Puybareau to Witchet. 'Could you not fetch your guitar, my dear, and keep us all happy?'

'You have a captive audience all to hand,' observed Monsieur Brocaire waving an arm towards the other tables. 'What artist could afford to neglect such an opportunity?'

'You're right,' said Tom. 'Go and get it, love. I'll have a word with the landlord.'

Witchet got up from her seat and trotted off to where the wagons were drawn up in the Grand Place under the surveillance of half a dozen watchmen. A small crowd of idle townfolk had strolled up to observe the goings-on. Having identified herself to the driver of her wagon she climbed aboard and collected her instrument.

She was making her way back across the Place when she overheard a man saying: '—and then on to Sisteron on Friday, eh?' Some quality in that voice touched her heart like an icy finger. She glanced round and saw two men talking with one of the wagon drivers. Although their backs were turned towards her she knew beyond all possibility of a doubt that they were the same two whom she had once seen emerging out of the pouring rain with a dead sheep slung on a pole between them. Her whole body began to tremble as if it were in the grip of some lethal fever. Clutching her guitar to her chest she broke into a stumbling run and did not stop till she had gained the sanctuary of the inn courtyard. There she came to a halt and stood, panting with fright, one hand gripping the neck of her dress as though it were a lifeline.

Tom caught sight of her, guessed something was amiss and hurried across. 'What is it, Witch? What's happened?'

She shook her head violently, and without saying a word, burst into tears.

Conscious of the curious eyes upon them he drew her back beside him into the shadow of the archway. Beneath his hand he could feel her shivering. 'What's happened?' he repeated. 'What's upset you?'

She just clung to him, trembling. He raised his head and gazed out over her shoulder down the street to the Grand Place. And suddenly he knew what had happened. 'The *briganti,*' he whispered. 'You've seen them, haven't you?'

Witchet gave a sort of choking gulp and shuddered convulsively.

'All of them?'

'Two,' she gasped. 'Those two. The first ones.'

'Where are they?'

'Back there. By the wagons. Oh, Tom, don't go! Don't go!'

'But you could have made a mistake,' he said.

'No, no. *Please,*' she begged, clutching at his arm.

'I promise I won't let them see me.'

'Please, Tom, no! They'll kill you!'

'Of course they won't. There are far too many people about for anything like that. You go on back to the table and wait for me.'

'What are you going to do? Warn the guards?'

'Yes,' he said. 'If it really is them, that's what I'll do.'

She scuffed the tears from her cheeks and drew in a huge, shuddering breath. 'Oh, be careful,' she implored. 'Be careful, my love.'

He kissed her on her damp cheek, turned her round bodily until she was pointing in the direction of the Puybareaus, and gave her a gentle shove. Next moment he was running back down the street which led to the Place, conscious only of a fierce and hungry excitement, of a tenseness like a cold steel spring coiled within his breast.

As soon as he came in sight of the assembled wagons he slowed his pace to a casual walk. Reasoning that Witchet would have taken the shortest route he began sauntering in the direction of their own carriage, covertly scanning the faces of the bystanders. Seeing no sign of either man he started on a rapid circuit of the Place, peering into each of the taverns as he passed.

On the third side of the square he came upon a narrow concealed alley which sloped steeply downwards in a series of irregular steps to the north bank of one of the two rivers around which the town was built. As he glanced down towards the distant water he saw, some twenty or so paces below him, a man urinating against a wall. Tom felt the skin at the back of his neck grow suddenly tense. The man finished what he was about and backed away, prick still in hand, then turned his head and looked back up the steps. A flicker of sunlight striking upwards from the surface of the river picked out the twisted outline of a scarred left eyebrow.

Tom caught his breath and ducked quickly aside. But the man seemed not to have noticed him. He wriggled himself back into his pouch and whistling tunelessly, continued his descent of the steps.

Tom waited until his quarry had almost reached the bottom then, keeping in close beside the wall, he darted in pursuit. Half way down he slid his left hand into his inner pocket and drew out his pipes. 'Like rats,' he murmured. 'Like I would kill rats. Without compunction.'

On the bottom step he paused, then edged forward and peeped cautiously round the corner. Beside a stone bridge some two hundred metres off to his right two boys were fishing. There was no one else to be seen, no sign of the man anywhere, but he noticed that one of the boys was gazing towards him apparently observing something that was taking place at the foot of the high stone wall which channelled the river. He stole silently forward and peered down.

Immediately below him Scar-brow was in the act of stepping off an iron boarding ladder into a rowing boat. Kneeling in the boat, unfastening the rope which was tethering it to one of the rungs of the ladder, was Montfort.

Tom's divided tongue flickered across his lips. 'One moment, if you please, Messieurs,' he called. 'I have something here for you.'

Startled, they both glanced up. 'What's that?' said Montfort. 'Who are you?'

'I have something here for you,' Tom repeated. 'From Signor Foscari.'

They saw his face and hands rippling in a golden web of reflected sunlight and then a sound which resembled no sound they had ever heard was coiling itself lazily around them like some strange and sinister tendril. For as long as it takes to count slowly up to ten they did not move at all, simply stared up at him as a dog stares up at its master waiting for his command. Then their arms began to twitch. A moment later their hands scuttled up their chests like spiders and started clawing at their necks as though they were struggling to prise loose an invisible garotte. The boat lurched violently and a succession of ripples fanned out across the sunlit water.

Within the space of a minute Scar-brow's face had contorted itself into a grimace of sheer mindless terror. His breathing had become a series of strangled gasps, his eyes bulged, and two trickles of blood were creeping out like thin dark worms from his flared nostrils. Montfort had half risen to his feet; his normally pallid features seemed to have been transformed into one enormous bruise; a grotesquely swollen tongue was protruding from between his teeth like a lump of raw liver and suds of a thin pinkish foam were dripping from his chin.

Through the frenzied pounding of the blood in their ears both men heard what sounded like the distant beating of giant wings. Before their eyes the light dimmed and brightened and dimmed again until all they could distinguish was the young man's face like a tiny circle of cold and silvery starlight at the end of a long dark tunnel. It grew smaller and ever smaller, until finally it faded and was gone.

The two boys heard the distant double splash, dropped their rods and ran back along the river bank to where Tom was standing gazing down at the empty boat. 'What happened, Monsieur?' they panted.

'I don't know,' he said. 'Can you see anything?'

They stared down at the water and shook their heads. 'It is very deep here,' said one. 'Were they perhaps drunk?'

'I think they must have been.'

'A drunkard is already three parts drowned,' said the other. 'That is what my grandfather says. Go and tell the Constable what has happened, Jules.'

'I will tell him,' said Tom. 'Where do I find him?'

'He will be in Madame Lassard's for sure,' said the boy. 'It is up in the Place, Monsieur. Next to Forège the saddler.'

Tom hastened back to the steps but as soon as he was out of their sight his pace slowed to a walk. His legs suddenly felt as heavy as though his shoes had been soled with lead and long before he reached the top of the steps he was obliged to sit down and force his head between his bent knees to prevent himself from fainting. The instant he closed his eyes the contorted faces of the two *briganti* seemed to float before his mind's eye like a pair of hideously deformed masks. His stomach heaved mutinously and his mouth filled with bile. He spat it out, rose dizzily to his feet, lurched over to the nearest wall and began handing himself along it like a drunkard.

When at last he reached the Place he had recovered sufficiently to be able to seek out the tavern which the Constable patronized. Having identified the man by his uniform he went across, told him there had been an accident and described its location. 'They are certainly drowned,' he concluded. 'There was no sign of them at all.'

'That makes five in eight years,' said the Constable. 'Five drowned at that same spot, Monsieur. Within an hour

74

the current will have carried them down to the grid. Drunk, you say?'

'I think so. I don't really know. I was just passing by when it happened.'

'Then you do not know who they were, these two?'

Tom shook his head.

'Well, thank you for telling me, Monsieur. It is not pleasant to be a witness of such things. But that is the way of it, hey? Lucille, a cognac if you please for this public-spirited gentleman.'

As Tom was making his way back towards the inn, Peter, one of the Arache brothers, hailed him from across the Place. 'Where the devil have you been hiding yourself, Thomas?' he demanded as Tom approached. 'Your lass has been worried sick about you.'

'I'm sorry,' said Tom. 'I was looking for someone.'

'A ghost was it?'

Tom stared at him. 'Why do you say that?'

'Well, you should see yourself, man. You've got a face on you like a fish's belly.'

'I came over a bit queer. I'm sorry if I've put you to trouble.'

They re-entered the inn courtyard just as the first course of the meal was being served. The diversion allowed Tom to make his excuses without having to fend off too many probing questions. As for Witchet she was so relieved to have him back safe that it was not until they were alone in bed that night that she plucked up sufficient courage to ask him what had really happened.

'It was them all right,' he said. 'Montfort and Scar-brow. So I paid them what we owed them.'

'What does that mean?'

'You can't guess?'

She shook her head.

'I killed them.'

Witchet stared at him in utter incredulity.

'You don't believe me?'

'You mean you found them and you told the guards who they were.'

'No, I don't mean that at all. I mean I did it by myself. I really killed them, Witch.'

'Oh, Tom, you *didn't!* You're just saying that.'

'Why can't you believe me?'

'Because.'

'Because what?'

'Because you're who you are, of course. Why, you aren't even armed. And you're Kin.'

Tom considered this as though it had never occurred to him before, and then he shook his head. 'I *was* Kin,' he said, 'but I'm not any more.'

'What are you *saying,* Tom?'

'No true Kin could have done what I did. Not even to those two rats. I did it in cold blood, Witch. Like a common executioner.'

For the first time Witchet found herself half believing him. 'But what *did* you do?' she said. 'I still don't know.'

Tom gazed at her but she knew he was not really seeing her at all. 'I hanged them,' he murmured. 'I hanged them both by the neck from a gallows inside my own head. And then I cut them loose and dropped their bodies in the river.'

Witchet gaped at him and then gave a little nervous hiccup of laughter. 'You couldn't have done that, Tom. Not really.'

'Really?' he repeated. 'Not really? If there's one thing I'm absolutely sure of, Witch, it's that I don't know what that word "really" means any more.'

The route the caravan was following brought them down from the Alpes by way of the Drôme valley to the great Rhône seaway. Fifteen days after taking leave of the Foscaris Tom and Witchet found themselves saying farewell to Monsieur Brocaire at Chabeuil. 'May the White Bird

76

protect you, my two songsters,' he said embracing them. 'If I had a cage big enough to hold you I would pop you both inside and then I would always have music to soothe my heart in the dog days. Remember old Anton Brocaire in your prayers. And take care.' So saying he gave them each a gold coin, patted Witchet on the cheek, and stumped away out of their lives.

The spare place in the wagon was taken by a sallow, thin-faced, bearded man who held the post of wine factor to a great merchant in Lyon. His name was Fernand Ory and his days were spent travelling the region, assessing the probable quality of the new vintage, and advising his employer accordingly. Much of his time was passed in adding and subtracting long columns of figures in a leather-bound ledger which was attached to his belt by means of a steel chain and was never allowed out of his sight. He kept himself very much to himself and none of the other passengers paid him much attention until, on the second day out from Chabeuil when the convoy was some forty kilometres from Vienne, Monsieur Ory suddenly collapsed in his seat.

Peter Arache who was sitting closest to him went to his assistance. A moment later he clapped his hand over his own nose and mouth, averted his head and cried: *'C'est la peste!'*

For a few seconds everyone else was simply too stunned to react. Then pandemonium broke loose. Passengers scrambled to their feet and leapt down into the road as though they were flinging themselves into the water from a blazing ship. Within the space of a minute, apart from the unfortunate victim himself, only Tom, Witchet and one rather deaf old man were still left on board.

The wagon rumbled to a halt and the alarmed face of the driver appeared framed in the little *guichet* demanding to know what the devil was going on.

Tom drew in a deep breath, made his way forward and

bent over the prostrate form of the wine factor. The man's blood-shot eyes stared up into his with a kind of fixed and desperate appeal, his chest laboured like a tinsmith's bellows, and a vile, sweetish stench arose from his lips.

With trembling fingers Tom contrived to release the man's cravat and undo some of the buttons on his shirt. As he drew the panels aside he saw that the whole of the exposed flesh had erupted in a sinister, circular rash like a smouldering ring-worm. He was gazing down at it in mingled disgust and fascination when the elderly man leant over his shoulder and muttered: 'Yes, yes. That's the Wreath of Araby, all right. I heard it was about in the south. Well, the Bird will surely come for you before nightfall, my poor friend. Not a doubt of it.'

'What's that?' demanded the driver. 'What does he say?'

'He says it's something called the Wreath of Araby,' said Tom, and turning to the old man he said: 'Is that a plague, monsieur?'

'Eh?'

'Is it plague?' Tom bawled.

'Certainly it is a plague, m'sieur. Two years ago in Corse over four thousand people died of it. They said it came over from Algiers, but I don't know anything about that.'

'Is there nothing we can do for him?'

'One can pray.'

The stopping of the wagon had brought the whole convoy grinding to a standstill. Soon a small crowd had collected in the road and the dreaded word *'peste'* was being heard on every side. Simon Arache climbed back into the wagon and handed down a box and two bed-rolls to his brother. 'We're off,' he said to Witchet. 'The wind's from the south and we reckon we'll get a passage on a barge up to Vienne from St. Vallier. Why don't you and Thomas come with us? It's only a couple of kilometres from here.'

Witchet beckoned Tom over and put the proposition to him.

'This hearse won't be going any further than Serves,' said Simon. 'They'll have to fumigate it.'

'And what about him?' murmured Tom, glancing back at the dying man.

Simon shrugged. 'If he's got the roses, Thomas, he'll be lucky to make it even as far as Serves. Well, are you coming?'

Witchet touched Tom's arm and as their eyes met she nodded.

The first thing Simon did on entering St. Vallier was to go into a tavern and buy a bottle of cheap cognac. At his insistence they all swilled out their mouths with the spirit and then spat it out into the ditch. He even advised them to sniff some up their noses but this proved too much for Witchet who compromised by pouring a little on to a corner of her skirt and sniffing that instead. Finally they each drank a generous tot and used what was left to rinse their hands. As a direct result of these measures Witchet all but lost her footing on the gangplank when climbing aboard the barge and shortly afterwards fell sound asleep on a pile of cork-oak bark.

An hour later she awoke from a sad, confused dream of which she could remember little except that she had been seeking for Tom and could not find him. For a bewildering moment she could not think where she was. Directly above her the huge brown mainsail bellied out quietly before the pursuing wind. From her viewpoint it looked more like some towering sandstone cliff than a sheet of canvas. Then she heard Tom's laugh and remembered. She sat up, shook herself and began rubbing the stiffness out of her arms and legs while she gazed out across the sapphire water at the sun-sculpted hills drifting slowly past.

Tom caught sight of her and came clambering over the cabin roof to join her. In his hand he held a bunch of yellow-green grapes. He broke off a part of the bunch and handed it to her. 'We're really in luck, Witch,' he said. 'They're going as far as Lyon and they say this wind will hold until sunset. That means we can be on our way to Bourges tomorrow.'

'And how long will that take?'

'To get to Bourges? A week. Ten days at the most.'

'And then?'

'Well, straight across to Normandy. We'll be in Alençon for sure before the end of the month. Can't you just see the look on old Dave's face when we roll up at the hospital and ask for Doctor Ronceval?'

Witchet smiled. 'For me the best moment of all will be when we step ashore in Tallon.'

'You're getting homesick, are you?'

'Ever since we left Nice,' she sighed. 'I can feel Tallon tugging at me like a tide. Stronger and stronger every day. Don't you feel it too?'

'Yes, I suppose I do,' he admitted. 'A bit anyway. But I remember feeling like that during my first days at Corlay. All those strange faces and people speaking a language I couldn't understand. Then I made friends with Dave and I discovered that he felt just as miserable as I was even though he did speak the language. After that things began to get better. Now I sometimes even find myself thinking of Corlay as home. I suppose all "home" means is the one place where you don't have to pretend to be someone you're not.'

'Then you're home now,' she said with a smile. 'You don't have to pretend with me.'

'Believe it or not, Witch, I never have.'

'No? What about those two *briganti*.'

Tom blinked at her. 'What about them?'

'Well, you didn't *really* kill them.'

'I told you exactly what happened,' he said. 'I wasn't lying. Maybe I shouldn't have done it but I did.'

'You told me you'd hanged them. You couldn't have done *that*, Tom.'

'Who says I couldn't?'

She picked off the largest grape on the bunch and pushed it between his lips. 'I do,' she said.

'Well, you're wrong,' he retorted. 'If I want to do something badly enough then I can do it. That's what I've discovered about myself, Witch. But what I still don't know is who is the self which can do it.'

'What do you mean?'

'It's like I told you before. It's as though there's a shadow me—another Tom who has his being in a different world from this one. And it's there in that other world that the real answers are waiting to be found. I'm sure of that.'

'I don't know what you mean, Tom. What answers?'

'To all those questions I used to chew over for hours on end with Dave and old Marwys. Things like—what was the true nature of the Boy's vision? What's time? Does the human soul really exist? What are the immortal harmonies which Morfedd is supposed to have discovered? We called those questions "the ultimate truths".'

'And the White Bird?' she said.

'That too,' he said.

There was a long, thoughtful silence. Finally Witchet asked: 'And if you do find your answers? What then?'

'I won't know that until I find them, will I?'

'But what is it you hope for?'

'Just to *know*, Witch. To become wise.'

'Like Francis, you mean?'

'Like no one else—well, except like Old Morfedd, maybe. You know, Witch, if I've ever truly envied the Boy anything it's that he was taught by the Wizard of Bowness. The times I've dreamt about that old man! I look up into his eyes—it's like looking up into windows filled with stars—and I feel a sort of terrible yearning hunger for something which I can't begin to express even to myself—

a sort of immortal longing like a load of sickness round my heart . . .' He broke off and grinned at her. 'Here, have some more grapes.'

Witchet took the bunch from him, snapped off a cluster of fruit and handed the rest back. 'Tell me about the Star Born,' she said.

'The Star Born? Oh, he's just someone in the Testament.'

'Well, I know *that,*' she said. 'What does he do?'

Tom laughed. 'He flies on the back of the White Bird to the Kingdom of the Unborn Stars.'

'Where's that?'

'How on earth should I know? Nowhere, probably. It's just a riddle, Witch. It doesn't *mean* anything.'

'But you told me you believed he was you. When you told me about the place you call the Land of Shadows. You remember.'

'I was just teasing you.'

'No, you weren't. You meant it. I know you did. And you told me you'd seen your father. You really scared me, Tom.'

Tom's eyes gleamed with reminiscence. He grinned. 'I seem to remember you hauling me back into this world very quickly.'

Witchet laughed. 'You don't know how lucky you were to have me around to do it.'

Fortune continued to favour them. Hardly had they stepped ashore at Lyon than they learned that a mail coach would be leaving for Roanne first thing next morning. There were still two places on it going begging. They took them without a second's hesitation and by the evening of the following day had reached the Loire.

A fellow passenger on the coach told them there was a canal boat service plying from Roanne right down to the coast at Briare and that from there they could easily get a passage across the sea of Orleans to the Isle of Normandy. He estimated that the journey from Roanne to Briare would take them about five days. 'I have done it myself many times,' he assured them, 'and believe me when I say that it is infinitely preferable to travelling by road. One simply cannot compare the two.'

They took his advice and made their way down to the *bassin* where the boats were moored. Within half an hour they had booked themselves two berths on the *Saint Sebastien*, a general carrier which was taking a cargo of melons and maize to Briare. Since the boat was scheduled to depart at first light, Tom and Witchet slept on board and awoke next morning to find that they were under way and already several kilometres north of Roanne.

There followed some of the most delightful days they had ever spent. The weather was glorious—the sun hot, the sky a fathomless deep blue—and Monsieur Argonne, his wife Celeste and their two children, Bernard and Augustine who comprised the whole crew of the *Saint Sebastien* were enchanting companions. The only smudge on an otherwise cloudless horizon was that starting from the very first day of the voyage Witchet began to feel sick in the mornings. Madame Argonne recognized the symptoms immediately and produced a jar of salty oatmeal biscuits which she claimed to be an infallible specific against *le mal du matin*. 'It will pass, *chérie*,' she said. 'How long is it now?'

Convinced that she knew when it had happened Witchet tried to reckon back to that magical evening on the hillside above Grasse. 'About seven weeks, I think,' she said.

'And you feel it up here already?' enquired Celeste, patting her own ample bosom.

Witchet nodded.

'Does he know, your Thomas?'

'Not yet.'

'He will be pleased.'

Witchet wondered. 'I hope so,' she said.

She could have spared herself the doubt. Tom was utterly enraptured when she broke the news to him two days later. 'But why didn't you tell me before?' he demanded. 'Didn't you know?'

'I wasn't sure,' said Witchet, adding as an afterthought, 'I've never had a baby before.'

'Nor me,' said Tom. 'Or at least no one's told me.'

But that night he was woken by sounds of muffled sobbing coming from Witchet's bunk. A bright shaft of harvest moonlight was slanting into the cabin as he clambered out of his own cot and leant over her. 'What's the matter, love? Aren't you feeling well?'

'My head hurts,' she complained tearfully. 'And I'm so hot.'

He laid his hand across her brow and found it wet with sweat. 'I'll get you something to drink,' he said. 'Have you got any of your medicine left?'

'What?'

'Your headache stuff. Where is it?'

'In my pack.'

Two minutes later he was back carrying a mug of water and a damp cloth. He set the mug down on the cabin floor and rummaged through her pack until he found the corked bottle of elixir which Kinsman Anthony of Holywell had prescribed for her migraines. He tipped a little of the medicine into the water, swirled it round and then offered it to her. With a faint groan Witchet lowered herself up on to one elbow, took the draught from him, swallowed it and lay back.

Tom removed the empty cup from her hand and wiped her forehead with the cool cloth. 'It could be that you've had too much sun,' he said. 'You were out in it almost all day.'

'Yes,' she agreed listlessly. 'I suppose so.'

'Would you like to change places? My bunk will be cooler than yours.'

'No, it's all right.'

'Shall I get you some more water?'

She did not answer and for a moment or two he supposed she must have fallen asleep, then she said: 'Tom?'

'I'm here, love.'

'Will you play me something?'

'Of course I will. What would you like to hear?'

' "Sea Witch".'

He stooped over her, touched her forehead with his lips then took out his pipes and played softly the song that he had composed after he had seen her emerging all silvery-wet from the moonlit sea on the beach at Perello. He followed it with a lullaby which was a legacy of their shared childhood. By the time the last note had faded on the air she was asleep.

Tom lay awake listening to her restless breathing and remembering the past and feeling his love for her like a sickness deep in his bowels. All his life he had accepted her worship of him as though it were his birthright, never questioning whether he deserved it or not. Now that she was carrying his child within her he felt ashamed of his male selfishness and for the first time for many a year found himself praying passionately to the White Bird to watch over her and keep her safe from harm. At that moment he could well have believed that they shared but a single heart between them.

By the morning Witchet's fever seemed to have burnt itself out but it had left her feeling tired and listless. She sat beside Tom on the cabin roof watching the two horses plodding away ahead of them down the tow-path. Glancing into her face he saw that her eyes were full of unshed tears. He reached up and stroked her hair. 'What is it?' he murmured. 'What's the matter?'

She shook her head and would not answer.

'Auguste says we'll be in Briare by mid-day tomorrow,' he said. 'He thinks we'll get a passage across the channel without any trouble. With luck we'll be in Alençon by tomorrow night.'

'I wish it was Tallon,' she sighed, and a single tear spilled over and trickled down her pale cheek.

Tom put his arm about her and held her tight against him. 'Tallon will be the very next stop,' he said. 'I promise you.'

'But what about Corlay?'

'Oh, Corlay can wait. We've got a lifetime ahead of us.'

'Do you really mean that?'

'Of course I do. I have a pressing desire to see Mother's face when we tell her she's going to be a granny.'

'Oh, Tom, I'm so glad. I can't tell you how glad I am.'

He laughed and kissed her. 'I'll let you be the one to break the news,' he said. 'How do you think Magpie will take it?'

He felt her suddenly go still in his arms. 'I dreamt about Dad last night,' she said and she shivered.

'Go on.'

'It was a sad dream,' she said. 'I don't really remember it.'

Tom guessed that she did but decided to let it go.

That night the fever returned and by noon the following day when they stepped ashore at Briare and bade farewell to the Argonnes, Witchet looked but a pale reflection of the girl who had boarded the *Saint Sebastien* at Roanne.

Celeste beckoned Tom aside. 'I am not happy about her, Thomas,' she confided. 'When you get to Alençon take her to the Kinsmen's Hospital and see what they say.'

'But that is just where we're going,' he said. 'We have a friend who is a doctor there.'

'That makes me feel much easier in my mind,' she said. 'I do not think it can be just the child makes her so. Away with you both and take my blessing with you.'

Despite Auguste's optimism they were unable to get a passage across to Normandy until ten o'clock the following day. By then it was clear to both of them that something was seriously wrong with Witchet. Tom had bought a blanket and she huddled up in it alternately shivering and sweating while the little packet boat butted its way across the narrow channel into the port of Mamers. As they were making their way down the gangplank to the quay Witchet's legs gave way beneath her and Tom had to carry her ashore in his arms.

He laid her down on a pile of sacks and was tugging loose the laces of her bodice when she came to and looked up into his face. 'I'm so sorry,' she whispered. 'Oh, Tom, I'm so sorry. I feel awful.'

A little knot of curious bystanders had gathered round. Tom asked them how far it was to the Kinsmen's Hospital.

'Ten kilometres, Monsieur.'

'Can I hire a cart here?'

'Georges Fresnay has a cart,' said a voice.

'And where do I find him?'

'Over by the fish market.'

The place was pointed out to him. He looked down at Witchet and his heart ached for her. 'Do you think you can make it, my love?'

She drew in a painful breath and nodded.

Tom put his arm about her and she rose unsteadily to her feet. 'Will someone keep an eye on our packs?' he said.

'I will bring them,' said a sailor. 'You are among Kinsfolk here, friend.'

They made their way slowly across the cobbled quay and eventually found the man who had the horse and cart for hire. Tom explained what it was wanted for. The owner looked doubtfully at Witchet. 'It is only a work cart,' he said, 'but you are welcome to it, Monsieur, if that is what you wish. For a crown it is yours until noon tomorrow. I will harness up the mare for you myself.'

Between them Tom and the sailor contrived to lift

Witchet into the cart. Tom tucked the blanket round her, arranged their packs to form a pillow, and stroked back the damp and lustreless strands of hair which had fallen across her face. 'It's not the carriage I'd have chosen,' he said with a worried smile, 'but it'll get us there and Dave'll soon have you put to rights.'

Witchet's lips quirked into a tremulous response and then, as though even this tiny effort had exhausted her, she closed her eyes.

The complex of stone buildings which constituted the Kinsmen's Hospital was clustered around the summit of a forest-clad hill. Once, long ago, it had been a seminary, then a military barracks, and finally a centre for healing. Evidence of each stage of the metamorphosis remained visible; the cloisters; the gravelled parade-ground; the dormitory wards and dispensaries; the hostels for the convalescent which were dotted about in quiet glades among the oaks and beeches.

Two hours after leaving the quayside at Mamers Tom drove his creaking cart under a wide arch whose keystone bore a spread-winged effigy of the White Bird and on across the gravelled courtyard to the main entrance. 'I'll be as quick as I can, my love,' he said. 'Will you be all right?'

He saw her head move in a faint nod of affirmation and he jumped to the ground and ran up the steps to the hospital.

A grey haired, blue-robed Kinswoman with the emblem of the Bird embroidered across her breast was seated at a desk in the hall making entries in a ledger. She glanced up as Tom approached and pointed with her pen to a row of wooden benches further down the hall where some half a dozen people were seated.

'I'm looking for Doctor Ronceval,' he said. 'Can you tell me where I can find him?'

She gazed at him and frowned. 'You have an appointment?'

'Please, madame. It is really urgent. My—my wife is out there. She is very sick.'

She peered in the direction of the door. 'She is outside now?'

'Yes. I've brought her up from Mamers. Please, madame, just tell me where I can find him.'

She turned in her chair and consulted a board on the wall behind her. 'Doctor Ronceval is on duty in the dispensary,' she said. 'Do you know where that is?'

'No.'

'Go out through this door, down the steps and turn to your right. The dispensary is the building at the far end in the corner of the courtyard.' Her last words were addressed to Tom's retreating back.

David Ronceval was supervising two apprentices who were distributing bundles of herbs among tiers of wooden drying racks when he heard someone call his name and swung round to see Tom framed in the doorway. For a moment he was too surprised to say anything then his face broke into a delighted grin. 'Tom! By all that's wonderful! Where on earth have you sprung from?'

'From the south. I've got Witchet with me. She's sick, Dave.'

'Witchet? Sick? Where is she?'

'Out in the courtyard. I brought her up from Mamers in a cart.'

'What's the matter with her?'

'I don't know. She's got some sort of fever, I think. You must come.'

'Of course I'll come.' David gave some rapid instructions to the two apprentices then seized Tom by the arm and hurried him back out into the courtyard. 'How long has she been sick?' he asked.

'About three days. To begin with we thought it was because she's starting a baby, but I'm sure it can't just be that.'

'Witch is with child? Really? By you?'

'Yes.'

'Congratulations, old friend! And how far has it gone?'

'She thinks about two months. *Could* it be that, David?'

'I suppose it's possible.'

As soon as they reached the van, David scrambled up and climbed inside. Tom followed close behind him. Witchet opened her eyes, saw who it was and smiled faintly. 'He found you then?' she murmured.

'Yes, he found me,' said David. 'What have you been up to, Witch?'

'I don't know.'

He took her wrist and felt her racing pulse, then with the tips of his fingers he began gently exploring the flesh at the angles of her jaw and along the sides of her throat. He coaxed down her lower eyelids and glanced at the inflamed tissue which had been exposed. Finally he examined her fingernails. Tom watched his friend's face intently and tried to read something from it but without any success at all.

David rose to his feet. 'The first thing is to get you into a proper bed, Witch,' he said. 'Then I'll ask Doctor Verelet to come and take a look at you. He's our expert on fevers. Come on, Tom, I'll need your help. We'll be back in a minute, Witch.'

He climbed down from the cart and walked a few paces away towards the steps to the main entrance. Tom hastened to his side. 'Well?' he said anxiously. 'Do you know what it is?'

'Where have you two been, Tom?'

'What?'

'Whereabouts in the south have you been?'

'Along the coast from Spain as far as Nice. Why?'

'Did you come in contact with any cases of plague?'

Tom felt as if he had been dropped into a glacial pool. His whole body seemed to turn to ice. His scalp cringed and the skin on his arms and legs erupted into shuddering gooseflesh.

'I guessed as much. How long ago was it?'

Still too appalled to speak Tom just stared at him.

'Would it have been about a week?'

Tom nodded.

'Do you know what it was?'

Tom's tongue seemed to have become completely paralysed. He opened his lips but no sound emerged.

David put his arm around his friend's shoulders and gripped him tight. 'I could be wrong, Tom. And even if I'm right she can pull through it. But you have to tell me everything you can. It'll save us time, and time is precious.'

It seemed to Tom at that moment as if he were once again leaning over wine-factor Ory and gazing down into those beseeching, death-haunted eyes. His own eyes were suddenly a-brim with tears. 'There was a man travelling in the same coach as us,' he muttered. 'One day he collapsed. When I opened up his shirt I saw red rings all over his chest. They said it was something called the Wreath of Araby.'

David gnawed his bottom lip. 'We daren't risk putting her into an open ward,' he said. 'She'll have to go to the isolation hostel. Come on, we'll drive the cart straight down there now and get her into bed. But whatever you do don't let her know what I suspect. I'm quite sure that wouldn't be any help to her at all.'

Still dazed with shock Tom climbed back into the cart. David took hold of the horse's bridle and led the way back across the courtyard, out under the stone arch, and down a winding path between the trees to a long, low building of grey stone. He vanished inside to reappear, almost immediately, accompanied by a burly bearded Kinsman who unfastened the tail flap of the cart, reached inside and scooped up Witchet into his arms as though she were a child.

Tom gathered up the packs together with Witchet's guitar and trailed dismally along in their wake down a long stone-flagged corridor into a sunny room at the far end of the building. Inside he found that two Kinswomen were already at work removing Witchet's dress. As they stripped the garment from her and then peeled off her underclothes Tom sought for the dread evidence of infection on her sweet, golden body. There were no signs at all. Within a matter of minutes she had been buttoned into a white linen nightgown and was lying stretched out in the plain little wooden bed with the covers drawn up to her chin. She turned her head and saw him gazing at her helplessly. 'Don't look so sad, my love,' she whispered. 'I feel better already.'

Tom forced himself to smile. 'I was just wishing we'd got that passage across yesterday. We've wasted a whole day.'

She drew an arm clear of the covers and held out her hand to him. For a moment he hesitated (the memory of that instant of instinctive cowardice was to haunt him for years) then, as her eyes flinched from the sting of his rejection he stepped forward, leant over her, and kissed her deliberately upon the lips.

Sustained by the medical skills of the Kinsmen Witchet contrived to hold her own against the disease. For two days and two nights there was no appreciable deterioration in her condition and Tom began to believe that she would recover. On the evening of the third day when she had dropped off to sleep he slipped out for a walk in the forest with David and asked him point blank for his honest opinion on her chances.

'Mine or Verelet's?' said David.

'You mean you don't agree?'

'He knows the disease better than I do, but I know Witch and I know you.'

'So what does he think?'

'He believes she'll come to the crisis sometime during the next thirty-six hours. It will be in three stages. During each stage her temperature will rise, then fall. The rash—the wreaths—will emerge during the second crisis.'

'And in the third?'

'Assuming she follows the usual pattern she'll go into a coma—*la crise suprême*. Verelet says it may last for an hour or two or even for a whole day. During it she'll have to be watched like a hawk to see she doesn't choke. When she comes out of it she'll be on the road to recovery. With the Bird's help we'll have her on her feet again in a week. In a fortnight you'll both be sailing over the sea to Tallon.'

'Is that really what he thinks?'

'He thinks she has an even chance, Tom.'

'No more than that?'

'No less, certainly.'

'Then how about you? What do you think?'

David looked into his friend's face, saw the shadows of strain and sleeplessness dusking the green eyes, and he felt a warm surge of affection welling up from the profoundest depths of his being. 'I'm sure she'll pull through, Tom,' he said.

In a long sigh Tom released the breath he was not even aware that he had been holding. 'And she'll keep the baby?'

'Well, it's hardly that yet, is it?'

'But will she lose it?'

'I really don't know, Tom. But even if she does it's not the end of the world, is it? You'll both have other children.'

'They won't be this one,' said Tom. 'This one is special.'

David smiled. 'You've *hueshed* it so, have you?'

'If only I had! I wouldn't be asking *you* if she'd pull through, would I?'

On their return to the hostel an hour later they met one of the attendant Kinswomen hurrying down the passage from Witchet's room. She was carrying a metal pan which she had covered with a cloth. As she passed them she murmured something to David and then rustled away in the direction of the surgery.

'What was that about?' asked Tom.

'She says Witch has had a flux.'

'What does that mean?'

'She's been losing some blood.'

'Blood!'

'There's no cause to panic, Tom. She's still all right.'

'What do you mean "all right"? How can she be if she's bleeding?'

'I mean *she's* all right.'

The import of the emphasis struck Tom like a blow on the throat. 'The baby,' he whispered. 'She's lost her baby. That's what's happened, isn't it?'

'I'm afraid she has,' said David sadly. 'I'm truly sorry, Tom. But it would have been a miracle if she'd managed to hang on to it. And who knows how her illness might have affected it? You go on in to her and let her see how much you love her. I'll go and find Verelet and tell him what's happened.'

A second Kinswoman was putting the finishing touches to Witchet's re-made bed. She glanced up as Tom entered and said with a sympathetic smile: 'Ah, she has been asking for you, m'sieur.'

Witchet lifted her head from the pillow. Her eyelids were red and swollen, her eyes dark as bruises in her pale, exhausted face. 'Oh, Tom,' she whispered, brokenly. 'Oh, *Tom . . .*' and the hot tears of misery welled up afresh, spilled over, and trickled down her wan cheeks.

At that moment Tom's love for her attained the intensity

of pure anguish. About her the room seemed to grow dark with shadows and her sad face became touched with a strange ethereal light which transformed it into a thing of wonder beyond his comprehension. His aching spirit reached out for her, enfolded her and cherished her. For a single breathless instant the air was all awash with the invisible presence of hovering wings. Then he was back again within his own mortal body, clasping her in his arms, and only vaguely aware that the Kinswoman had dropped to her knees beside the bed and was babbling some inconsequential nonsense about *'L'Oiseau Blanc'*.

A short while later David reappeared with Doctor Verelet who was carrying a wooden medicine chest. By then Witchet's pallor had given way to a hectic flush; her eyes were fever-bright and her breathing had become a rapid, shallow panting. The Doctor took a reading of her temperature and felt a pulse in her neck. 'There is no question,' he said. 'We have here the onset of the first crisis.' He took a small green bottle from his box, poured some drops of a yellow liquid into the glass of water which stood on the table beside the bed and said to Witchet: 'Come, drink this, my dear.'

David helped her up. She took the glass in both hands, closed her eyes and swallowed the draught in two gulps.

Doctor Verelet took the empty glass from her, measured out a second dose and placed it ready to hand on the table. 'You must see that she drinks this in one hour from now,' he told David. 'That will be sufficient for the first crisis.' He patted Witchet on the shoulder and glanced across at Tom. 'This will be a long night, Thomas,' he said, 'but I assure you we shall all greet the dawn.'

In the event both statements proved true. As the daylight faded from the room and the shaded lamp began to people the walls with shadows Tom sat at Witchet's side and they played the game of 'Do you remember?', reaching ever further and further backwards in time to their childhood on the western shores of the Somersea. When he recalled the coming of Marwys the Wanderer Witchet said: 'My otter. Give me my otter, Tom.'

'You mean you brought him?'

'Yes. He's in my pack. At the very bottom of the inside pocket.'

Tom got up and hunted through her belongings until he found the little wooden figure of an otter with a salmon gripped in its mouth which Marwys had given to her on the night before he had taken Tom away with him to Corlay. He put it into her hot, dry hand. 'I had no idea you'd brought him with you,' he said. 'You never told me.'

Witchet held up the little figure so that the lamplight glanced from the surface of the polished wood and a huge shadow otter lifted its head warily upon the whitewashed wall. 'Every time you went away to Corlay I used to climb with him up into the cherry tree. I left him there to watch over you till you'd got safe to Chardport. If anything had happened to you he'd have rescued you.'

'A guardian otter,' said Tom with a smile. 'He did his job well even though he's a bit on the small side.'

'Size has nothing to do with it,' said Witchet. 'He's a spirit otter.'

'Ah.'

'And he'll go on looking after you when I'm not here.'

Tom stared at her. 'What are you talking about? We'll be on our way home to Tallon within two weeks. Dave told me that today.'

Witchet was silent.

'And you heard what Doctor Verelet said.'

'Have they told you what's the matter with me?' she murmured with her eyes closed.

'They're still not sure. There are so many different fevers. Hundreds, Dave says.'

'Doctor Verelet knows what it is.'

'Has he told you?'

'No. But I know that he knows.'

'He knows you're going to get better. That's all that matters.'

Outside in the forest an owl hooted lugubriously and by and by another answered it. After a while Tom reached out, released the talisman from between her fingers and set it down quietly beside the empty glass on the bedside table. Then he slid her arm in beneath the covers and resumed his vigil.

Shortly before midnight Witchet successfully weathered the first crisis. Tom watched as the Kinswomen sponged her down and deftly replaced her soiled nightdress and the sweat-soaked bedding. While they were doing it David came in. 'You must go and get some sleep, Tom', he said, 'or I can see us with another invalid on our hands. I'll take over from you now. Use the bed next door if you'd rather.'

'You promise you'll call me if she needs me?'

'Of course I will.'

'And what about Verelet?'

'I've arranged to have him sent for if it's necessary. But I'm sure it won't be. She'll come through the next one on her own. We know she will.'

'And the third?'

'That too, old friend. Trust me.'

It seemed to Tom that his head had scarcely touched the pillow before David's hand was on his shoulder shaking him back to consciousness. He jerked upright and was astonished to see bright sunshine streaming in through the open window. 'What's happened?' he gasped. 'Is she all right?'

'Yes,' said David. 'She's awake and they're tidying her up. Verelet's in with her now.'

'How was it?'

'Just as we'd expected. Her temperature peaked again at

about five o'clock and then the rash broke. Come on, let's go and get something to eat.'

'I'll just go in and say hello to her first.'

'Give her another ten minutes, Tom.'

'Why do you say that?'

David spread his hands. 'Only that during these major crises the patient tends to lose control—bowels, bladder and so forth—you know what I mean. We had to clean her up three times during the night. What with that and the rash she doesn't look at her best just now. I'm pretty certain she'd rather you didn't go in till she was a bit more presentable.'

Tom gazed meditatively at his friend and then slowly shook his head. 'You're wrong, Dave,' he said. 'Witch and I aren't much good at pretending with one another. I'm pretty sure she's guessed what's the matter with her and the sooner she knows that I know too, the better for both of us. Blood, shit, and spots. If you ask me I'd say this is the moment when she needs me to tell her I love her.'

'Perhaps you're right,' said David. 'I just didn't want you to get too much of a shock. I remember how you used to say you couldn't bear the sight of sick people.'

'I've grown up a lot since then,' said Tom, shrugging on his jacket. 'On your way, Kinsman. I'll join you in the kitchen in five minutes.'

But for all that the sight which greeted Tom when he edged open the door to Witchet's room well nigh stopped his heart in mid-beat. The girl he loved was lying face downwards on the mattress as naked and red as a freshly skinned rabbit. Her legs were splayed wide, two linen-masked Kinswomen held her gripped fast by the ankles and Doctor Verelet was bending over her administering an enema with a large metal syringe. As Tom closed the door behind him, Verelet eased the nozzle clear. One of the Kinswomen heaved Witchet up by the hips and the other slid a metal pan beneath her. Witchet uttered a sort of whimpering groan and then, as Verelet coaxed her back-wards into a crouching position, a torrent of foul air and fouler liquid poured out of her into the pan.

Overwhelmed by a terrible impotent pity, Tom ran forward and put his arms about her quivering shoulders.

Her head drooped like a broken flower. 'Go 'way,' she muttered. 'Go 'way, Tom,' and then she was racked by another noisome spasm which made his own gorge heave in futile sympathy.

In a few minutes it was all over. Swabbed clean with spirit and buttoned into a fresh white gown Witchet lay back against the pillows and even managed a faint smile. 'Poor love,' she whispered, 'I'm sorry you had to see me like that.'

'How do you feel now?' he asked.

'Drifty mostly.'

'What does that mean?'

'Like a boat without a rudder. I can't seem to think straight.'

'Could you ever?'

'Where's Dave?'

'Having his breakfast.'

'Have you had yours?'

'No, not yet.'

She placed her hand on his arm and gave him a feeble push. 'Go and have it,' she said. 'Then come back and talk to me.'

'I love you, Witch,' he said. 'I love you more than anyone in the whole world.'

'I know you do,' she murmured. 'Now go and have your breakfast.'

He stooped, kissed her on the top of her head, and went off to find David.

Shortly before noon Witchet's temperature began to climb once more. For a while she fretted about restlessly, seeming unable to make herself comfortable, and complained that her head was hurting. Then, without warning, she began to hallucinate. Convinced that her mother and father were standing at the foot of her bed, she sat up, stretched out her arms towards them and talked to them quite lucidly for several minutes. Then she sank back on the pillows and wept so bitterly that Tom's torn heart was racked anew. He sponged her burning, sweat-blistered face with a cool cloth and found that his own eyes were blurred with tears. 'I'm here, Witch. I'm here. I'm here,' he murmured.

But this time she would not be consoled and he was suddenly assailed by her own melancholy fancy of a little rudderless boat drifting out on to the dark waters, turning slowly this way and that at the behest of unknown currents, but always slipping further and further away from the shelter of the shore into the gathering dusk. So poignant was the vision that he gathered her up in his arms and held her tight against his breast while the tears ran down his cheeks unregarded.

David came over to him, touched him gently on the shoulder and removed Witchet's pillows. 'Lay her down now, Tom,' he said, 'and turn her head to one side.'

Tom saw that Witchet's eyes had closed and he suddenly realized that she had gone limp in his arms. He laid her down and shuddered. 'She's not . . . ?'

'She's gone into coma,' said David. 'I told you this would happen.' He indicated a steadily throbbing pulse in Witchet's throat. 'She's all right, Tom. Really she is.'

Tom stared at the quiet face which was still glistening wet from her own sweat and his tears. 'Wherever you go, my love, I'll go there too,' he muttered. 'I promise you'll not be left to drift on your own.' He stooped and touched the softly fluttering pulse with his lips then sketched the Sign of the Bird across his heart.

Early in the afternoon Doctor Verelet carried out another

examination and instructed David to sponge Witchet from head to foot with alcohol to bring down her temperature. While this was being done Tom noticed that the appearance of the rash had altered—the rings were no longer clearly defined but had spread and merged to form a series of irregular blobs and patches. He asked whether this was a good sign.

'We believe so, yes,' said Verelet, 'but it is impossible to say for certain. No two cases are ever exactly alike. There are so many variable factors. Nevertheless, in this particular instance I am inclined to accept it as a hopeful indication.'

'So how long will it be before she wakes up?'

Verelet shook his head. 'It could be in one hour: it could be in twelve or more. There is no sure way of telling.'

'But she *will* wake up?'

'Of course she will,' said David.

Tom glanced across at Doctor Verelet. 'Do you agree, Doctor?'

'She is young. Her heart is strong. I believe she has an excellent chance of making a complete recovery.'

But as the day slowly wore on and Witchet showed no sign of emerging from her coma Tom became increasingly anxious. He began pacing restlessly back and forth across the room until the Kinswoman who was watching at the bedside begged him to stop because he was preventing her from hearing the patient's breathing. Finally David succeeded in persuading him to come and drink a glass of wine with him in the kitchen.

They set off down the corridor and had just turned into the passage which led to the domestic quarters when Tom suddenly stopped dead in his tracks. David glanced round and saw that his friend's face had gone as grey as ash. Before he could ask what was the matter Tom spun round and fled back the way they had come. David set off after him and had just gained the corridor when he saw the distant door of Witchet's room open and heard the Kinswoman calling: 'Doctor Ronceval! Doctor Ronceval! Come quickly!'

David ran as though his heels had grown wings and reached the doorway almost at Tom's shoulder. 'What's happened?' he gasped.

The Kinswoman's eyes were wide with fright. 'She does not breathe.'

'Go and fetch Doctor Verelet!' he cried, thrusting his way past her. 'Hurry!'

He dragged aside the covers, laid his ear against Witchet's chest and tried to detect the beat of her heart above the pounding of his own. Then he began a rhythmic pressing with both hands upon the ribs below her left breast.

Tom watched him with a kind of desperate helplessness, glancing back and forth from his friend's tense, abstracted face to the tell-tale pulse point on Witchet's throat. The yearning cry which had snatched him back to her side was already no more than a fading memory, the faintest echo of an echo, and yet there she was, lying before him, her lips just parted, a tiny silvery trace of spittle at the corner of her mouth, her cheeks still faintly flushed. He shut his eyes and cried her name soundlessly through the empty caverns of his mind, pleading *'Witch . . . Witch . . . Witch'* with such an intensity of desolation that he knew she could not fail to hear him, knew that her soul must come winging back like a dove to its nest. But when he opened his eyes he saw that he had deceived himself. No longer was it possible that the girl he loved would return alone and unaided. There was only one road left to him.

The Kinswoman hurried in with Doctor Verelet. In a matter of minutes the doctor had confirmed what David already knew. 'I am most deeply grieved, Thomas,' he said sorrowfully. 'She was the sweetest of maids and truly brave. The Bird will rejoice over her.'

Tom stared at him. 'But the Bird has not got her yet.'

'Alas, my poor Thomas. She is dead.'

Tom shook his head stubbornly. 'Not so, Doctor.'

Uncertain how best to respond Doctor Verelet glanced down at Witchet's naked body. In so doing he perceived that the rash had faded and was now scarcely visible at all. 'This I have never seen before,' he murmured. 'It is most curious.'

White faced, David walked over to Tom, put his arm around him and suddenly burst into tears.

Tom patted his friend's shoulder. 'It's all right, Dave,' he said. 'You did everything you possibly could. Now you must leave me alone with her for an hour.'

David shook his head. 'I can't do that, Tom. I can't.'

'But you *must,* Dave. If you don't I'll lose her.'

Dave turned helplessly to Doctor Verelet as if to say, 'What can I do?'

'Please, Doctor,' said Tom. 'Every minute is precious now.'

Doctor Verelet shrugged. 'Very well, Thomas. You shall have your hour. Come, David.'

David gripped Tom by both arms. 'But you don't *understand,* Tom,' he whispered passionately. 'It's not like it was in Tallon. By now her brain . . . *Please,* Tom. Don't do it.'

Tom shook his head. 'I've tried going your way, Dave,' he murmured. 'Now I must go my own. Nothing you could say would stop me. I mean that.'

'Then I'll sit outside the door till the hour's up.'

'Whatever you wish.'

Doctor Verelet and the Kinswoman let themselves out into the passage. Tom walked to the door with David. They kissed each other and then with a last despairing shake of his head David went out and closed the door behind him.

Tom turned back to the bed and looked down at the still form upon it. Then he drew his hands in a long and tender caress all the way down her body from her shoulders to her toes. 'Stay for me, my love,' he whispered and he reached into his jacket for his pipes.

He was running down the grassy track that skirted the line of the shore before swinging inland among the marshes at the mouth of the creek. He knew the path well, but the sickly pre-dawn light had given it an unfamiliar appearance which twice cause him to stop and gaze about seeking for some remembered point of reassurance. And ever and again he scanned the surface of the dark waters which stretched away beyond the misty creek and beyond the dim and far-off headland till they merged with the leaden sky and were lost to his view.

When he reached the place where the track turned he halted and called her name aloud, peering this way and that in an effort to discern what lay beneath the quilting of va-pour which was spread like a milky shroud across the face of the creek.

As though in answer to his summons a faint breeze sprang up. It wafted aside the mist-smoke and, scarcely a dozen paces from where he was standing, he beheld the nebulous outlines of a little boat. It had come to rest on the margin of a reed bed and was rocking up and down on the slow, dark ripples.

He sat down on the wet turf, dragged off his boots, and waded out. Before his hand had even touched the boat he knew it for hers, for it was thus he had seen it in his mind's eye and he sensed her soul's presence still lingering upon it like the faint and inimitable perfume of wild flowers. He took hold of it, towed it back through the shallows and dragged it up on the shore. Then he sat down with his back resting against the hull and began pulling on his boots over his cold, wet legs.

Beside him the breeze whispered through the sedge and the dry stems rapped gently one against another like sticks tapping upon stones. He turned his head.

An old man, cowled and caped in leather, was striding towards him along the path which wound beside the creek. The mist was lapping about his waist, and in his right hand he carried a long wooden staff with which he was testing the surface of the barely visible track. When he reached the point where the path altered course he paused, glanced across at the little boat, then strode over to it and prodded it with his stick. 'A well made craft,' he observed. 'Is it yours, Thomas?'

'You know well enough whose it is, old man. So why do you ask?'

'Ah. She has come then? I had not thought it would be so soon.'

'So why are you here?'

'I felt your need, Thomas. Nothing more.'

'Then tell me where I shall find her.'

Again the old man tapped the boat with his stick. 'And when you do? What then?'

'I shall take her back with me, of course.'

'In this?'

'Yes. If there is no other way.'

'For those who have the courage to seek them there are always other ways, Star Born.'

'You question my courage, Morfedd?'

'No. But is your soul truly set upon it?'

'I have taken my vow, old man. It is for that I am here.'

The old man gave the boat a last rap with the butt of his staff and nodded. 'So. It shall be as you wish. You have the pipes?'

'Next to my heart.'

'Give them to me.'

Tom dipped his hand into his breast, drew out the pipes and handed them to the old man. He set them to his lips, played a few notes and then frowned. 'What have you done with these?' His voice was cold, accusing.

'Done with them? Why, nothing.'

Without warning the old man suddenly raised his staff and brought it down so hard across Tom's back that he all but knocked him to the ground. 'Fool!' he shouted. 'Dolt! You have locked a ball and chain about your own leg!' And he drew back the stick again preparatory to taking another furious swipe which Tom prudently avoided by skipping backwards out of range.

'What are you talking about?' he protested, rubbing at his bruised arm. 'I swear I've done nothing.'

'Then who are these?' shouted the old man, waving his staff towards the path at Tom's back.

Still contriving to keep a wary eye on the raised stick Tom glanced over his shoulder and saw two figures hurrying down the track towards them. The light was poor and they were still some way off, but even so something about them was all too dauntingly familiar. He looked back at Morfedd and suddenly he knew what the old man meant. 'I think they are the two I killed,' he said. 'The ones who raped Witch.'

'Killed? How killed?'

'I hanged them.'

For a moment the old man seemed taken aback. He stared at his protégé. 'Hanged them?' he repeated. 'In that world or in this?'

'In both, I think.'

Something which might almost have qualified as reluctant admiration gleamed like a bright spark in the old man's eyes. He nodded. 'So that was how you chose to break your most sacred vow.'

'I did what I had to do, Morfedd.'

'Maybe. Maybe. But it is like to cost you dear, Star Born. You will not be quit of them so easily this time.'

'What do you mean?'

'Wherever you go in this world there must they go too. They will never leave you. Like it or not you have taken upon yourself the responsibility for their ultimate salvation.'

Tom gazed at the old man as the full implication of his words slowly dawned. 'Can they harm me?' he said at last.

'Not directly. But be warned, Star Born. Though you hold their destiny in your hands, their needs will not be your needs.'

Tom turned just as the two bandits came hurrying down the track towards him. 'Well-met, young master! Oh, well-met indeed!' panted Scar-brow. 'And a very good day to you, most reverend sage. This is truly a most fortunate meeting.'

'Your humble servant, sir,' said Montfort, bowing from the waist towards Tom. 'We have come with all possible speed. I trust we have not delayed you unduly.'

Wholly at a loss for words, Tom stared at them. There was no evidence at all that he could see of the havoc he had wrought upon them and yet he could not bring himself to do more than acknowledge them with a tiny, frigid nod of his head. But it was enough. Scar-brow flung himself down on the wet turf, clutched Tom's knees and blubbered: 'He does not reject us! Oh, bless you, young master! Such kindness! Such magnanimity! On your knees, Nikko! Down in the dirt before our young lord and master!'

Montfort gave an embarrassed cough and murmured: 'Pray forgive him, my lord. He is a trifle overwrought. But I can vouch for his loyalty.'

Morfedd stepped forward, swung his staff and whacked Scar-brow across the buttocks. 'That's enough of that,' he said. 'Back on your feet, you dog!'

Scar-brow released Tom instantly and scrambled back to Montfort's side where he stood bobbing his round head up and down and grinning inanely.

The whole bizarre episode had so totally unnerved Tom that he had all but forgotten what had brought him to this place. Now he glanced down, caught sight of Witchet's

little boat and was appalled. 'Where is she?' he demanded
of Morfedd.

'Far from here. By now she will have entered the Valley.'

'But that's not possible! It's a full day's journey!'

'You are too spendthrift of your time, Thomas. What is
but a minute to you may well be an hour to her. And you
have wasted many precious minutes.'

'Give me those pipes, Morfedd.'

'They have lost their virtue.'

'So you say. But there are some things which even you
do not know. Who was it told me to seek for my own
truth?'

'He did not tell you where it is to be found.'

'I know where to find it. The pipes, Morfedd.'

When the old man made no attempt to prevent him, Tom
reached out and took the pipes. No sooner had he grasped
them than he knew what he must do. In this world of shadows one thing alone had substance, the rest was dreams.
He closed his eyes, and as if he had been lowering a bucket
into a deep well, drew up from far down within himself
one solitary pellucid image of the lost reality. Breathing his
own spirit into it he transformed it into music.

Storms raged; great black wings beat up against the
darkness; a thousand nameless creatures of the night howled
and bayed about him; but adrift on his little raft of faith
Tom knew nothing of it, would not let it be. And so the
seas grew calm, the dark wings fluttered into silence and
the night beasts slunk away back into their lairs. He lowered the pipes, opened his eyes once more, and found that
he was standing not in the rocky valley which he had been
half expecting but on the quayside at Tallon.

Bright sunshine was flickering off the lapping water,
gilding the hulls of the moored boats with a shifting mosaic
of light and shade. Silver-white sea birds circled shrieking
overhead and the voice which above all others he longed

to hear was calling *Tom! Tom! Tom!* He turned his head and saw her running towards him along the quay, her fluttering hair gleaming golden in the sunlight, her arms reaching out to enfold him. For an eternal moment he held her there, trapped in the enchanted web of his song, and then the spell broke. Shadows like tongues of black flame began to lick at the tissue of the vision. Soon the only remnant left was that which held her own face seeking for his and then that too was gone.

'I swear I know that one, Nikko. I've always had a good memory for a face. D'you remember that time we sheltered in a barn up above Pareuse? She was there.'

'I don't recall it.'

'Sure you do. Those dumb actors.'

'Actors? What actors?'

'That bunch of macaronis, Nikko. The day we took the Draguinan coach. You remember.'

'What are you talking about? What coach?'

'When Gorjo bought it.'

'Did you say "Gorjo"? I knew a Gorjo once. We fought at Mulhouse together. He was in Combray's troop. He saved my neck at Drax. What did you say happened to him?'

'Oh, forget it.'

'No, no. Tell me. I'm really interested.'

'Tell you what?'

'What happened to Gorjo.'

'Gorjo? Who the hell's Gorjo?'

'Might have been before your time. We joined up together. Gorjo was the best hand with a talon I ever saw. He could split the mark two times out of three at fifty paces. He used to win money at it . . .'

The voices faded, became jumbled and inconsequential, until they were nothing more than a swirl of fragmented whispers lacking all pattern, all cohesion.

'Morfedd?'

Faint as a breath the old man's voice was at his ear: 'I am listening, Star Born.'

'Where is she, Morfedd?'

'Not in the past then?'

'Didn't you see what happened? It all broke apart. I couldn't hold her.'

'That was their doing. I warned you, Thomas. Their needs are not your needs.'

'Then how do I find her, Morfedd?'

'You must use them. They are all you have left.'

'Do they know where she is?'

'Perhaps. Perhaps not.'

'But I *will* find her?'

'If she can be found then surely you will find her.'

'Why do you say "if"?'

'Life and death are but a part of the eternal process of becoming, Thomas. The dead leaf shields the new leaf's bud. You do not need me to tell you that. Seek, Star Born. All is waiting to be won . . .'

Before him lay the high road. Bone white, straight as a taut string it stretched out across the noon-day plain to the castle gate. In the blue sky above a single cloud blossomed. Far beyond were the distant, snow-streaked mountain peaks. 'All that's missing is the lizard,' he muttered.

'What's that, my lord?'

He spun round to find Montfort and Scar-brow hovering solicitously at his shoulder. 'Is *she* in there?' he demanded.

'My lord?'

'Witch. Is she in there?'

'And who is Witch, my lord?'

'The girl who was on the quay.'

Montfort's expression was a grotesque parody of mingled commiseration and incomprehension. 'Who knows, my lord? Shall we ask this fellow?' He put two fingers to his lips and blew a piercing whistle blast. The air above the road appeared to tremble. As it grew still again Tom saw that someone was limping painfully towards them.

'Shall we put him to the question for you, young master?' asked Scar-brow eagerly.

Tom shaded his eyes and surveyed the approaching figure. He saw the man's cheeks and forehead had been clawed with thorns, his leather jerkin ripped and tattered in a dozen places, and he knew who it was. He stepped forward. 'Stay, soldier. Do you remember me?'

The man blinked and shook his head.

'We came face to face once on the road to Draguinan.'

'If you say so, sir.'

'Do you remember the girl in the actors' cart? The girl with fair hair?'

The man rubbed his forehead with a lacerated hand. 'What about her?'

'Have you seen her? Has she passed this way?'

The man screwed up his eyes. 'You wouldn't by any chance be a piper and have "Tom" for given name?'

'Yes, I'm Tom. What of it?'

'It tallies. The lass was asking after you, see? Said if I was to see Tom the Piper I was to tell him she couldn't wait much longer.'

'When was this?'

'Last week some time. Tuesday or Wednesday as I recall.'

'*Last week!* Did she say where she was going?'

The man shook his head. 'Seemed like as if she thought you'd know,' he said. 'Tell him I can't stay for him much longer, that's what she said.'

Tom's eyes darkened with a sort of numb despair.

'Ask him if she had anyone with her, my lord,' prompted Scar-brow.

'Aye, there was one other with her,' said the man. 'A priest or somesuch. An old man. He carried a wooden staff.'

Tom gaped. 'Was he bearded? Did he wear a cape and hood?'

'Aye, that's the one.'

'And he was *with her?*'

'They travelled the road together.'

Tom stared at him incredulously. 'You wouldn't be lying to me?'

'Not I, sir. I reckon as I owed you a truth.' With that he lifted his hand to his brow in a token salute and limped away to melt once more into the shimmering air out of which he had come.

Tom turned to Montfort. 'What game do you think you're playing with me?'

'Game, my lord? We do but serve you in fealty. We are oath-bound.'

'It is our pleasure, too, my lord,' said Scar-brow, bowing low.

'You know who I am?'

'You are our liege-lord, master.'

'Who has ordained it so?'

The two men looked at one another and then at Tom, but said nothing.

'Answer me?'

Scar-brow suddenly sprawled himself face down in the roadway and began embracing and kissing Tom's boots. 'It was all Nikko's fault, master,' he blubbered. 'He said you must not have the wench or we'd lose you.'

'He lies,' said Montfort disgustedly. 'He always lies, my lord,' and he kicked his grovelling companion in the ribs.

'It's true! It's true!' howled Scar-brow. 'He pushed her boat out so's you shouldn't find it. I tried to stop him, my lord. Truly I did.'

Tom bent down and dragged him up on to his knees. 'So where is she?' he demanded grimly. 'Tell me now or I swear by the Holy Bird that you'll both hang for a second time.'

Scar-brow scuttled backwards like a crab, his eyes darting all ways at once. 'Tell him, Nikko,' he wailed. 'He means it, man! He means it!'

Montfort's face had turned as grey as the dust beneath his feet. 'The wizard has her,' he muttered. 'Him you call Morfedd.'

'That cannot be,' Tom whispered and reached for his pipes.

With a squeal of terror Scar-brow flung himself back at Tom's feet. 'No, no, my lord!' he wailed. 'Nikko speaks true! The wizard summoned up the wench!'

Tom gazed from one to the other. 'Summoned her?' he repeated dully. 'How summoned her?'

Scar-brow scrambled up. 'He stood on the shore and commanded her to come to him,' he panted breathlessly. 'We hid in the reeds and watched him do it, didn't we, Nikko? Her boat came sailing in out of the mist.'

'That's the way it was,' said Montfort. 'Then the two of them set off together.'

'Set off? Where?'

'Inland.'

'And you both swear that it was Morfedd?'

'There aren't two like him, are there?' said Montfort. 'He was the one all right.'

Tom recalled the old man's sudden fury on learning of the presence of these two. Did he suspect that they had seen him summoning Witch? Tom had no means of knowing, but his perspective of the old man had shifted dramatically. At one stroke the benign counsellor had been transformed into the mage who manipulated others for his own inscrutable purposes. And, if others, why not these two rogues as well? 'You say you serve me,' he said to Montfort, 'but to what end? What would you have of me?'

A glance flickered between them like a darting swallow. 'We seek only your love, my lord.'

The idea was so grotesque, so utterly inconceivable that,

in spite of himself, Tom laughed out aloud. Whereupon Scar-brow, grinning like a lunatic, began to caper about clapping his hands, winking, and nudging his companion with his elbows until even the dour Montfort was seduced into a lop-sided grin. The impromptu performance concluded with an inept attempt at a handstand which left Scar-brow spreadeagled in the dust, giggling and hiccupping helplessly.

Tom gazed down at him, shook his head in utter incomprehension, and then set off along the road towards the castle.

He had covered no more than fifty paces before he heard them scampering after him. 'My lord! My lord! Wait for us! We can help you, my lord!'

Tom slowed his pace. As they came up with him he said: 'If this is some trick to delay me, you'll pay dearly for it, I promise you.'

Scar-brow licked his dusty lips and grinned nervously. 'We think we know where he was taking her, my lord.'

'Go on.'

'But an hour's journey from here there is a place they call the Eye-Stone.'

The shadow of a cloud, shaped like a wingless dragon, slithered up the outer wall of the castle and then drifted off towards the distant mountains. Tom felt the world lurch drunkenly around him and then rock back into watchful stillness. 'I know the place,' he said.

'We have seen the wizard by the Stone many times,' said Montfort. 'And we know the maid was with him.'

'And if she's not there I'll have wasted another hour.'

'We are doing our best to help, my lord.'

'So you say,' said Tom.

'Do you but follow us,' said Scar-brow, 'and have a care where you're setting your feet.'

With Montfort leading the way they struck off at a rapid pace along a small side road and were soon scrambling

114

down a steep track into a wooded gully. At the bottom flowed a shallow stream which they crossed by means of stepping stones. As they were making their way along the narrow track on the other side the light began to thicken perceptibly. A mist like a dense, cold sea-fret came rolling in across the reed beds which had begun to take over from the dripping, moss-mantled trees and the dank undergrowth. Within minutes Tom had altogether lost sight of Montfort, and Scar-brow had become an insubstantial shadow bobbing ahead of him in the gloom. In an effort to close the gap he quickened his pace, and next moment caught his foot in a snare of bramble and pitched headlong into a clump of briers.

By the time he had freed himself there was no sign of the others anywhere. He called out to them but the mist clogged his throat and his voice emerged as scarcely more than a husky whisper. He sucked at his scratched hands and set off along the barely discernible trail wondering how long it would be before they turned back to look for him or whether he was the victim of some plan they had devised to delay him even further.

The mist ebbed and flowed around him, coiling itself into strange and fanciful shapes, while a spectral sun, no brighter than a harvest moon, drifted in and out among the billowing vapours overhead. Once or twice he thought he heard water-birds splashing nearby and, once, a sound like wet sails flapping, but when he stood still and listened there was nothing. Next moment, in its arbitrary way, the curtain of fog shifted and thinned. Scarcely twenty paces from where he stood he beheld, rising up out of the marshy ground, a wooden framework composed of two tall posts with a third spanning them across the top. Dangling from this beam were two noosed corpses.

As though he had been nailed to the spot Tom stood and gaped up at them. Suddenly one of them began to move. An arm jerked stiffly outwards until it was pointing directly at him. The legs began to twitch. Then the other arm. A moment later all its limbs were jerking wildly up and down as if in a parody of that same mad caper Scar-brow had launched himself into on the road. In its gyrations it bumped against the second corpse which twisted slowly around until it seemed to be regarding the performance with the identical lop-sided grin that Montfort had favoured. Just when the point seemed to have been reached where the original performer had dived into a handstand, the mist rolled back and brought the *danse macabre* to a timely end.

A vision of what was about to come crawling after him out of the marsh effectively unlocked Tom's limbs. With his heart bursting he fled along the track, slipping and sliding on the wet stones, clutched at by brier-claws, splashing through puddles, until suddenly he was clear of the fog and collapsed, shivering and gasping, on the lower slope of the hill where once he had stood with Maria. As he fought to recover his breath he heard voices hailing him and scrambled to his feet to see Montfort and Scar-brow emerging from the mist behind him.

'Well met, my lord! We have been looking for you everywhere.'

Tom backed off shuddering. 'Go away,' he muttered. 'Let me alone.'

'But that's not possible,' said Montfort advancing upon him. 'You are our liege lord.'

'So I release you from your fealty,' Tom panted. 'You are free. Go.'

'He still does not love us, Nikko,' said Scar-brow dolefully. 'What can we have done wrong?'

Tom shivered violently. 'Why did you take me there?'

'It was the shortest way to the Stone,' said Montfort. 'That's what you wanted, wasn't it?'

'Nikko's right, my lord,' said Scar-brow. 'We've saved you hours and hours.'

'You knew what I'd find there, didn't you?'

116

The two men glanced slyly at one another and Scar-brow suddenly stuck his tongue out of the corner of his mouth, laid his head on his left shoulder, gave a puppet-like jerk of his arms and exploded with laughter. 'A joke, my lord,' he spluttered. 'Just a little joke.'

'You make me sick,' said Tom.

'That's *good*, my lord,' cried Scar-brow. '*Very* good. You have to *feel*, see? First a bit of a laugh; now a bit of a puke. We're really getting somewhere, aren't we, Nikko?'

Montfort shrugged. "He's got a long way to go yet.'

'But he's made a start, hasn't he? A fair start?'

'I don't know what you're talking about,' said Tom.

"Ah, but you *do*, my lord,' said Scar-brow. 'Otherwise none of us would *be* here, would we? You see, my lord, the fact of the matter is you need us as much as we need you. You tell him, Nikko.'

Montfort eyed Tom dubiously. 'To be free is to know yourself.'

'That's it, my lord!' cried Scar-brow. 'I couldn't have put it half so well. Through knowing *us*, you'll know *you*. Get it?'

Tom looked from one to the other. 'I killed you,' he said, slowly and deliberately. 'I killed you both. Do you know that?'

'But of *course* we do, my lord,' said Scar-brow, grinning broadly. 'And a very neat little job you made of it too, if I may say so. Isn't that right, Nikko?'

'Highly commendable,' Montfort conceded.

'And do you know *why* I did it?'

'With respect, my lord,' said Montfort, 'the only question which concerns us here and now is—do you?'

Tom stared at him. 'I did it for Witch,' he said.

'Is that so?' said Scar-brow. 'This wench you're looking for? Well, that really does surprise me. She never struck me as that sort. Just shows you how wrong you can be, doesn't it? Mind you, I suppose it's possible you might have made a mistake, my lord. In the heat of the moment and all that. It wouldn't have been too difficult, would it?'

'There was no mistake.'

'Well, it's not strictly my business, my lord, I'll grant you that. But if, like you say, she really *was* responsible I think we'd have heard about it by now. Seeing as she's over on this side, I mean. Right, Nikko?'

'I told you he'd got a long way to go,' said Montfort.

'So the sooner you find her and get things sorted out, the better for all of us,' said Scar-brow sententiously. 'Do you know your way from here?'

Tom nodded.

'Then hadn't you better be making a move, my lord? If you want to get there by daylight, I mean. I can't say as I'd fancy being out on that hill alone after dark.'

Tom glanced up at the sky and saw to his profound dismay that the sun was already well down on the horizon. 'An hour!' he cried. 'You told me it would only take an hour!'

'True enough, my lord. But then we didn't reckon on you losing your way. It's not fair to blame us for that.'

Tom choked back the retort which rose to his lips, turned his back upon them and set off along the stony winding track towards the summit, certain that he would soon hear their footsteps padding after him. But when he glanced round he saw they were still standing where he had left them. Scar-brow waved his hand and called: 'Good hunting, my lord!' then both men touched their foreheads in ironic salute, turned and vanished into the mist.

The air became cooler as he trudged upwards. A breeze awoke and began to stir among the withered grasses. As it licked a cool tongue across his perspiring brow he paused for breath and looked back. He saw the sun like a golden claw clinging to the rim of the world and the mysterious sea-fret sketched out like a coppery fleece all along the coast. Inland the shadows had already mustered. Of the castle and the distant mountains there was no sign at all.

As his gaze moved round from point to point he conceived the singular notion that this whole strange world existed only through him, that he and he alone was its reason for being and that no one, no single thing which did not constitute some part of his own life's experience could ever enter it. Yet it was *real*. The ground beneath his feet was real; the cool air which filled his lungs was real; and the briers whose jealous thorns had ripped his flesh were things of savage substance.

His apprehension clutched, and lost its hold, and clutched again. *Know yourself. Be free.* A whisper down the dim star-dusted tideways of his past. Old Morfedd's words. But who was Morfedd? Was he just some part of *him*, some dream, some hungry need that had called the old man into being? If so, then who had summoned Witch? Who was it that had stood upon this shadowy shore and drawn her drifting spirit in? The questions rippled out across the void of thought and were not answered. As the last gleam of the sinking sun splashed his long-limbed shadow out across the hillside, he turned once more and broke into a stumbling run.

Witchet was not waiting for him by the stone and there was no sign of Morfedd. Even the stone itself was not as he remembered it. Where he recalled at least a score of holes he now saw that there were only two, and that what he had once taken for grey granite was, in fact, a dull, yellowish sandstone. Yet the similarity to some gigantic skull was, if anything, even more remarkable. The two empty sockets gazing sightlessly out to sea were dark with mystery. As he drew closer the conviction grew in him that Witchet *had* been there; that Montfort and Scar-brow had not lied. He sensed the frail ghost of her presence as earlier he had sensed it lying upon the boat. It was as though the vacant air still retained the impress of her spirit as the wild

grass holds for a time the shape of the wild bird which has
lain among it.

Then he heard the wind whisper in the empty sockets: *Tell
him I can't stay for him much longer . . . tell him . . . tell
him* and he was overcome by such a poignant longing for her
that it was like a deathly sickness. He clambered on to the
top of the rock and standing there alone in the twilight he
cupped his hands to his mouth and began to bawl her name
at the top of his voice, howling *'Witch! . . . Witch! . . .
Witch!* like a dog howling at the moon until he had no breath
left in his body. Then he waited for the answering call, willing it to come winging back to him out of the gathering
shadows. But there was no response. As the realization that
he had finally lost her slowly settled upon his heart like a
cold grey dust of desolation he sank to his knees and wept
more bitterly than ever he had wept in his life before. The
tears dripped warm on to the stone like drops of blood dripping from some deep and mortal wound.

'I warned you the road would be a hard one, Star Born.'

His eyes half-blinded with grief, Tom raised his bowed
head, saw Morfedd standing there on the rock beside him
and was too choked with misery to speak.

The old man gazed down at him and shook his head.
'You are like a child, Thomas. You grieve for shadows.'

'Where is she, Morfedd?'

'Patience. Patience. The time is not yet ripe.'

'Did *you* bring her here?'

'The Bird brought her, Thomas.'

'You did not summon her?'

'She came. She is here. Where would you have her be?'

'So let me see her.'

'Have I not said you shall? Come now, stop these foolish
tears. We have urgent work to do.'

The old man sprang nimbly down and set off at a great
pace across the hillside. Still shuddering in the aftermath
of his grief Tom hurried in pursuit.

The tall, cloaked figure fluttered on ahead of him like some great dark moth hovering just at limit of his vision. The slope of the hill grew rapidly steeper and then, without warning, dropped away into a sheer cliff. From below rose the muffled thunder of waves breaking upon rocks. The old man glanced back, beckoned briefly and vanished down a narrow track.

Fearful of losing him Tom broke into a run. Just as he reached the defile the moon emerged from behind a high tatter of cloud and by its feeble light he saw Morfedd striding away down the path ahead of him. At the same instant he felt his heart turn over in his breast. He knew where he was! It was exactly as though, in a single step, he had passed through an invisible door and had emerged upon the other side to find himself back on Quantock Isle. This was the path that led down to the rocky cove known to the Combers as 'the Jaws'. In their childhood he and Witch had trodden it uncounted times, searching for the treasures that the storms cast up. He could have walked it with his eyes closed.

When he reached the bottom he found the old man leaning upon his staff and staring out towards the moon-silvered rocks which gave the cove its name. He turned as Tom approached. 'You'll know this place, Thomas.'

'Of course I do. Why have you brought me here?'

'To purchase our freedom, Star Born. Yours and mine both.' He raised his staff and pointed out across the water. 'See there.'

Tom screwed up his eyes and was just able to discern something glimmering faintly in the dark lee of a half-submerged rock. The blood in his veins seemed to congeal into ice. 'Is it . . . ?' he whispered, and found he could not utter Witchet's name for terror of making it be so.

The old man shook his head. 'She is neither of this time nor of this place, Star Born. Go quickly now and bring what you find back here to me.'

Tom walked down to the water's edge, drew a deep breath, and waded in. The swaying weed pulled at him like fingers; the small waves rose coldly until they were lapping about his chest; and the brine crept into his torn hands and stung like nettles.

The head of the corpse was almost on a level with his own face. Its blind eyes twinkled coldly in the moonlight and the long-drowned head lolled on a pillow of sea wrack. Conscious of little more than a sort of weary pity, Tom took hold of it by its spongy shoulders and towed it slowly back to the shore where Morfedd was waiting.

Together they dragged it clear of the water and laid it on the moonlit shingle.

The old man picked up two flat stones, thumbed down the reluctant eyelids over the sightless eyes, and laid a stone on each. 'Now you must speak the Kinship rites for the dead, Star Born.'

'I can't,' Tom whispered. 'I've broken my vow.'

'You can. You must. Do you not know whose body this is?'

Tom's teeth were chattering so hard from cold and shock that it was all he could do to mutter: 'My father's.'

'Then speak the words quickly, Thomas, or surely she will be lost to you and all will have been for nothing!'

So Tom knelt down beside the body of the man he had never known in life and offered its sad flesh to the earth and its soul back to the White Bird who had lent it. Then he drew the Sign over the wound where once the Falcon's bolt had pierced his father's breast, but he could not bring himself to touch the cold brow with his lips. He dragged in a gasping breath and looked up at the old man. 'How can we bury him here, Morfedd?'

'Such is not within our power, Thomas. We have done what had to be done. The rest has all been done by other hands long ago. Let us return the body to the waves and be quit of this place.'

He stooped, pulled Tom to his feet, and together they dragged the corpse back to the water's edge where the ripples welcomed it.

The old man thrust it out with the butt of his staff then turned and laid his hand on Tom's shoulder. 'That was most bravely done, Star Born,' he said. 'Truly you do not lack for courage.'

In the moonlight Tom's face was as pale as the dead man's. 'You will take me to her now?'

'I will do more than that, Star Born. Much more.'

'I want nothing more.'

'We shall see. We shall see. You have the pipes still safe?'

'They are here.' Tom touched his breast.

'All is well. Now give me your right hand.'

Tom held out his hand and the old man grasped it firmly. Then raising his staff he began flailing it rapidly up and down and back and forth in the moonlight as though he were fighting off a host of invisible assailants or weaving some arcane and intricate cage upon the shore. As Tom watched and wondered he perceived that the rocks about them were growing fainter and fainter until at last they had no more substance than a dimly remembered dream. Then, as though they had never existed at all, they were gone and in their place was a slowly swirling vortex of inchoate shadows in which he seemed to glimpse flickering images drawn from his own recollections—the towers and turrets of Corlay; his mother's face; golden Alice lying naked in the bracken; fragments of landscape, of sea and cloudy sky; and Witch emerging like some slim and silvered naiad from the moonlit water—a whole multitude of brilliant revelations strung out like living heads along the necklace of his songs. His senses reeled. Awareness hung over him, posed like some huge and brooding wave. All this was *him,* was *his;* he and he alone had brought it into being! He tore his hand free and cried out: *'Let me be!'*

Darkness. Darkness within darkness. Darkness so profound, so absolute that he knew he had finally reached his journey's end. As though invisible strands of gossamer were softly caressing his face he felt her dreaming spirit floating near him and he scarcely dared to breathe lest he should lose her. Then, like a subtle frost-flower blossoming upon a frozen window-pane, the pattern of his destiny began gradually to unfold itself upon his comprehension. Every thread of his life's web was centred on this point. Here at last, as Morfedd had promised, he had found his own truth. He could redeem her only by fulfilling the charge which had been laid upon him before his infant soul had even begun to quicken in his mother's womb. He reached into his breast for the pipes, held them up before him in the darkness, then set them to his lips and began to play.

If pure crystals of sound could ever be imagined then such, most surely, were what the Star Born quarried from within himself. Nor did they fade and die. Each cluster of notes seemed to hang suspended, trembling in the velvet blackness, till the next one floated out to join it. Fragile as snowflakes, each one perfect of its kind yet each a fragment of a sublime harmony incomparably more intricate and marvellous than itself, they drifted, singing, far away out upon the trackless tideways of empty space beyond all human knowing.

Such was The Song of Songs. Old before the Word was young: older than Time, or Nature's laws, or analytic thought. A dream envisioned by Man; his noblest aspiration; the purest Principle of Beauty.

Who shall say whether Tom was truly aware of what he did? The Singer and the Song cannot exist apart. Knowledge of the Self, once gained, is but to know there is no Self to know. I am the thing I make: the thing I make is I.

And so he played on, lost in his own miraculous dream of perfection, until out of the singing, ringing darkness a faint and nebulous light began to filter back. Like a silvery pollen dust it settled upon his hands and upon his face and upon the pipes, and thence spread slowly outwards in an insubstantial sheen. Dim shapes began to condense out of the shadows—a stone archway opening upon a flight of steps which rose beyond until they were lost behind a shifting curtain of shade.

He knew that she was within there, listening; knew that if he could only find the key to unlock those doors of shadow he could draw her back to him. It was the instant of his final *huesh*. The anguish of yearning he had felt then came rushing back and possessed him so fiercely it was like an iron grapnel hooked clean through his body into his beating heart. At that moment, with no conscious volition on his part, he found that his song had merged into that magical *Lament* which the Boy had played on those same pipes in the last moments just before his death. The two pure streams flowed together and became one, each complementing and completing the other as light complements darkness: darkness light.

There was a gentle sighing like a murmur of approbation; an area of the shadow grew more dense; and as though she had been distilled out of the very darkness itself he saw her, moving silently and hesitantly down the steps towards him like a sleepwalker. Just as she was about to pass through the archway he thought he heard the faint and distant echo of Morfedd's voice murmuring: *'Remember, Star Born, life and death are but a part of the eternal process of becoming . . . '* Then the whisper grew thin, faded like a ghost at cock-crow and was gone.

She stood before him as she had stood once before. As the last notes of the *Lament* died away he reached out for her hand, grasped it and felt it marble cold. He touched her cheek and her breast and in all he felt that same deathly chill that struck cold into his own hand. He put his arms around her, drew her close and felt her stir against him as his eager spirit cherished hers. 'My own love,' he murmured. 'My own sweet Witch. All you need to do now is to take my hand and follow me.'

He led her down a long arcade in which shafts of moonlight lay like drifted snow across the stone pavement. And this too was all as familiar to him as a dream which he had once dreamt and then forgotten. But he knew they must come to a place where a flight of steps led down to a stone quay and there would be a boat, because that was how it had always been, waiting for him.

And so it was. He stood with her hand lying passively in his, looked down and saw the boat rocking upon the quiet, starlit water. In the distance he could just discern the faint lines of mist cloaking the other shore where they would disembark. Yet even as he beheld it he knew that something was amiss. And then it came to him. *Her own boat.* In his mind's eye he could see it lying where he had left it far away among the reeds at the edge of the creek. Between the two parts of his dream lay a gulf too wide for him to bridge and in that gulf doubt rose up like a black tide. It was as if a crack had opened, and as he struggled to close it, shadows slipped through.

He hurried her down the steps. They had reached the quay and were half way to the boat when two figures emerged from a concealed passageway and he clearly heard Montfort saying: 'Didn't I tell you he'd try to give us the slip?'

He tightened his grip on Witchet's hand, drew her closer to him and moved resolutely towards the edge of the quay.

'Didn't you find her?' called Scar-brow. 'Wasn't she at the Stone?'

Tom ignored them. He reached the steps where the boat was tethered and discovered to his dismay that it was full to the gunwales with rain-water, though he had seen no sign of this when he had looked down upon it from the terrace above.

Scar-brow sidled up to him and peered down. 'Well, fancy that,' he said. 'Hey come and take a look here, Nikko!'

Montfort joined them. 'What is it?'

'Well, you remember, don't you?'

'Remember what?'

'When we got the drop from his lordship here. That's the very boat. I'd swear to it.'

'Empty it,' said Tom.

Scar-brow looked round at him and grinned. 'And here was me thinking you weren't going to acknowledge us, my lord.'

'I'm ordering you to empty it.'

'And why should we do a thing like that?'

'I don't have to give you reasons. Do it.'

The two men eyed one another speculatively, then Montfort said: 'We'll strike a bargain, my lord. We'll do it if you'll take us back with you.'

'That's impossible.'

'No, it's not,' said Scar-brow. 'She'll take three easy, won't she, Nikko?'

Tom stared at him. 'But not four.'

'Who's talking about four? Come, my lord. Your hand on it.'

They stretched across in front of Tom, slapped each other on the palm and turned to him. 'All for one and one for all,' said Scar-brow. 'Let's have your paw, my lord.'

Reluctantly Tom proffered his hand to seal the bargain. The moon shone down brightly upon them but cast no shadows upon the stones.

Montfort descended the steps and manoeuvred the waterlogged boat round with an oar till they were both able to get a grip on the prow. Then they lugged it slowly backwards, one step at a time. The water cascaded out over the stern and a smell like that of ancient, rotting leaves rose to the quayside where Tom stood watching with Witchet's hand clasped in his.

When the two men had succeeded in hauling the boat clear of the water they tipped it over on to its side and let it drain out on the steps. Then they righted it again and allowed it to slide back. While Montfort held it fast by the tethering rope, Scar-brow stepped aboard and slotted the dripping oars into the rowlocks. 'She's all yours to command, captain,' he said. 'Welcome aboard.'

Tom gazed out across the expanse of dark waters and then back at the boat. 'I'll take one of you with me now,' he said, 'and then I'll come back for the other. I give you my word on it.'

Montfort gave a mirthless chuckle. 'You've already given us your hand on it, my lord. So we all go together or she goes back to the bottom. The choice is yours.'

Tom looked at Witch. Her eyes, dark as the dark waters, seemed to be fixed upon some distant point on the other side. The choice was already made. He led her down the steps, climbed into the stern of the boat and drew her down beside him.

Montfort stepped aboard and thrust the boat away from the quay. The oars dipped. Scar-brow winked at Tom. 'It's like I've always said, my lord. We need each other, see? You help us, we help you. That's all there is to it.'

A mist was beginning to rise from the surface of the water. It drifted around them like wisps of pale grey smoke, bringing that same foetid smell of wet, decaying leaves to Tom's nostrils and striking such a deathly chill into his bones that he tightened his arm about Witch and held her closer.

They moved steadily further away from the shore and it was not long before the quay had disappeared completely. They were alone in the midst of the still, black waters with only the melancholy creaking of Scar-brow's oars for company, and the moonlit fog coiling itself around them, and the ever-present smell of decay.

'What will you do when we get there?' Tom asked.

'Now there's a question, my lord,' said Scar-brow. 'It couldn't be that you're thinking of running out on us? Not after all we've done for you.'

Tom shuddered.

'That wouldn't be friendly at all,' said Scar-brow. 'Not seeing as how it was you got us into this fix in the first place. Right, Nikko?'

'You only got what you deserved,' Tom retorted. 'If I hadn't done it someone else would.'

'Ah, but you *enjoyed it,* my lord. That's the bare facts of the matter.' Scar-brow leant forward and leered at him roguishly. 'Ten times better than a good screw, wasn't it, eh? Isn't that the truth now?'

Tom cringed away from him. The smell of corruption on the man's breath was so strong it made his head swim. And suddenly he saw that Scar-brow's whole face was undergoing a most revolting transformation. The flesh on his round, bristly scalp had begun melting away like wax, leaving odd-shaped whitish islands of bone showing through. Something thin and grey emerged wriggling from the inner corner of his scarred left eye and hung downwards like a candle drip. Yet he still went on talking away with a kind of hoarse panting urgency as though he were totally unaware of what was happening to him.

'You see, my lord, you didn't *have* to kill us—you *chose* to, like I took a fancy to dip my wick in that little wench of yours. That's what men like us do, my lord. It's what makes us all blood brothers, see? We grab what we want and screw the whole world stiff. It's our nature. Listen to me, my lord—' In his eagerness to make his point he let go of one oar and reached out with a hand that was now nothing more than a claw of bone and tendon as if intent upon grasping Tom by the wrist.

With a strangled yelp of terror Tom flung himself backwards out of range. The overladen boat canted wildly and next moment he was in the water. He went right under, kicked out, and rose choking and spluttering to the surface to find himself alone. Scar-brow, Montfort and the boat had vanished without so much as a ripple left to show where they had been. He opened his mouth to scream for Witchet then saw her head rising to the surface beside him. He turned over on to his back, kicked off his boots and threshed himself round till he was able to grasp her by the shoulders. Then he struck out for the shore.

He had no guide other than the pale globe of the moon which floated high overhead half-hidden in a vaporous haze too thick for the stars to penetrate. Soon he had lost all sense of time and swam on with his eyes almost closed, counting the steady rhythm of his strokes as one might count the slow heartbeats of one who lies in a deep swoon. So numb had his hands become that he could scarcely feel her at all, and had it not been for the dark outline of her head and the faint whisper as the water rippled past he could almost have believed that she too had slipped away and vanished like the others.

Gradually the mist grew thicker, the moon lost its shape, dissolving into an area of vaguely circular brightness, and he guessed that he was at last approaching the shore. From some deep inner reserve he had not known he possessed he summoned up the strength to kick out once more. Almost immediately he felt one of his heels touch the bottom. Half a dozen more strokes and he could stand. Too weary to do anything else he stumbled backwards, towing her behind him, till the water was lapping about his ankles. Then he sank to his knees, heaved her unconscious body up against his chest and staggering like a drunkard, tottered half a dozen paces up the beach till he tripped and collapsed across her.

* * *

Something warm and wet was licking his face, lapping across the brow and down the curve of his jaw below his right ear. He tried to lift his hand to push it away but his arm would not move. By an immense effort of will he contrived to roll his head sideways. The tongue was gone. Next moment it was back again, even warmer and wetter than before, this time licking across his closed eyes. ' 'way,' he whispered. 'Go 'way.'

'Tom? Tom?'

The voice came to him as if from an immeasurable distance, tiny and so far away that it was like hearing someone shouting his name from a remote hill top, yet even so he recognized it.

'Tom? Can you hear me, Tom?'

'Of course I can hear you, Dave,' but the words formed themselves only in his mind, not on his tongue.

'Bran bags,' said another distant voice which spoke in French. 'More hot bran bags.'

Sacs . . . *son* . . . *showed* . . . *brot* . . . The words were sliding away from him, slipping through the mist . . . *missed* . . . *Witch* . . .

'Tom! Tom!'

'Witch,' he whispered. 'Witch . . . love . . . cold . . .'

'Wake up, Tom!'

He willed his eyes to open and there was the face that he knew to be Dave's, hovering before him like a dark and friendly cloud.

David watched the pupils of his friend's eyes quiver then slowly shrink and become steady. It was when the irises appeared to shimmer like green stones lying at the bottom of a pool that he realized he was seeing them through the lens of his own tears.

'Dave?'

Too overwhelmed with relief to speak David simply nodded.

'I got her, Dave.' The voice was as faint as the whisper

of sun-dried sand trickling in the dunes, scarcely recognizable as even the phantom of Tom's voice. 'I got her back . . . in the end.'

David leant over him and kissed him. 'Dear friend,' he murmured. 'My own true, dear friend.'

He saw the twinned tip of Tom's double tongue emerge and slide slowly across his lower lip, then the exhausted eyelids had fluttered down over the deeply sunken eyes and he had drifted away from him again.

They brought bags stuffed with bran hot from the oven, peeled back the covers and laid the bags between his legs and against the sides of his thin, naked body. Within an hour his pulse had quickened, his temperature had begun to climb and a faint flush of colour could be seen on the lobes of his ears and at the tips of his cheeks.

Doctor Verelet examined him and gave orders for rectal feeding to be discontinued. 'The White Bird must love him dearly,' he observed, 'for surely it has worked a miracle here.'

'He will live, won't he?' asked David.

'I believe so, yes.'

David looked across at the unconscious figure on the bed then followed the doctor out into the passage and closed the door behind them. 'I'm sure he believes that she is still alive,' he said.

'Why do you say that?'

'He whispered something about how he'd got her back.'

Doctor Verelet plucked at his lower lip and frowned. 'Then we must keep him in ignorance until he has regained some of his physical strength. He is in no condition to withstand any severe emotional shock. Tell me, how long is it now?'

'Almost four weeks.'

'Incredible. Quite incredible. Well, we shall have to humour him for as long as possible. I will speak with the Kinswomen.'

'But what can I tell him?'

Verelet pondered. 'Tell him that he is in a condition of extreme vulnerability to her infection, and on that account, for the time being, is forbidden all contact with her. Say that those are my express orders.'

'I don't like it,' said David.

'I like it no more than you do, but what is the alternative? Two things have kept him alive this past month—your stubborn faith that he would recover, and his own indomitable spirit. To tell him the truth now could destroy his spirit. Then all that will be left to sustain him is your faith. Alone I do not think it will suffice.'

'And when he does learn the truth? What then?'

Doctor Verelet spread his hands in a gesture expressive of total ignorance. 'That, my dear David, is something we shall discover only when it happens.'

For twenty-four hours Tom hovered on the border between two worlds. Watching at his bedside David was reminded of a time when as young pupil Kinsmen at Corlay they had once found a bottle lying on the beach of 'L'Index'. They had put a message inside it and thrown it out into the sea of Nantes only for the waves to toss it back at their feet. After a dozen abortive attempts they had grown weary of the game and had left the bottle lying on the sand where they had found it. Now it seemed to him that he was watching Tom being obstinately returned to life almost in spite of himself, as if some invisible tidal current were saying: 'No, not yet. Not this time.' And back he would come. His eyelids would flutter open, his eyes would slowly clear and he would look up into David's face as if he could not quite believe what he saw. Then away he would drift again and David would see his eyes moving restlessly behind his closed eyelids as though he were watching things visible only to himself.

On the afternoon of the second day a marked change took place. In his own mind David likened it to the tide having finally withdrawn and left Tom stranded on the shores of Life. He entered the room where his friend was lying to find him fully awake, propped up on pillows, finishing off a concoction of raw eggs and honey beaten up in warm milk which the attendant Kinswoman was deftly spooning into him. David laughed delightedly. 'Better that end than the other, eh, Tom?'

'What does that mean?' The voice was still weak and husky but it was at least more recognizable as Tom's voice than the ghostly whisper of the previous day.

'Hasn't Sister Margaret told you?'

'She hasn't even told me what I'm doing here.'

David offered up a silent prayer. 'You've been ill, old friend. Really ill. We'd almost given you up.'

Tom stared at him. 'Ill?' he repeated woodenly.

'You went into a sort of coma. We couldn't bring you round.'

Tom slowly withdrew his thin, wasted hand from beneath the blankets and fingered the dark beard which now covered his chin.

Watching his face David saw doubt and wonder skitter across it like the shadows of wheeling birds. 'A beard suits you,' he said. 'It could do with a trim though.'

Tom transferred his attention to his hand, staring at it as if he had never seen it before. 'How long has it . . . ? Have I . . . ?'

'Four weeks tomorrow.'

'Four weeks!'

David nodded.

Tom withdrew his other hand and masked his eyes. 'Four weeks,' he repeated. 'Four *weeks!*'

'It seems like yesterday, does it?'

Tom slowly shook his head. 'But it doesn't make sense,' he groaned. 'Tell me what happened.'

'How much do you remember?'

Tom said nothing.

David sat himself down on the end of the bed. 'I can only tell you what *I* know,' he said. 'When I went back into the room after the hour was up I found you lying on the floor. I was really scared, Tom. I couldn't feel your heart at all. I wasn't even sure you were *breathing!* So I rushed out and got Verelet and he discovered that you *were* alive but in a state of profound catatonic trance. We carried you in here and kept watch over you. When you still hadn't come round after three days we had to start feeding you through your bottom. We've been doing that for the past three weeks. Then, yesterday, one of the Kinswomen noticed you were moving—up till then the only time you'd moved was when we shifted you round every two hours. She ran out and called me. And here you are, back with us again, as large as life and half as handsome.'

'Where's Witch?'

The question came so suddenly that David was taken completely off his guard. 'What?' he stammered. 'What did you . . . ?'

'Witchet. Where is she?'

'Oh, *Witch*. I thought you—But of course you don't know, do you? We moved her out into a convalescent hostel. We couldn't risk you catching plague from her. You wouldn't have had any resistance to it.'

Tom gazed into his face. 'But she *is* all right?'

'Oh, she's fine, fine,' David assured him glibly.

Tom closed his eyes and let out his breath in a profound sigh which David silently reciprocated.

'When can I see her, Dave?'

'Not for a few days yet, I'm afraid. But of course that's entirely up to Verelet. He says you've got to get your strength back first. And he's right, Tom. You only have to take a look at yourself. Why, man, you'd scare her to death if she saw you now.'

Tom contrived a pale smile. 'The beard? I'll get rid of that tomorrow.' He stretched out his right hand and grasped David's. 'It sounds as if I owe you my life, Dave.'

'Not just me,' said David. 'It's been shared out among a lot of us. You were a sort of challenge to us all. Now you'd better get some more sleep before the next meal. From now on they'll be stuffing food down your throat every four hours.'

'I've got so much to tell you,' whispered Tom. 'You simply can't imagine.'

'It'll keep a while, old friend.'

Tom nodded. 'Oh, yes. It'll keep all right,' he said, and closed his eyes.

During the next three days David learnt something of what had taken place in the world which Tom called 'the Land of Shadows'. As he pieced together the strange story he began to understand why his friend never appeared to question the fact that Witchet was still alive. And yet Tom would not allow that world to have an objective reality. 'It exists,' he said. 'I know it *exists*, Dave. But it exists *in me*. They *all* exist in me. Morfedd, Montfort, Scar-brow— even my own father.'

'Do you know why?' asked David.

'Because some part of me needs them, I suppose.'

'Even those two murderers?'

'Yes. Even them.'

'But why, Tom?'

'To teach me something about myself, maybe. To make me realize what breaking my Kinship vows really meant. When I killed Montfort and Scar-brow I was really trying to kill part of myself—but it was *that very part of me* which *made me* kill them. It's the one thing I've done that Witch has never been able to believe. She just can't understand how *I* could do it. But *they* understood all right. And by doing what I did I took some of their own guilt upon myself. That's what Morfedd meant when he said I'd made myself responsible for them. I suppose I had to acknowledge that—to accept it—before I could free myself from them.'

'And you think that's what you've done?'

'How can I tell? Perhaps if I ever went back there I'd find them again—or they'd find me. But in this world I'm quit of them. I'm sure of that.'

It was after that conversation that David sought out Doctor Verelet and told him he could not keep up the pretence that Witch was alive. 'The longer it goes on the worse it gets,' he said. 'As it is I don't suppose he'll ever be able to forgive me for the way I've lied to him.'

'So you wish me to tell him?'

'All I know is that somebody must, and I just *can't.*'

'Physically he is making an excellent recovery,' Verelet observed, 'and though for my own part I would have preferred to wait for two more days, I can well appreciate your dilemma. I think it will be best if we confront him together, David. I will explain to him that you have been carrying out my orders and are in no way to be held responsible for the deception. Come, let us go and do it straight away. It will not be pleasant but at least it will be done.'

They found Tom sitting in a chair beside the window writing something in his notebook. His pipes were lying in his lap. He looked up as they entered and smiled at David. 'I've just got back part of the Song,' he said. 'It really is something extraordinary, Dave. Would you like to hear it?'

David glanced round at Doctor Verelet who said: 'That will be a great privilege, Thomas. But first I have something very important to say to you.'

Tom regarded him questioningly but did not say anything.

'It concerns Witchet.'

Tom darted a sharp look at David. 'What about her?'

'I have an admission to make to you, Thomas. When you eventually recovered consciousness you told David that you had succeeded in finding Witchet—that you had brought her back with you.'

'What about it?'

'When David informed me of this I was convinced that your physical condition was so critical that to disabuse you of your belief might well have proved fatal. Consequently I gave strict orders that you were not to be informed of the true situation. You must understand that this was entirely my own decision. David had no part in it other than in carrying out my express instructions.'

Tom stared at him. 'True situation?' he whispered. 'What is it you're trying to tell me?'

Doctor Verelet met his eyes without flinching. 'Witchet is dead, Thomas. She died that evening four weeks ago before you went into your trance. She was interred in the hospital graveyard the following day. Such is ordained practice in all plague fatalities.'

Tom said nothing at all. He looked from Verelet to David and then down at the pipes and the notebook which were lying in his lap.

'What he says is true, Tom,' said David miserably. 'I was the one who spoke the last rites over her. When I did it I thought I'd soon be speaking them over you too.'

'Believe me, Thomas, the decision to withhold this knowledge from you was not taken lightly. I considered that your own life was hanging from the single thread of your faith that she was still alive. I dared not risk breaking that thread before you had regained at least a modicum of physical strength.'

Tom raised his bowed head and looked at David. His

eyes were dark with shock. 'A month ago,' he muttered. 'You say you buried her a month ago?'

David nodded.

'She was so cold, Dave. So cold. And where is she now?'

'What do you mean, Tom?'

'I brought her back with me. I *know* I did. But where is she now? Where did she go?'

With a sudden involuntary shudder David realized what he must be thinking. 'Oh, *no*,' he said. 'That simply isn't possible, Tom.'

'What is it troubles him?' murmured Verelet.

'He believes her spirit will have returned to her body.'

'But there *is* no body, Thomas. Witchet was cremated. Only her ashes were interred. With plague victims we have no other option. I am sorry. I thought you understood that.'

Tom turned his head away. He laid his bent arms along the window-sill and let his face sink down upon them. For perhaps a minute there was absolute silence in the room then, without warning, a tempest of unutterable misery had snatched him up and was beating him like a broken branch. So elemental was that grief that neither David nor Doctor Verelet dared to intrude upon it. With one accord they tiptoed out and closed the door quietly behind them.

Some two hours later David returned and found the room empty. He guessed at once where Tom had gone and having confirmed his suspicion by speaking to one of the Kinswomen he set off along the woodland path towards the cemetery.

By now the sun had gone down but the western sky was still bright and a light fleecing of golden-pink cloud was skeined high above the forest. The air was warm, there was no breeze at all, and the only sound was the twittering of birds and the muted crackling of dead twigs and beech mast being crushed underfoot. But so still was the air and so tense and apprehensive was David that even these faint sounds seemed almost intolerably loud in his ears.

The path led into a birch grove at the end of which stood a white-painted iron gate to the enclosure where the hospital dead lay buried. David had walked more than half way through the grove and was approaching the gate when suddenly he came to a complete standstill.

Later that night, attempting to describe what had happened to him next, he said to Tom: 'It was exactly as if someone had put a hand gently and firmly in the middle of my chest and stopped me going any further. I knew I was at liberty to turn round and go back the way I had come, but I was not being allowed to go on. So I just stood there and waited. And then I heard the singing. That's the only way I can describe it. But I knew it wasn't ordinary singing. It was as though the trees were doing it—the trees and the grass and the sky and the air—all of them together. It wasn't like any music I'd ever heard in my life—not even yours. It seemed to lift me right out of myself and for a moment I seemed to be aware of the whole world turning round beneath me. But I didn't really *see* it—*I was a part of it*—part of something so much greater than myself that I knew that I—Kinsman David Ronceval— was less than even a speck of dust, a stupid little fret and a worry, just not important at all. And I was so happy at that moment I would gladly have died. Then it slowly faded away and I was myself again and I could move. I walked on, looked over the gate and saw you there with the pipes in your hand. And I knew it was all right—that what had happened to me was just a faint echo of what had happened to you, and from that moment I wasn't worried or afraid for you any more.'

For a long while Tom considered this in silence. Finally he sighed and said: 'If that had happened yesterday I suppose I would have said that what you'd heard was The Song of Songs—the music the Star Born played to unlock the frozen stars and bring his dead love back to life. But that's just a fairy tale—or maybe a sort of poetic version of the truth. Those stars are in *us*, Dave. I know that now, just as I know that without Witch the Song would never have come to be. She's here, Dave, there's no doubt about that at all. *She's alive, in me, now,* and that's the only truth. I have given her just as much immortality as I had in me to give her. If I could have given more she'd be sitting here beside us. But it wasn't Witch I had to bring back to life—it was myself. I made her into my excuse for living. I think I knew it too—knew it right at the end when I looked down at that boat and was afraid to go back and look for hers because, deep down inside myself where the *real* truth lay—the truth Morfedd warned me of—down there I knew it was already too late and that her boat wouldn't be there any more.'

'What are you going to do now, Tom?'

'Well, first of all I must go and see Francis. Then back to Tallon. After that, who knows? Rocquevaire maybe.'

'Why Francis?'

'I've got something to say to him. He lent me the Boy's pipes, remember? I don't need them any more.'

'Would you like me to come with you? I'm overdue a leave.'

Tom shook his head. 'I think it's time I started getting used to being on my own.'

'There'll be plenty of time for that later,' said David. 'So you might as well put up with me as far as Corlay.'

They left Alençon at the beginning of October and landed at the port of St. Brieuc on the Isle of Brittany two days later. A tradesman's wagon gave them a lift to the village of Corlay and from there they walked the few remaining kilometres up to the castle.

The afternoon was spent renewing old friendships with teachers and pupils and then, with a murmured apology to his friend, Tom slipped away, climbed the winding turret stairs to Brother Francis' quarters and knocked at the door. It was opened by a manservant who asked him his business.

'I've come to speak with Brother Francis,' said Tom.

'Who is it, Peter?' inquired a familiar voice from within.

'Thomas of Tallon, sir,' Tom called out.

'Thomas? Come in, my boy, come in!'

As Tom entered the lamplit room the man who, above all others, had come to personify Kinship throughout the western world rose from behind his desk with hand outstretched in welcome. 'This is indeed an unexpected pleasure, Thomas. And what brings you back to Corlay?'

Tom shook the proffered hand and felt a twinge of the old familiar awe he had always experienced in Francis' presence. 'You would probably say it was the wish of the White Bird, sir,' he said with a smile.

'It is what *you* would say that interests me, Thomas. Come, sit yourself down. Peter, two glasses of the white, if you please, there's a good fellow.' Francis stepped out from behind his desk, ushered Tom into a chair beside the fire and seated himself opposite. 'And how is your mother, Thomas? Is she keeping well?'

'I haven't seen her for the past year, sir.'

'Then you have not come to us from Tallon?'

'I've come from Normandy.'

'Normandy, eh? Then I surmise that you have been paying a visit to your friend David Ronceval.'

Tom admitted this was so.

'And how is David?'

142

'Oh, he's fine. He's here with me now. We made the journey from Alençon together.'

'I shall look forward to meeting him. So tell me what you have been doing with yourself, Thomas, for I am certain you have not been idle.'

The challenge of summarizing the events of the past year was altogether too much for Tom. 'I've been travelling,' he said. 'First in Spain and then along the south coast of France.'

'And composing?'

Tom nodded.

'Excellent. You must certainly perform for us while you're here. We have none of us forgotten your *donation*, Thomas.'

The servant appeared bearing a tray on which were two glasses and a bottle. He set the tray down on a small table between them, poured out the wine and silently withdrew.

Francis handed a glass to Thomas, then lifted his own and said: 'Your health, Thomas.'

'And yours, sir.'

They both sipped at the wine and Francis fixed Tom with that eye which still bore the scars of the fearful night almost a quarter of a century before when Corlay had been sacked. 'I gather you have something you wish to say to me, Thomas. But unless you are expecting me to read your thoughts, you will have to tell me what it is in plain words.'

Tom traded look for look. 'Do you mind if I ask you a question, sir?'

'What question is that?'

'Why did you lend me the Boy's pipes?'

Francis chuckled. '*I* did not lend them to you, Thomas. That was the Bird's wish.'

Tom looked completely nonplussed.

'It was an act of the purest impulse, Thomas. Done on the spur of the moment. Are you answered?'

'Then it was not because of the Testament?'

'The Legend of the Star Born, you mean? The Lost Singer of the Song of Songs?' Francis shook his head. 'My dear Thomas, I have never for one moment believed that *you* are he.'

'But what if I should prove to you that I am?'

Although Francis had not moved an inch it was as though the distance between them had suddenly increased immeasurably. 'And how, may I ask, would you do that?'

Tom reached inside his breast and drew out the pipes. 'By playing you that very Song of Songs that Morfedd speaks of.'

Francis stared first at Tom, then down at the pipes he held in his hands and finally at the glass in his own. In those few brief seconds it seemed to him that he re-lived whole years of his life. He became again the young Advocate Sceptic travelling the self-same path the Boy had trodden on his way to York: watched Gyre wasting to death in his lonely island cell: crouched beside Tom's father in the Falcon dungeon in Broadbury: crawled through the hungry flames into this very room: rose again from the dead. All this he saw as if it were being cast into the scales before his eyes while on the other side of the balance lay nothing more than this pale-faced boy, Jane's son. And yet he felt the needle quiver, sensed it drifting back and forth poised between the two. All he had to do was to say the word, to make an act of faith, to *believe*. And he could not do it. He was too old and altogether too much was at stake. He shook his head. 'This is neither the time nor the place for a demonstration of your skills, Thomas. But I thank you for the offer.'

Tom stroked the pipes slowly across his arm. 'I had not thought that you would be afraid,' he murmured. 'There is no need to be afraid.'

Francis noted the subtle change in the tone of the boy's voice and chose to ignore it. 'Was that all you wished to say to me, Thomas?'

Tom shook his head. 'I came here to tell you that you have chosen the wrong path,' he said. 'What you are doing to Kinship is wrong.'

Francis frowned. 'Wrong?' he repeated. 'Can it be that I have been singled out to receive the blessing of some profound spiritual revelation, Thomas? If so, what is it?'

Tom did not even notice the irony. He laid the pipes down in his lap. 'The Song would have spoken directly to your soul,' he said. 'My words will not reach half so far.'

'Nevertheless, I should be most interested to hear them.'

Tom raised his eyes until he was gazing straight at Francis. 'The White Bird of Kinship is a dream,' he said. 'It is our dream of human perfection, of everything that can be achieved when the human spirit is set free from fear. But it is a *human* dream—something we all carry within ourselves. It's not up there'—he waved his hand in the air—'but in here'—he touched his own breast. 'The White Bird is within me, within you, within every man, every woman, every child, and that is where it must be worshipped. It can only exist through people—through the human imagination. That is where it will work its miracles. That is what Morfedd knew, what he taught the Boy, and that is what you have forgotten, Brother Francis. You are taking the boy's wild Bird and locking it up in your churches and your cathedrals and convincing the Kinsfolk that that is where it belongs. You have clipped its wings so that it can no longer soar up into the skies and carry them with it. You have changed it into a thing of words, into a creed. It is no longer real. And that is why I say to you that you are wrong.'

He picked up the pipes and tilted them back and forth

so that the lamplight rippled along the polished barrels. 'After I had played the Song to you I was going to return these to the reliquary. Now I know that they don't belong there. And I don't belong here either. But one day you will remember what I've said to you tonight and you will find that you are grieving for something you have lost—for The Bride of Time and her Child, for the Song the Star Born sang, and for the wild White Bird of Kinship.'

He stood up, restored the pipes to his pocket and said: 'Goodbye, Brother Francis. I do not suppose that we shall ever set eyes upon each other again in this life.'

The door closed behind him. Francis heard his footsteps growing fainter and fainter in the distance. Long after they had faded into silence he was still sitting there, gazing down into the fire and not seeing it.

A November wind with an edge to it like a blade of blue steel was whistling down from the northern fells, harrying the long tidal inlet of the Windersea and stripping the leaves from the trees which clothed the slopes of the hills above the little town of Bowness in the Fifth Kingdom. The leaves swirled up and were blown about the bright sky like flocks of golden birds which by their flight give a shape to the air.

A girl child and a young man came walking across the slope of the hill, following a sheep track. When they reached a place from which the peaks of Scafell were visible far in the distance between a cleft in the western hills, the child pointed upwards across the rocky slope to where an ancient oak tree stood by itself and she said something to her companion. The young man reached into his knapsack, took out a coin and handed it to her. She seized it, scampered away across the hill side and vanished among the trees on the eastern flank of the hill.

The young man struck off across the slope until he reached the tree. Although it was obviously very much alive, it must at some time in the past have been struck by lightning for it was hollow and there were still traces of charring visible on the inside. Some rusty iron nails had been hammered into the fire-blackened wood and from these a number of small objects were hanging—little figures of people, of animals and birds modelled out of baked clay; scraps of paper with names written on them; a copper bracelet; a curl of reddish hair.

The young man contemplated these things curiously but did not touch them. He crouched down, unshouldered his knapsack, and having extracted from it a metal trowel he began to excavate among the dead leaves, the twigs and the acorns which had accumulated within the hollow base of the tree. After an hour he had succeeded in burrowing down between the roots to the depth of his own arm. He laid the trowel aside upon the heap of soil and stones, sat down with his back resting against the gnarled trunk, brushed the dirt from his sleeves, wiped his hands clean and looked about him. He saw the wind flittering the grass into ever-changing patterns like eddies in water, and he saw a flock of wood-pigeons busily stripping the blood-red berries from a holly tree on the edge of the forest, and he saw the dead leaves swirling across the sky. And the wind blew cold around the trunk of the tree and made his eyes water.

He opened his knapsack again and took out a cylindrical container made of glazed earthenware. He unfastened the cap and drew from within the container a set of twin-barrelled pipes. He held them up before him, blinked the wind-tears from his eyes, then put the twin mouthpieces to his lips and began to play.

Presently the wind dropped. The pigeons flew away into the forest. The dead leaves drifted down out of the sky and lay still.

The young man stopped playing. He carefully wrapped up the pipes in some sheets of paper which he tore from a notebook and replaced them inside the earthenware cylinder. Then he screwed the cap down, lifted the container and slid it down into the hole which he had dug. Working first with his bare hands and then with the trowel he replaced all the soil and some of the stones he had excavated. Finally he scattered the twigs, the acorns and the dead leaves back on top.

When at last everything had been completed to his satisfaction he climbed to his feet, picked up the knapsack and slung it over his shoulder. Then without even so much as a backward glance he strode away across the hillside along the track by which he had come.

PART II

The Cartwright Papers

(Editor's Foreword)

I have heard it said that nobody ever kept a journal of their life without entertaining the secret hope that one day it would be published. If that is true then my father, James Cartwright, must surely have been an exception to the rule. He was always an extremely private person and there is no doubt at all in my mind that the journal which he kept for so many years was intended for no eyes but his own. He never spoke of its existence and, I suspect, simply forgot about it once it had ceased to have any importance in his life. For nearly half a century the five manuscript volumes lay buried at the bottom of a box in the attic of my parents' home and it was not until my wife and I were clearing out the house after my mother's death in 3844 that I stumbled across them. The only one of the volumes which is of more than family interest is the last. This covers the first four months of 3799 (the year in which the first volume of my father's variorum edition of the Avian Apocrypha was published). The story it unfolds is so curious, and in the light of all that has ensued, of such supreme historical interest, that I have no hesitation whatsoever in offering it to the public in precisely the form in which I first discovered it.

Thomas R. Cartwright
New Bristol
October, 3846.

*The journal of Robert James Cartwright M.A., D.Phil.,
sometime Fellow of St. Malcolm's College, Oxford.*

December 31st, 3798

Lunched with the Master in Senior Common Room. Also
present Miss Coley, Miss Phipps, McIntyre, Henderson,
Abrahams and the Bursar (bean soup; cold roast pork;
stewed plums). The Master in excellent spirits (brandy??)
after meeting of Hebdomadal Council at which it was announced that the Estimate for the coming year has been
accepted *sans caviller* by the Ministry. General air of self-
congratulation. McIntyre like dog with two tails at prospect
of more apparatus for his department. Over coffee chatted
to Miss Coley about variorum ed. of A.A. Both agreed
such an undertaking could well constitute a life's work.
She offered her assistance in collating texts to some of
which it appears that she has privileged access. I countered
with offer to let her look through the galley proofs of *Piper
at the Gates*. Conversation concluded with my accepting
her invitation to accompany her to New Year Service at St.
Francis'. I am to call for her at 11.30.

(Later)

Is it conceivable that I shall ever again find myself making
so extraordinary an entry in this prosaic record of my life?
Already it is three hours past midnight—the City clocks
have just finished striking the hour—but never has sleep
been further from my thoughts. So let me now, quietly and
soberly, describe as best I may the events of the past four
hours.

Shortly after eleven o'clock I put on my stoutest shoes,
donned my scarf and heavy overcoat and, umbrella in hand,
set out for Miss Coley's lodgings in Scrivener Street. The
snow which had been falling intermittently since about four
in the afternoon had eased off, but a few flakes were still

visible drifting down in the aura of the gas lamps. There were lights on in many of the downstairs windows and I detected the sounds of music and laughter as people prepared to see the New Year in. I passed several families who were obviously making their way towards the cathedral—the children masked and dressed in traditional costume to represent the various Birds, the Boy and the Apostles. I felt a surge of gratitude to Miss Coley for having persuaded me to join her in what would be my first Midnight Service for more years than I care to recall.

She was already waiting for me in the hall of her lodgings, dressed in a grey woollen coat trimmed with dark fur and a hat and gloves to match. The ensemble was altogether charming and I was moved to tell her so. Her response was to inform me with a laugh that she had not thought I was the kind of man who noticed such things. My response to *that* was to offer her my arm!

As we descended the steps into the street the summoning bell from the cathedral began to toll and we walked briskly to join the stream of the faithful who were hurrying across Broad Place. I thought to ask Miss Coley whether she made a regular practice of attending the New Year Service and she assured me she did. 'In York it is the crown of the year,' she said. 'Everybody goes.'

'You are from York?' I said. 'I did not know.'

'From Boroughbridge,' she replied. 'And I'll wager you've never heard of it, Mr. Cartwright.'

'Ah, but I have,' I returned with a smile. 'Not only is Boroughbridge mentioned in the Carlisle manuscript, it also features in my own version.'

'Then I must certainly make a point of reading it,' said Miss Coley, 'for I would not wish you to make any mistake over my birthplace.'

We had scarcely been ushered to our seats at the rear of the centre nave before the bell ceased tolling and the Kinsman Prebendary announced the opening carol *All Hearts*

Shall Beat as One Heart. To a rustling of hymn sheets the organist played his introductory chords and then the whole congregation rose and launched themselves into song. Beside me Miss Coley's full-throated contralto soared like a bird. Encouraged by her example I forgot my customary inhibitions and sang with a zest I had not experienced since I was a boy. From that moment I found myself in the grip of a most strange and curious excitement the like of which is all but impossible to convey in words. It was as though by the mere act of relinquishing my habitual reserve I had exposed some sensitive area of my psyche to the power of that very mystery which, nominally at least, I had come to celebrate. Yet the sensation was every bit as much physical as mental. It was almost as if my skin had become imbrued with an electrical charge from one of McIntyre's mysterious machines. I felt it as a distinct tingling over the whole outer surface of my body, while at the same time my visual and auditory senses seemed to have become quite exceptionally acute. As the carol ended and I resumed my seat I caught Miss Coley's eye and from its brightness and from the fine flush upon her cheek I guessed that I was not the only one to be in a state of heightened awareness.

Apart from an unfamiliar variant reading from the *Revelations* of St. Francis the service took its customary course and then, following hard upon the last stroke of midnight the great bells of the cathedral unleashed their tremendous voices across the rooftops of the waiting city. We all rose to our feet and I made the obligatory token gesture of Kinship to those on either side of me—a brief handclasp for the elderly gentleman stationed upon my left and, for Miss Coley, what would certainly have been a decorous raising of her fingers to my lips had she not suddenly turned full face towards me and, smiling broadly, pressed *her* lips upon my left cheek! Before I could respond she had turned away from me and was saluting the lady upon her right in similar fashion. It is, I think, a fair comment upon my state of mind at that moment that her vivid impetuosity did not strike me as being in any sense either perverse or unseemly—if anything quite the reverse!

After a minute the bells fell silent and the Prebendary announced the second hymn—that beautiful old carol *High Upon the Walls of a Northern City*—the third verse of which was to be rendered as a soprano solo with instrumental accompaniment. I do not know how many of us were present in the cathedral but it must have been close upon two thousand and we all sang the opening verses as though our very lives depended upon it. Then a flute and a recorder repeated the melody and a boy's pure silver voice soared upwards to the skies. It was a truly magical moment—one that tugged at the heartstrings. I found myself recalling those mysterious words of the Carlisle m.s. *'I believe there's a master-key, Peter. One to unlock the whole world. I call that key the White Bird'*—and I could not help reflecting upon the gulf that separates that passionate, primitive vision of human kinship from our formalized Modern Authorised Version. Raising my eyes to the High Altar I briefly contemplated the distant figure of the Bird spreadeagled upon the Cross and felt strangely troubled without quite knowing why.

At the conclusion of the carol the Bishop spoke briefly and movingly to the text: 'Lo! He shall return and all things Old shall be made New,' and ended with the ritual Blessing of the kneeling congregation: 'Let the Blood of the Boy ransom us: Let the Bird of Dawning hover over us: Grant us the Bliss of Kinship for Eternity.' As the choir responded with the seven-fold 'Amen' the Bishop, flanked by two candle-bearing acolytes, proceeded towards the High Altar where he knelt with arms outstretched in supplication while the lamplight winked and flickered richly among the encrusted jewels of his splendid vestments. Finally the organist struck up the superb *Jubilate* which has been speculatively ascribed to the elusive 'Thomas of Tallon' and once more the cathedral bells crashed out their joyous message from the tower high above our heads.

I retrieved my hat and my umbrella from beneath the pew and rose slowly to my feet preparatory to joining in the shuffling exodus. I then observed that Miss Coley was still kneeling with eyes closed, rapt in her devotions. Not wishing to interrupt them (and feeling, in truth, a trifle *de trop*) I stepped out into the aisle on my side of the pew and waited quietly in attendance upon her. In a matter of a minute or two—though at the time it seemed somewhat longer—she raised her head, gathered up her gloves from the shelf before her and rose to her feet. As she turned towards me I caught upon her cheek the gleam of what I can only suppose to have been a tear. 'Forgive me,' she murmured. 'I have kept you waiting.'

I smiled and shook my head to signify that there was absolutely no cause for apology and side by side we made our way out into the keen, reverberating air.

By now the majority of the congregation had dispersed, though a fair number were still clustered on the cathedral steps wishing each other a happy and prosperous New Year. It occurred to me to invite Miss Coley to accompany me to one of the tea-shops in the High Street which I knew had Civic Licence to remain open until the small hours on this particular annual holiday.

'Thank you, Mr. Cartwright,' she replied, 'but I am not over-partial to tea. Now had it been a glass of brandy . . . or do I shock you?'

'Not in the least,' I assured her. 'The Three Fiddlers in Falcon Street is renowned for hot toddy. That would be just the thing to bring some life back into frozen toes. If we strike off across the Precinct by way of Dean's Gate we shall find it directly upon our way.'

We descended the steps and took the snowy path towards the gate. The frozen, trampled snow was very treacherous underfoot and I offered my arm for support. Just as we were about to enter the narrow, dimly-lit lane which allows pedestrian access to the cathedral from Falcon Street an old man with a long white beard emerged from the shadows, peered at us, muttered something inaudible and strode off towards the cathedral. A moment later a group of laughing children scampered past us. They were all in fancy dress and had presumably been present at the Service. Leading the group was a boy clad in the costume of the Piper. He was closely followed by a soldier (St. Gyre?) and an 'old' man of at least ten years of age who had, no doubt, been playing the part of St. Peter the Tale-Spinner. As they disappeared round the corner ahead of us we heard a plaintive little voice wailing: 'Wait for me! Wait for me!' and we turned to see an infant (whether boy or girl was impossible to tell) got up to represent the White Bird. On its head was a long-beaked papier mâché mask and its body and limbs were sheathed in a remarkable knitted garment of white wool on to which had been stitched a rudimentary tail and a pair of cardboard wings. These appendages it was beating up and down in its frantic efforts to catch up with its companions.

As it drew abreast of us it missed its footing and tumbled headlong into the snow. Miss Coley was down on her knees in an instant. She lifted it to its feet, brushed off the snow and cried: 'Fly, Bird! Fly!' whereupon it pointed its beak in the direction of Falcon Street, spread its 'wings' and—*vanished!*

I had hoped that by writing the thing down—seeing it stated baldly in words written upon the page—I would perhaps succeed in convincing myself that it had never happened—that what I 'saw' I did not see—that I had, quite simply, imagined the whole inexplicable episode. I have tried telling myself that I beheld the child trot off down the path and disappear round the corner just as its companions had done—I *wish* to believe that, and yet I cannot. And the reason I cannot is that Miss Coley knows it happened just

as I have described it. One moment the child was there in
her hands and the next it was not. She looked down at the
snow upon her gloves and then she looked up at me. 'Mr.
Cartwright,' she said, 'am I dreaming?'

'I was about to ask you the same thing,' I replied.

'Then tell me what happened,' she said.

'You picked the infant up, brushed the snow from it,
and said: "Fly, Bird! Fly!" I told her. And suddenly I
found that I was shivering so violently that I could scarcely
contrive to enunciate the final words.

Miss Coley scrambled to her feet and seized me by both
my forearms. 'It *happened*, Mr. Cartwright!' she said
fiercely. 'We both *know* it happened! Never let us forget
that! *Never!*'

'You don't think we can both simply have imagined it?'

'I *know* we have not. See, there are the marks where it
fell. My gloves are still wet from the snow. If I imagined
it then I am imagining *you* at this moment and *you* are
imagining *me*.'

'Then how do you explain it?'

'Birds fly,' said Miss Coley. 'It was a bird. It flew.'

'It was a *child*, Miss Coley!'

'At that moment, Mr. Cartwright, it was the White Bird
of Kinship. *That* is the truth of the matter. Come now, let
us pull ourselves together. I think we are both sorely in
need of that refreshment you spoke of.'

I allowed her to take me by the arm and conduct me
down the path into Falcon Street. In truth I think I was a
good deal more distressed by what had occurred than she
was, and it was not until we were seated at a corner table
in the Residents' Saloon of the Three Fiddlers with rum-
mers of steaming punch before us that I began to feel sufficiently recovered to begin fumbling at the margins of the
problem. 'The light *was* very dim in the lane,' I ventured,
'and the colour of the child's costume . . .'

Miss Coley removed her gloves and laid them on the

table before her. 'Go on, Mr. Cartwright,' she said. 'I assure you I am listening.'

'You don't think that perhaps a fortuitous combination of those two circumstances . . . ?'

'I have already told you what I think.'

'And you can *accept* that?'

'It depends upon what you mean by "accept". Certainly I feel no overwhelming compulsion to pretend that it did not happen. On the contrary I know very well that it did.'

'You do not feel the urge to seek for a more rational explanation?'

'If by "rational explanation" you mean do I feel it necessary to deny the firm evidence of my own senses, no, I do not.' She dipped her spoon into her glass of toddy, raised it to her lips, blew gently upon it and then sipped it delicately, all the time regarding me levelly with her cool grey eyes as if defying me to gainsay what I had witnessed.

'I am an historian, Miss Coley,' I said. 'I do not believe in miracles.'

'I too am an historian, Mr. Cartwright,' she retorted. 'And I do not think that miracles will care very much whether I believe in them or not.'

We appeared to have reached an *impasse*. It was clear to me that I would not budge her from her stance. It was equally clear that she did not feel any overwhelming compulsion to budge me from mine. 'Has anything like this ever happened to you before?' I asked.

'No, Mr. Cartwright, it has not.'

'Then how can you accept it so calmly?'

She picked up her glass in both hands, raised it to her lips and breathed gently upon it. A faint cloud of fragrant steam filled the space between us. 'We are both students of the *Avian Apocrypha,* Mr. Cartwright,' she said. 'What else is that if it is not an extensive catalogue of the miraculous?'

I shook my head. 'It is also the reason why the stories

157

were excluded from the Canon, Miss Coley. Such truths as the *Apocrypha* contains must be understood as metaphorical rather than literal.'

'And who, pray, is to decide that?'

'It has already *been* decided.'

Miss Coley coloured faintly. 'That is the coward's way out,' she said. 'I do not care to believe that something did or did not happen eight hundred years ago just because someone in authority tells me I must do so. I prefer to make up my own mind. What took place tonight seems a perfect case in point.'

I had no prepared answer to that but I still had one card left to play. 'As historians we are both aware that the human memory is notoriously unreliable,' I said. 'In the interest of evidential accuracy if nothing else, would you be prepared to commit to paper a brief account of what has taken place tonight?'

She did not answer immediately and I thought to add: 'It need not take you very long.'

She gazed at me contemplatively. 'And would this be for your benefit, Mr. Cartwright, or for my own?'

'For both, I hope. I certainly intend to write my own account.'

'Tonight?'

'The moment I return to my lodgings.'

She appeared to consider this. 'Very well,' she said at last, 'I will do so too. It will be interesting to compare the two versions. Thank you for suggesting it.'

'And perhaps we could meet somewhere for lunch tomorrow and bring them with us.'

'Do you really mean tomorrow—or today?'

'True, true. I had forgotten it *is* today already. Are you agreeable?'

She nodded and I raised my own glass in a silent toast to the project.

We are to meet at the Mutton Chop in Bridge Street at 1.30.

January 1st, 3799

I had been seated at my reserved table for a good twenty minutes before Miss Coley appeared. She apologized profusely that she had forgotten to wind up her wristwatch before retiring.

'And what time was that, Miss Coley?' I asked her.

'Oh, about four o'clock, I think. But do please call me Margaret—after all it is my name. And with your permission I shall call you James.'

The waiter approached and took our order. When he had retired I reached down beside my chair, extracted the proofs of *Piper at the Gates of Dawn* from my briefcase and handed them to her across the table. She glanced at the title page and smiled. 'For a wild moment I thought this was your detailed account of our last night's adventure,' she said. 'Thank you very much, James. I'm sure I shall find it fascinating reading. Do you mind if I mark it?'

'Do so, by all means,' I said. 'It is a spare copy.'

'Can I ask why you chose this title rather than *Old Peter's Tale?*'

'I'm not really sure,' I replied. 'It seemed to have a slightly more numinous quality than the other. And John Hollins has approved.'

'He has seen it, has he?'

'In manuscript only. But he has undertaken to notice it for *The Antiquarian,* when it appears. No doubt he is saving up his adverse opinions until then.'

She opened her handbag, placed my proofs inside it and removed two sheets of notepaper which she handed to me. 'I hope this is what you wanted,' she said. 'Have you brought me yours?'

I retrieved the single sheet of foolscap on which, some two hours previously, I had abstracted the bare facts from the description which I have already given, and I passed it over to her.

She had finished reading mine before I was half way through hers, yet she had commenced her description only at the moment when we had both stepped out of the cathedral porch. The difference was that she had endeavoured to include some indication of her subjective feelings whereas I had stuck rigidly to observed fact. Even here we were at variance for she appeared to have forgotten the old man and had counted four children in the initial rush (one of whom, she stated, was a girl) whereas I had supposed them to be three young boys. Yet now my attention was drawn to it I became almost certain that the error was mine and that here her recollection was correct. She also mentioned that the child (the Bird) had been wearing red shoes and white woollen mittens, two details which had quite escaped me. But for the crucial instant we were both in complete accord. Where I had written "vanished" she had "vanished from between my hands". For the rest, apart from some minor differences in the actual wording of the conversation which had passed between us immediately afterwards, the substance of the two accounts was to all intents and purposes identical.

'Well?' she said. 'Is it what you expected?'

The waiter chose that moment to appear at her shoulder with a plate of soup which he set before her. By the time I too had been served and the man had retired, Margaret had either forgotten that she had asked me for my opinion, or assuming that I would regard her query as mere rhetoric, had moved on. 'Since we are both sure in our own minds that it *did* happen,' she said, 'is it not time for us to ask ourselves *why* it happened? To my way of thinking all miracles have one thing in common—they are never purposeless.'

'If it *was* a miracle,' I murmured.

She raised her eyes and gazed steadfastly into mine. 'You think otherwise?'

I shook my head. 'I simply don't know *what* to think, Margaret. You have read my account of what I *believe* occurred: I have read yours. They appear to tally in every important feature. But is that really enough?'

'Enough?' she echoed. 'What more could there be?'

'Might we not perhaps attempt to identify the child and question it?'

'Are you serious?'

The truth is I did not know whether I was or not. I think I had seized upon the notion as a way of delaying that final step across the frontier into the *terra incognita* which lay beyond. And yet I sensed that my answer could well prove my undoing: that her seemingly simple question constituted the tip of an iceberg whose concealed bulk would effectively knock the bottom out of any hopes I entertained of retaining her respect. Mentally I weighed the two alternatives in the balance and discovered, somewhat to my surprise, that I valued her good opinion of me a good deal more highly than I had supposed. 'The idea had simply crossed my mind,' I said lamely. 'I do not imagine that it could prove either practical or productive.'

Margaret smiled faintly and returned her attention to her plate.

But having taken my first hesitant step over the border I was now eager to explore what lay beyond. 'Are you not going to tell me why *you* think it happened?' I asked. 'Or am I wrong in presuming you to have detected a purpose lying behind it?'

'I was hoping that you might help to reveal one, James. I believe there *is* a purpose, but I have not the slightest idea what it could be.'

'Perhaps the purpose was to bring us here together,' I suggested slyly. 'Or is that altogether too prosaic a motive?'

'On the contrary, it had occurred to me too,' she said. 'After composing my account for you last night I tried asking myself what would have happened if we had chosen some other path. Was it purely fortuitous, or was it part of some pre-ordained pattern?'

'And what conclusion did you come to?' I asked curiously.

'None really. But I could not, in all honesty, see our "experience" as existing in some way apart from the New Year Service.'

'Do go on.'

'I simply feel that the two events were related. If I can comprehend the mystery of either I shall understand both.'

'I too found the Service profoundly moving,' I said. 'I owe you a deep debt of gratitude for having invited me to accompany you. But was it in any radical way different from previous ones which you have attended?'

Margaret laid her spoon in her empty plate and touched her lips with her napkin. 'Only insofar as *I* was different,' she said.

'I don't follow you.'

'I have just begun my twenty-ninth year,' she said. 'I believe that at the commencement of each seven year cycle we enter upon a new period of spiritual growth. I think it quite likely that I was in a particularly receptive frame of mind last night. Was I alone in that?'

The waiter reappeared wheeling a trolley on which were the grilled cutlets we had ordered. The interruption allowed me a moment in which to reflect upon her question. I recollected most clearly my fumbling attempt to put into words that wholly unfamiliar sense of heightened mental and physical awareness which I had experienced in the cathedral a bare twelve hours earlier, and it occurred to me to wonder whether she herself could possibly have contributed towards it. Yet by no stretch of the imagination could I relate what had happened to me then to what had happened to us both afterwards. The two experiences had even less in common than had that absurd little creature in its knitted woollen costume and cardboard wings with the Divine Symbol of Human Kinship which hovered above the High Altar. Yet, even so, I sensed that there *was* a connection, nebulous and fanciful though it might be, and tracking back through my recollections I found I had stumbled again upon the moment when the soloist had sung the third verse of the carol and my eyes had wandered upwards to the distant figure hanging upon the Cross. A single ghostly thread seemed to link the two—the remembrance of my own acute sense that something infinitely precious had been lost in the great gulf of years which separated the Old Kinship from the New.

'May I be allowed to share it?' asked Margaret, calling me back to earth.

'I am sorry,' I apologized. 'I was day-dreaming. I remembered thinking last night how strange our Modern Church would seem to those early Kinsfolk—Gyre, Orgen, Old Peter and the rest. Indeed, I wonder if they would even recognize it.'

'They would certainly have recognized what happened to us afterwards.'

I considered her words for a moment and then nodded. 'Yes, I think you might well be right. They saw a different world from ours.'

'I think not,' she said. 'I think they saw the same world but with different eyes.'

'Is that not the same thing?'

'Far from it. The world is shaped by our expectations of what it contains.'

'In a metaphorical sense, I have no doubt you are right.'

'Ah, now you have put your finger upon it, James. What for us today can only be accepted as a metaphorical truth was for them true in the literal sense. That is the difference between us and them. They *knew* that miracles occurred, whereas you and I are still fighting tooth and nail to deny the literal truth of what happened to us last night.'

'We are?' I said. 'But I was under the impression that you had accepted it without demur.'

'Superficially, yes. But deep down in those regions of the mind where belief is transmuted into true faith, there I can assure you the battle is still being fought. Had our roles been reversed last night I think I might well have been even more sceptical than you were. As it was I had the evidence of at least three of my senses to contend with—you had only two. I was still holding the child by the wrist when it happened: you only *saw me* holding it.'

'You *felt* it vanish?'

'My fingers closed upon the empty air.'

I picked up my knife and fork and then laid them aside again. 'Do you remember saying, just after it had happened, that it *was* a bird—the White Bird, in fact?'

Margaret nodded.

'What did you mean by that?'

'It was the only way I could explain it to myself,' she said. 'Three thousand years ago I suppose I would have said it was an angel. In the twentieth century I might perhaps have called it a ghost. But at no point in time could I ever have have persuaded myself that it was a pure illusion—a mere figment of my imagination.'

'I wonder what McIntyre would have called it?' I said, and made a belated attack upon my lunch.

'McIntyre would never have seen what we saw,' she said. 'He is Kin in name only. In private he regards all faith as superstition. He has told me so himself more than once.'

'He has his own faith in what he calls "scientific logic",' I observed.

'There he would doubtless be prepared to make an exception, but he would be careful to stress a distinction between his sort of belief and mine.'

At this point the conversation drifted off into a general discussion of our professional colleagues which, though fascinating in itself, had no direct bearing upon the events which had drawn us together. After lunch we strolled as far as the Parks then parted and went our separate way.

Friday, January 3rd 3799

I arrived at the breakfast table to find a large envelope lying beside my plate. Mrs. Berenson informed me that it had been delivered half an hour earlier by a young lady. Since any female below the age of thirty-five is a young lady to Mrs. Berenson I guessed (correctly) that the message bearer had been M. herself. It was the proofs of *Piper* together with a long letter (written the previous evening) which I perused with absorbed interest while I was abstractedly breaking my fast.

The greater part of the communication was taken up with critical observations upon my proofs—mostly matters of detail—and contained a number of extremely perceptive cross-references to the *Kentmere Psalter*. Her general tone throughout was one of warm approval, and her unstinted enthusiasm both for the *Variorum* project itself and for the manner in which I had tackled it in *Piper* gave me undeniable pleasure. Praise from one's professional colleagues is the only kind of praise which is truly worth having. But when I reached the final page of her letter I found my pleasure being transmuted into something more closely akin to astonishment. Rather than risk misinterpreting her words I shall copy them here.

. . . I cannot allow myself to close without making some attempt to convey to you my profound conviction that your own work contains the answer to the question you posed yesterday—namely: *Why did it happen?* Your own suggestion (I am perfectly well aware that it was tinged with irony) was that the marvel might conceivably have been engineered to bring us together—something I myself had already considered and had discounted on the grounds that we were already acquainted before it happened. What I failed to appreciate—or did not then appreciate sufficiently—was that we were the two people present at the Service (perhaps the *only* two *adults* present!) who were capable of making an *imaginative historical identification* with the ancient mystery of Kinship. But that in itself was not enough. What was lacking was some manifestation—some miraculous demonstration if you will allow it—of the incontrovertible *truth* of The Mystery—something which would, at a single stroke, demolish the intellectual barriers of our own familiar modes of perception and allow us access to a world whose wonders have been denied to so many for so long. We both know (none better!) that the History of Kinship is really the History of Franciscanism—that our Modern Established Church has been constructed upon the ruins of the Old Faith whose bones are everywhere evident beneath the tissue of living flesh. Is it not possible that you and I have been chosen—and I do not use that word lightly—to track the stream of Kinship back to its source and there, by clearing away the weeds which have been allowed to choke it, to let the pure truth flow free once more and nourish the hearts of men?

Perhaps, swept forward on the flood tide of my enthusiasm, I have been carried too far and too fast for you to follow me. If you are even now discounting what I am trying to say as "female hysteria" may I beg that you ask yourself the one vital question: *Did it really happen?* If your answer is *yes,* then read again what I have written and see whether it does not make sense.

Yours in all sincerity,
Margaret Coley

Since transcribing that passage from her letter I have turned back the pages and re-read my account of what occurred in the cathedral Precinct. I am convinced that, whatever it was, it *did happen.* More I am not prepared to say.

January 4th

Spent most of the day in the Mortenson working on my fourth lecture. The central heating has been turned down to the barest minimum requisite for human survival which does nothing to aid my powers of concentration. Before leaving I penned a brief note to M. thanking her for her letter and for the kind things she had said about *Piper*. On the way home I made a detour by way of Scrivener Street and posted my note through her letter box. The town looking very messy with heaps of half-melted snow still blocking many of the pavements. Arrived back to find a letter from Mother awaiting me—the usual dismal catalogue of minor domestic catastrophes. Consoled myself with an hour's flute practice (Paquati: Sonata No. 4). Picquet with Mrs. B. after supper.

Monday, January 6th

Completed fourth lecture and commenced work upon fifth. Dropped in to S.C.R. ostensibly to stake my claim to the Small Lecture Room for Wednesday mornings of next term, but really, I must confess, to see if M. was in evidence. Henderson stood me a glass of sherry to which I responded in kind. Scratch S.C. lunch of cold roast beef and pickles. Decided to call round at M's lodgings and invite her to accompany me on a stroll in the Parks to be followed by tea at the Mitre. Informed by her landlady that M. had left for Yorkshire on Saturday and was not expected back until the end of next week. Glimpsed my own note to her tucked into the letter board in the hallway. Feeling inordinately frustrated and depressed, walked back via Dean's Gate to the cathedral Precinct and stood for a while contemplating the place where the 'miracle' occurred. As far as I can judge the precise spot is now occupied by a large piece of canine excrement! However, it is possible I was mistaken. Spent evening writing letters to Mother, Jennifer, and Dr. Forrest. A poor sort of day.

January 9th

On an impulse decided to attend Choral Evensong in the Cathedral. Congregation approximately one-twentieth of the number present on New Year's Eve. Average age appeared to be about sixty! Service conducted by Minor Canon suffering from severe head-cold. Found myself meditating upon M's observations concerning the History of Kinship. *Can* she be right? And, if so, where did things go wrong?

While kneeling in prayer found I was suddenly recalling her pale face turned up towards me as she demanded: 'Mr. Cartwright, am I dreaming?' The memory of *that* moment was far more real to me than the reality of the Service.

As I was leaving the cathedral I again caught sight of that strange old man I had seen on N.Y's Eve. This time he was hurrying in the direction of Lowe's Gate and I lost sight of him almost immediately. On my return home I started composing a letter to M. but abandoned it in frustration when I discovered that I did not know what I wished to say. Tonight I feel thoroughly out of sorts with myself.

Saturday, January 11th

Have passed the whole day following up the suggestion in M's letter. Working backwards from the Grand Council of Turin (3243)—chosen as my datum line because it established the First Official Canon. I find I have filled three foolscap sheets with notes and have come to no satisfactory conclusion. Nevertheless, I am becoming persuaded that M. has stumbled upon something extremely important. Today, for the first time since I was at work upon the Carlisle m.s., I have felt supremely content and in tune with myself.

January 12th

Spent today deep in St. Francis' *Revelations* and the *Letters to Brother Matthew.* What a giant of a man Francis is! Setbacks and disasters which would have completely broken a thousand others seem to act upon him like a rejuvenating tonic. An organizer of unsurpassed genius. Truly he, and he alone, is the architect of Kinship. *Si monumentum requiris, circumspice!* And what a magnificent edifice he has bequeathed to us! Bertrand of Zurich surely came closest to the truth with his observation: 'A saint among men: a man among saints.' If only more of Francis' own writings had survived. What would I not give to see the manuscript of *The True History of the Boy* written in his own hand. Did he ever complete it? And, if so, what became of it? Strange how even Dom Sarega's marvellous *Life* is silent on that point.

January 14th

I was hard at work delving into Vol. I of Franscombe's *History of Kinship in the United Kingdoms* when Mrs. B. knocked at my door and announced that I had a visitor. To my surprise and delight this proved to be none other than M. She had arrived in Oxford late last night, read my note, and discovered from her landlady that I had called round to see her. I prevailed upon Mrs. B. to provide us with some tea and apologized to M. for the untidiness of my room. Her smiling response was: 'This is nothing. You should see mine!'

We talked briefly about her holiday and then she glanced across at the books scattered about my desk and asked me what I was working at. When I told her her face lit up. 'Then you were not repelled by the last page of my letter? Since you did not mention it in your note I was afraid you might have been.'

'I was surprised certainly,' I replied, 'but I followed the suggestion in your final paragraph and—no doubt as a result—I am persuaded that you were justified. For the past three days I have been hard at work burrowing down into the roots of Kinship.'

'And?'

'All paths lead back to St. Francis—to be precise to January 3019. Beyond that it dissipates into myth, magic and hearsay.'

'Or into miracle.'

'Well, let us say into the Apocrypha.'

'Is that where you would assign what happened to us?'

'That is *argumentum ad hominem,* Margaret,' I protested. 'I can work only with the tools of my trade. Those, as we both know, are the surviving historical records.'

'But the bulk of the Apocrypha was written in the three centuries following 3019,' she objected. 'It was only debarred from the Canon in '243. Some of the stories weren't excluded till as late as '382. And what about *Morfedd's Testament?*'

'What about it?'

'Well, surely you are prepared to concede that it *did* exist?'

'I am prepared to concede that *something* existed. After all, Francis himself refers to it on several occasions. But whatever it was it has not survived.'

'Has it never occurred to you that it might have been deliberately destroyed?'

'During the sack of Corlay, you mean?'

'Or afterwards. Perhaps many years afterwards, when its continuing existence could have been seen as detrimental to the image of Kinship which Francis was striving to establish.'

'It is an interesting hypothesis,' I said. 'But since there is no supportive evidence I should not care to have to argue the case for it in a court of law.'

'Nevertheless, James, I am convinced that is what happened. Only consider. Of the three genuine relics of the Boy which we know reached Corlay—his pipes, the *Testa-*

ment of *Morfedd,* and Francis' own *History*—not a single one has survived. If it were not for those three books of the Apocrypha—the Carlisle manuscript, the *Book of Gyre* and *Old Peter's Tale*—and some questionable scraps of material surviving in the Secular Archive in York, who would believe that the Boy Thomas had *ever* really existed in the flesh? What we have left to us today is the idealized image which Francis and those who came after him have substituted for the real thing. Don't you see? Francis' church has succeeded in doing to Tom precisely what the Old Faith did to their Jesus of Nazareth. And for the same reasons.'

I stared at her. Her cheeks were flushed, her eyes shining, and her hands clasped together so tightly in her lap that the knuckles showed white. There was about her a vibrancy—an *intensity*—that I found extraordinarily affecting, but to which I could evoke no adequate response within myself. I found I was recalling that supreme passage from the last of the *Revelations* where Francis speaks of the one he calls 'the Maid' who appeared to him in a vision shortly before his death and from whom he begged forgiveness for his 'failing in faith', and I was sorely tempted to do the same. However, before I could reply, there was a knock at the door and Mrs. B. appeared bearing a loaded tray. During the to-ing and fro-ing which ensued the opportunity was lost.

Over tea I told M. how I had re-visited the site of our 'miracle' while she was away and she responded by telling me that she had spent a day in York endeavouring to retrace the steps of the Boy's last days on earth as they are outlined in *Piper at the Gates*. 'By far the most poignant moment was when I reached the Station on the City wall,' she said. 'It was snowing when I got there and the place was completely deserted except for one old man crouching over a brazier who had the job of preventing people from desecrating the shrine. I leant out over the parapet more or less where St. Peter must have stood and I tried to imagine what it could have been like on that New Year's Eve eight hundred years ago. The snow was falling in great soft feathery flakes just as it must have been then and I thought of all those silent upturned faces awaiting the miraculous Advent, passionately willing it to happen, until suddenly the sound of the Boy's piping was there turning their dreams into reality. Only for me there was no sound of piping, just the sniffing of the old watchman and the snow falling on the metal plaque which said: "Any Person Defacing this Monument will be Prosecuted. By Order." I asked the old man if many people visited the Station and he said there were a fair number in the summer, but in the winter they favoured the Tomb in the cathedral because it was warmer. Even so I was glad I had done it. I felt I owed it to poor Tom's uneasy spirit.'

I reached out, lifted the volume of Franscombe from my desk and turned to the index. 'Did you know that there are at least five "authentic" sites listed for the Boy's death—one of them in Doncaster?'

'Yes, I know,' said Margaret. 'There's one at a place called Hammerton Bridge, half way between my home town and York.'

'The place where they first encountered Gyre, if we are to believe the Carlisle version.'

'Do *you* believe it?'

'Does it matter whether I do or not?'

'I think it does. I think it matters a great deal.'

'In what regard precisely?'

'In the light of what happened to us both on New Year's Eve.'

I closed up the book and restored it to its place on my desk. In doing so I dislodged the sheet of notes I had been working on prior to M's arrival. It floated to the floor at her feet and she leant forward and retrieved it. In the act of handing it back to me she glanced down at it and her eye was caught by something. 'May I?' she asked.

'By all means,' I said with a smile. 'But I defy you to make sense of it. It's just a collection of loose ends.'

She nodded and returned her attention to the paper. After a minute or so she said: 'What are the numbers in brackets after the names?'

'The Roman numerals refer to St. Francis' *Revelations*: the Arabic to the *Letters to Brother Matthew*. The figures themselves I culled from Langley's *Lexicon*. They represent the number of actual references to that particular name in the two texts.'

'And the initials "B.T."?'

'They stand for those two enigmatic references to "The Bride of Time" in the second *Letter*.'

'Then why the cross-reference with "the Maid"?'

'Ah,' I said. 'You may well ask. I have been idly speculating whether "the Maid" and "the Bride of Time" might not conceivably have been one and the same person.'

'The girl who perished in the holocaust?'

I nodded. 'There is no doubt in my mind that she came to stand for something very special in Francis' life, to personify some moment of profound spiritual crisis. She is like a shadow haunting him. Try as he will he cannot wholly exorcise her memory. In the end, in what I think is unquestionably the most moving passage in all the *Revelations,* he calls upon her to forgive him for his "failing in faith". Yet we are never told precisely what he meant by those words.'

'So you believe she really did exist?'

'Oh yes, certainly I do. Why? Do you doubt it?'

She shook her head. 'No, no,' she said. 'I am quite sure she did. I believe she is the link between Francis and the Old Kinship. If we could find her then she would lead us back to the Boy who died upon the walls of York.'

'A substantial claim indeed; unfortunately there is no evidence to support it.'

Margaret looked down at the page of notes she was holding and then she handed it back to me. 'I think I know where we might find her,' she said.

'Really? And where is that?'

'In a manuscript in the New Exeter archive.'

'And what manuscript is that?'

'One of the ones Pardoe dismisses in his *Catalogue*— *The Witch's Tale*.'

'*That!* Are you sure it even exists?'

'Oh, yes. Certainly it exists. I've seen it.'

I gazed at her. 'You've *examined* it?'

'No. I was only able to glance at it. But what I saw was quite enough to convince me that it is no thirty-fourth century forgery.'

'Then why was Dean Pardoe so certain that it was?'

'Because it conflicted so totally with his own pre-conception of what it *ought* to have contained. Pardoe's principal concern was never with *historical* truth, only with what he believed to be in the best interest of the Church.'

'And what do you suppose he found in the text which made it so offensive to him?'

Margaret shook her head. 'All I know for certain is that he dismissed it as a palpable forgery and an obscene and rubbishy fairy tale of no literary or scriptural merit whatsoever.'

'A round enough condemnation even by his standards!'

'Yes. Until you recall that he used almost those identical phrases to dismiss the Carlisle manuscript.'

'I had forgotten that,' I laughed. 'The Venerable Dean was certainly a man of very decided opinions.'

'And of formidable social influence,' said Margaret. 'He virtually compelled Sir George Harcourt to refuse any other scholar access to the New Exeter archive. For the past eighty years that manuscript has been locked away in the Castle library.'

'Then how on earth did you come to set eyes on it?'

'Lady Felicity—Sir George's grand-daughter—is a friend of mine. We were at Durham together. Two years ago I spent a week's holiday with her. I persuaded her to let me take a peep at it.'

'Good heavens, Margaret, I really had no idea that you moved in such illustrious social circles.'

She tossed her head disparagingly. 'If I can obtain Felicity's permission, would you be prepared to go down to New Exeter with me and examine the manuscript?'

I was so astonished that it was several seconds before I managed to say—'I am truly flattered that you should suggest it, but I—'

'I am not *flattering* you, James. Heaven forbid! I really would need your expert help and your authority.'

'But even if *I* were to agree, would Lady Harcourt?'

'Yes, I think so. I doubt whether the Dean's fiat carries the weight it did in Sir George's day.'

'And when would this expedition take place?'

'I had thought of suggesting April—that is if you are agreeable.'

I glanced at her sharply. 'Then this is not something which has just occurred to you?'

She laughed—a truly delightful sound. 'Oh, no, James,' she said. 'I must confess that I became resolved upon it during that day I spent on my pilgrimage round York.'

At that moment the bells of St. Bartolph's began to chime the hour. Margaret jumped to her feet protesting that she had no idea it was so late. I walked her back to her lodgings and then hastened home to commit to paper this account of what has indeed been a most fascinating afternoon.

January 17th

Spent hour this afternoon at the Univ. Press discussing various technical details with Philby, among them the revised acknowledgments list. All settled amicably. P. anticipates despatching sheets to binders by third week of Feb. Returning via Willsher Street I happened to glance in through window of Cutler's Pantry and saw M. in animated conversation with a man I did not recognize. I hurried past reflecting how little I really know of her or she of me. Yet having shared that one extraordinary and unforgettable moment of intimacy with her I feel that I am now, in some wholly inexplicable manner, closer to her than to any other person in the world.

Continued working on fifth lecture until dinner. Afterwards, at her invitation, played my flute to Mrs. B. and her sister (3 *Songs of Summer*, Tallon arr. Darwin). Performed quite well, I think.

Oxford; January 29th

My thirty-third anniversary found me in Aldershot whither I had been peremptorily summoned by an express appeal from Jennifer ('Father *very* ill! *Do* come!'). Arrived late on Tuesday afternoon (21st) after an exhausting journey—steam coach to Wycombe: paddle-packet to Guilford: coach to Aldershot: raining heavily all the way. Find my sister greeting me with the news that it has all been a false alarm and that Father is now completely recovered! My joy somewhat muted in the circumstances. The following day I myself go down with a severe chill and spend next two days confined to bed alternately shivering and sweating. Weird hallucination Wed. night that the old man from Dean's Gate was standing at the foot of the bed glaring at me! Jennifer the personification of abject contrition: Father (in rude good health) vastly amused: Mother exhaustingly solicitous. Up again on Friday: more or less fully recovered by Saturday. Announce intention of returning to Oxford on Monday. Mother protests loudly that Monday is my birthday and that she has invited our Cousins Welby round for the evening on purpose to celebrate it. Departure postponed until Tuesday. At breakfast on Monday Mother presents me with a silk cravat; Jennifer with a small packet tied up in pink ribbon. Unwrap it and discover a most exquisite little antique wooden carving of an otter with a salmon in its mouth—the whole barely the length of my middle finger but quite perfect in its animation and detail—a true work of art. I do my best to express my profound pleasure and gratitude and ask Jennifer where she found it. 'In that funny little shop at the corner of Leechwell Street. I saw him hiding in a corner of the window last October and somehow I knew you'd like him. He was a bit scratched so I polished him with beeswax to make him shine. Doctor Margetts thinks he could date right back to the 31st Century.'

My little otter is standing here beside me on my desk watching me write this. I laid down my pen at that point and picked him up. I could almost swear I felt him move between my fingers. A true creature of the wild!

January 31st

Literally bumped into Prof. Hollins on the steps of the Mortenson. We passed the time of day and he asked me when *Piper* was expected out. Just as we were about to go our separate ways I thought to ask him whether he had heard of a manuscript entitled *The Witch's Tale*. He scratched his chin. 'It sounds vaguely familiar. Wasn't it one of old Pardoe's burnt offerings?'

'Burnt offerings?' I echoed.

'Lord, yes. The old devil used to buy stuff up by the cartload and then incinerate it. Heaven knows what we didn't lose while he was on the rampage. The astonishing thing is that as much has survived as it has. But what makes you ask?'

'Oh, I heard a vague whisper that it might still exist.'

'Really? Then it's certainly worth following up. If Pardoe damned it, it's almost bound to be of genuine antiquarian interest. Quite possible a classic into the bargain.' And with a grin and a cheerful flourish of his umbrella he was off.

Later I proceeded to the Schools and posted my lecture timetable.

February 7th

Tedious Faculty meeting (8–9.30). Afterwards passed a pleasant half-hour chatting to M. and Miss Phipps. Invited M. to attend Magdalenian concert in Chapter House (March 1st) whereupon she laughed and told me it had been on the tip of her tongue to invite *me!* Mutual delight and astonishment. Learned that she has recently joined the Aeolians. I suggested we might get together for an evening's music-making during the week and we have settled on Friday. I am to call for her at 8.30.

February 14th

Have just returned from escorting M. back to her lodgings after what has been a truly delightful evening. As we were turning out of Prospect Place (prior to short-cutting back to her lodgings via Milliner Street) I caught sight of the old man who had issued from Dean's Gate on New Year's Eve. I recognized him at once from his dark, old-fashioned carter's cloak with its matching shoulder-cape. I was on the point of drawing M's attention when he turned aside and disappeared down one of the alleys (Brideswell?) towards Merton. I was immediately reminded of my second sighting of him in the cathedral Precinct when M. was away in York, and of my strange, feverish hallucination in Aldershot, both of which I had forgotten.

When we came abreast of the alley I paused, peered down it, and found that it was deserted.

M. enquired what had engaged my attention and when I

told her she glanced up at me with a puzzled expression and said: 'But there *was* no old man in Dean's Gate.'

'Well, not *in* it, exactly,' I said. 'He emerged just before we entered. Don't you remember? I specifically mentioned him in my account.'

'Are you sure you did, James?'

'Positive.'

'I don't recall it.'

'That's probably because you didn't notice him.'

'James, are you *certain* you mentioned him? I could have sworn that your description began at the moment when we both turned into the lane.'

It was now my turn to be assailed by doubt. 'I made you a factual abstract from the more detailed account in my journal,' I said. 'I may possibly have confused the two accounts in my own mind.'

'Yet you have never mentioned him to me before.'

'There seemed no reason to,' I said. 'Anyway, I thought I had. And I'm still not entirely sure that I didn't.'

'Can you describe him?'

'Of course I can. He is extremely patriarchal. Long white beard and moustache. Bushy eyebrows. And he wears one of those old-fashioned carters' cloaks—the long leather kind with a hood and a shoulder cape.'

'And you say he emerged from Dean's Gate lane just before we entered it?'

'He must have done. I don't see where else he could have come from.'

'Did he *do* anything?'

'He glanced at us and muttered something or other. But surely you must have seen him, Margaret. After all he passed within a yard of us.'

'That is just what I find so hard to believe,' she said.

'Are you trying to tell me I *imagined* him? But I swear I've just seen him *again*—for the third time—a bare two minutes ago.'

'Here?'

'Here on this very spot. He turned down there.'

She gazed into the deserted alley and then shook her head. 'I'll get out your account and check it when I get home,' she said. 'What will you give me if I'm right and you're wrong?'

'I'll treat you to tea in the Mitre tomorrow.'

'Not tomorrow,' she said. 'I could manage Sunday though.'

I have just checked to see what I wrote on New Year's Day and find that apart from the details of his dress it is exactly as I had supposed. In spite of that I still feel decidedly uneasy about the episode.

February 16th

M. greeted me in the Mitre with the news that she has received permission from Lady Harcourt for us to examine the manuscript. Lady H. will be abroad for the whole of April but is apparently prepared to allow us access to the library during her absence if we will give her notice of when we intend to make our visit. M. asked me what reply she should make.

'What reply have you in mind?' said I. 'For I am perfectly certain you have one.'

She smiled. 'I had intended to suggest the week commencing Friday the 11th.'

'A whole week? Isn't that rather excessive?'

'It would allow us to do some sightseeing. And the weather is often at its best in April. But of course if it is inconvenient . . .'

'No, no,' I said. 'I can think of no prospect I should enjoy more, nor of any colleague I would rather share it with.'

She gave me a quick, appraising glance and I perceived a faint flush mounting to her cheek. Anxious to put her at her ease I remarked: 'By the way, John Hollins seems to think you may have stumbled across something of real value.'

'Professor Hollins? Oh, James you haven't told *him* about it?'

'I simply mentioned it *en passant*. He was under the impression that Dean Pardoe had destroyed the manuscript. Have I done something wrong?'

Margaret frowned. 'I do wish you had not told him, James. It may turn out to be completely worthless and then we shall both be made to look foolish.'

'I have obviously given you entirely the wrong impression,' I said hastily. 'I did not even tell him I was sure the document existed. I believe I said I had heard a vague rumour to that effect. I am truly sorry if I spoke out of turn, Margaret, but you did not tell me that you wished it kept a secret.'

She shook her head. 'I don't suppose there's any harm done. It's just that I want this to be *our* discovery—*our* triumph.'

'Ours?' I echoed. 'But it will be *yours*, Margaret! Had you not told me about the manuscript's existence I should still be completely ignorant of it.'

'And had you not shown me the proofs of *Piper at the Gates* I should never have dared to mention it at all,' she replied. 'One thing led to the other.'

'And both are entangled with that inexplicable encounter in Dean's Gate.'

Margaret nodded. 'Oh, by the way,' she said. 'I looked up your account of what happened as soon as I got back the other evening. It contains no mention at all of any old man.'

'Well, he is there as large as life in my journal,' I said, 'and I'm perfectly satisfied in my own mind that I did not imagine him.'

A waitress brought us our tea and Margaret set about performing the duties of hostess. I experienced a warm glow of pleasure as I watched her, and the prospect of spending a week in her company became extraordinarily attractive to me. I resolved there and then to learn more about her and, for once in my life, I was moved to act upon my impulse. 'Apart from the facts that you are twenty-nine years of age, that you hail from Boroughbridge, and that you are a specialist in the political history of the United Kingdoms during the 33rd and 34th Centuries I still know next to nothing about you, Margaret. Can I persuade you to tell me a little more about yourself.'

'About myself or about my past?' she replied with a smile.

'Are they so different?'

'Well, let us start with the past and see where that takes us. Here are some facts for you. My father is a lawyer. I have a brother, two years older than myself, who is Town Clerk in Malton, and a sister two years younger than me who is married to a doctor in Doncaster. We all went to school in Boroughbridge and I won a scholarship to Durham where I read Modern History. After graduating I taught History for two years at Carlisle Academy and then spent a happy year working on my thesis in Edinburgh. After that I applied for a lectureship in Winchester. I was there for two years then I got my post at St. Malcolm's. And here I am.'

'And here you are,' I agreed. 'What made you choose history?'

'That is more a question about myself than about my past,' she said. 'Do *you* know why *you* chose it?'

'The past has always held a great attraction for me,' I said. 'For one thing I am free to interpret it as I choose— to discover its patterns for myself—secure in the knowledge that it is all over and done with.'

'Do you really believe that?' she asked.

'That it is over and done with? What else could it be?'

'I think it lies in wait for us just as much as the future

does. Sometimes I almost persuade myself that it *is* a part of the future. It is only the present that has no form, no reality.'

'I'm prepared to agree that the present is the moment of historical evolution,' I said, 'but I am still pragmatist enough to credit it with existence.'

'Then it exists only because *you* wish it to,' she said. 'When I was a child I knew that what we call "reality" did not *really* exist at all. The trouble was that everyone else pretended it did and told me to stop making things up. But it was *they* who were making things up, not I. They even refused to believe me when I told them I saw the stars in daytime. They just did not see the same world as I saw.'

'So you chose to study history because that at least was something you could all agree upon?' I suggested with a smile.

She shook her head. 'Not at all,' she said. 'I chose it because of the Boy. I fell desperately in love with him when I was ten years old. But my Thomas was not the one they told us about in Sunday School, he was the one in the Apocrypha. *That* is why I decided to study history.'

'It seems a long way from the Boy to the political intrigues of the 33rd and 34th Centuries.'

'That's not my fault,' she said. 'It's ours.'

Something in the way she said this made me enquire what it was she was hoping we would discover in the New Exeter manuscript.

'I am hoping we shall discover the truth,' she said simply.

'The truth about what exactly?'

'About what went wrong with Kinship, and why we two should have been singled out to uncover it.'

'You really think we have?'

'Yes,' she said, 'that is exactly what I think.'

'Are you saying you have traced some connection between this manuscript and what happened to us on New Year's Eve?'

'*We* are the connection, James. You and I. And what is even more to the point I do not think that we could turn aside from it now however much we might wish to.'

Was it just the manner in which she said those words which, at that moment, almost had me believing that she was right? It is a curious and rather daunting reflection.

February 20th

While returning from concert practice this evening by way of Martyrs' Bridge in company with M., Miss Edgeway (a friend of M's) and Peter Barnaby of Oriel, I again caught sight of the old man of Dean's Gate. He was standing on the tow path gazing up at us and I at once plucked M. by the sleeve intending to draw her attention to him. She was at that moment engaged in animated conversation with Miss Edgeway and it was some seconds before I could gain her attention. In that brief interval the old man had slipped away into the mist and shadow. Fortunately Barnaby was prepared to agree that he too thought he had glimpsed someone standing on the tow path otherwise M. might well have been forced to conclude that I am suffering from some form of persistent hallucination.

February 26th

On my way home from delivering my third lecture I dropped into Padgett's and while browsing along the shelves I came across a first edition of Dean Pardoe's *Leaves From an Antiquarian's Notebook*. Apart from slightly foxed endpapers the copy was in very fair condition and I was happy to pay the fifteen pence asked for it. This evening, leafing through it, I came upon this:

In July of the following year (3714) I had occasion to visit the Isle of Quantock and was fortunately able to take advantage of a long-standing invitation to visit my old friend the Rev. William Cuthbertson who for many years has held the living at Aisholt. I was thus vouchsafed the inestimable pleasure of renewing my acquaintance with Mrs. Cuthbertson and meeting their three charming daughters, celebrated collectively (and justly) as 'The fair flowers of Quantock'.

During the course of the week which I passed so agreeably in William's company I had many occasions to converse with him upon the subject of our shared passion, for not only has he become one of the leading authorities upon the early history of Kinship in the Southern Kingdoms but, over the years has accumulated a truly magnificent collection of Avian curios and primitive cult artefacts many of which date back to the earliest years of the 31st Century.

Pride of place in his little museum is shared by two splendid pieces. The first is a small wooden spread-winged image of our Saviour, of great antiquity and supreme artistry, which William is convinced must have originated from the studio, if not the actual hand, of the anonymous 'Master of Corlay'. It is certainly a magnificent work and will surely someday grace one of our great national collections though, perhaps understandably, Cuthbertson is reluctant to commit himself upon this. The second gem is a simple headstone on which beneath a crudely fashioned but forceful Avian symbol is engraved the legend 'POTS and SUSAN THOMSON, MAY 3018'. This ancient memorial was unearthed several years ago by workmen who were excavating the foundations for a new house in the little coastal town of Tallon. It was through his acquisition of this treasure that William came to learn of the cache of documents lying in the library of New Exeter Castle— the seat of the Harcourts. The story is curious and well worth the telling even though one is never quite certain how much credence to give to such tales.

As soon as William learned of the discovery of the headstone he hastened to the site where it had been unearthed, purchased it on the spot and made arrangements for it to be transported to Aisholt. This was done the next day and the stone was laid out across two wooden trestles in the coach-house in readiness for the labour of removing the accumulated grime of many hundreds of years. That same evening one of the servants who had just returned from visiting her family in the village rushed into the Cuthbertsons' parlour in a blubbering fright crying out that she had just heard a most piteous weeping coming from within the locked coach-house. The girl was in a state of such abject terror that William was obliged to take a lantern and go by himself out to the coach-house. He heard nothing untoward, but upon unlocking the door he found, to his great astonishment, that the headstone was lying upon the ground and the two stout wooden trestles had been flung several paces aside. He set down the lantern, returned the trestles to their original places and was just stooping over the stone preparatory to restoring it to its position when he felt such a deathly chill strike into his bones that, in his own words, 'it seemed as if my heart had frozen in mid-beat'. Sinking to his knees beside the stone he prayed aloud for the souls of the two Kinsfolk and vowed that their bones would be laid to rest in peace within his churchyard together with all the solemn rites which were their due. Accordingly next day he rode back to Tallon and instructed the workmen to excavate the area immediately adjacent to that where they had unearthed the stone. Within a short space they had uncovered a shallow grave containing two skeletons. Thus William was able to keep his promise, and the bones were duly interred in Aisholt churchyard where they have lain peacefully ever since.

Some months later William was inspired to write an account of the whole curious episode for the *New Exeter Chronicle* to which he was in the habit of contributing an occasional column upon subjects of local antiquarian interest. A few days subsequent to the publication of his article he received a communication from a Mr. Abraham Wilpert who it transpired held the post of curator of Lord Harcourt's library. By an odd coincidence on the very day when he had happened to read William's story, Mr. Wilpert had been engaged upon the task of cataloguing certain ancient documents and his eye had been caught by those very same two names which William had recorded as being inscribed upon the headstone. The paper in question was a list which had been drawn up at the express command of Robert, Earl of Exeter (2962–3034) and detailed the names of some twenty-seven unfortunate Kinsfolk who had fallen victims to the troops of the Secular Force during an armed incursion into the First Kingdom in the year 3018.

Through the correspondence which ensued between William and Mr. Wilpert a warm friendship sprang up. This led ultimately to their joint founding of "The New Exeter Antiquarian Society" which I am happy to say is still flourishing. It also led to William paying a number of visits to the Castle during which he was able to examine the Harcourt Collection of ancient texts, several of which are of considerable historical value. Unfortunately the one upon which he himself set such high store has since proved to be yet another of those meretricious pseudo-histories which were popular in the 33rd Century. Thanks to the good offices of Bishop Hoxton I have since been afforded the opportunity to scrutinize the contents of the archive and have accordingly been in a position to advise Lord Harcourt as to the worth of his collection.

I wonder what caused poor William Cuthbertson to pin such high hopes upon that 'meretricious pseudo-history', and what became of his private museum? Perhaps in April we will be able to pay a visit to Aisholt and discover the truth for ourselves.

Sunday, March 2nd

In a week which has been largely taken up with strenuous rehearsing for the concert I seem to have found no time to keep up this journal and even in retrospect there seems to be little of note to record. As is so often the case the actual performance was rather less satisfying than one had hoped, though I thought the audience was particularly appreciative of M's solo rendering of *Where the Wild Rose Blossoms* and of the Portina *Serenade* in which I like to think I took full advantage of my flute *obbligato*.

At the reception afterwards M. introduced me to a Mr. Giles Opie whom I at once recognized as the gentleman I had seen taking tea with her last month in Cutler's Pantry. He is a lecturer in the School of Transcendental Medicine and, according to M., a leading authority upon regressive hypnosis.

'You are a metempsychosist, Mr. Opie?' I enquired.

'Do you mean in the Classical sense, Mr. Cartwright?' he replied with a smile.

'Is there any other?'

'Certainly there is. I would class myself as a non-valent hierarchist—a follower of Mundi. You have read Hagendorf's *Being and Non-Being?*'

I shook my head. 'I am afraid I am just another of your orthodox Avians, Mr. Opie.'

'We are all that, Mr. Cartwright, otherwise none of us would be where we are today. But you really should read Hagendorf. You must ask Margaret to lend you the copy I gave her.'

'Has she read it?' I asked curiously.

He nodded and seemed on the point of saying something further when we were interrupted. Mr. Opie was drawn away to talk to someone else and I was appropriated by Mrs. Berenson and her sister.

                                                          March 6th
Today for the first time I took advantage of the spell of beautiful weather to stroll in the Parks with M. after lunch. Many of the daffodils are out already and there is a faint but hopeful mist of green on several of the trees. We discussed arrangements for our forthcoming expedition to the west county. I mentioned that, if the opportunity were to arise, I would not be averse to paying a brief visit to Aisholt on the Isle of Quantock and explained how I had been intrigued by the reference I had discovered in Pardoe's reminiscences. 'Then let us take the steamer from New Bristol to Tallon,' she suggested. 'It is a charming little seaside resort only a few miles from Aisholt. If you are agreeable I am prepared to write to the Harbour Hotel in Tallon and ask them to reserve us rooms for the night of the 11th. We can then pay our visit to Aisholt en route to New Exeter on the Saturday.'

I protested that this would be putting her to a great deal of trouble for what was, after all, nothing more than an idle fancy, but she seemed genuinely delighted at the prospect and I was only too happy to leave matters in her capable hands.

Our perambulation taking us past the Medical Schools I was reminded of my brief conversation with Mr. Opie at the reception. 'I believe you have in your possession a book that I ought to read,' I said. 'Or at least that is what Mr. Opie thinks.'

'*Being and Non-Being,*' she replied. 'Giles gave it to me some weeks ago after I told him about our experience in Dean's Gate.'

'Oh, really?' I said and the tone of my voice betrayed my consternation. 'I did not realize that you had spoken of that to anyone apart from myself.'

'You mean you have not?' The surprise in her voice was at least the equal of my own.

'Not to another soul,' I assured her.

'But why on earth not, James?'

'I have no really intimate friends in Oxford,' I said. 'None I would care to confide in.'

'But you went home to Aldershot at the end of January. Did you not speak of it then?'

I shook my head.

'I really am astonished,' said Margaret. 'If I did not know better I would almost suppose you were ashamed of it.'

Wisely I chose to let that pass. 'May I be allowed to know what Mr. Opie made of our experience?' I asked.

'Giles believes it happened,' she said. 'As a matter of fact he offered to regress me to the moment when it occurred.'

'And did you agree?'

'I could see no point in such an exercise. I know *what* happened and no amount of hypnotic regression could tell me *why* it did.'

'Then I take it he had no satisfactory explanation to offer you?'

She glanced up at me out of the corner of her eye. 'Giles believes it happened because we both *needed* it to happen,' she said.

'Does he indeed?'

'Yes,' she said. 'That was the reason he asked me to introduce you to him after the concert.'

'And I thought it was on account of my virtuoso *obbligato* in the *Serenade.*'

Margaret laughed. 'Did you like him?'

'I hardly had a chance to form an opinion before he was whisked from my side and replaced by Mrs. Berenson and her sister. However, as I recall our brief exchange, he said nothing to which I could possibly take exception, unless it was when he referred to you as "Margaret". That suggested to me a degree of intimacy which I did not care to contemplate.'

'Oh, I've known Giles for years,' she said. 'We met at Winchester in '97. He is a practising homosexual.'

'Already I find that I like him a great deal more than I did,' I said. 'So much so in fact that I am now prepared to ask you if you are aware that he is also a practising non-valent hierarchist?'

'Do you know what that is?'

'No,' I confessed. 'Do you?'

'It is a belief in a system of spiritual hierarchy by which the asomatous identity (non-being) is preserved through many hundreds of re-incarnations (being).'

'Thank you,' I said. 'Now I shall not need to borrow the book.'

But she has insisted upon lending it to me nonetheless and I have reciprocated by loaning her my copy of Pardoe's memoirs.

March 11th

On my way home from a late afternoon tutorial I plainly saw the old man from Dean's Gate turning into the cathedral Precinct scarcely a hundred paces ahead of me. I immediately quickened my stride and had reached West Gate within half a minute. To my astonishment the only persons visible to me were a lady with a young child and two gowned scholars one of whom (Hinchliffe) I happened to recognize. As they approached me I saluted them and inquired of H. whether, in the last minute or so, he had been passed an elderly gentleman wearing a long dark cloak and cape.

He glanced at his companion and they both shook their heads. 'No one at all has passed us, sir,' said Hinchliffe.

'There was a Chapter Beadle,' observed the other, 'but that was at least five minutes ago'.

'Then I must have been mistaken,' I said. 'Forgive me for troubling you.' I stepped aside and they walked past me out into the street.

I was still planted there, prey to heaven knows what doubts and indecisions, when I became aware that the woman and child were almost upon me and that the child— a little girl of some four or five years—was regarding me curiously. On the point of turning and continuing on my way some strange impulse made me doff my hat and, having excused myself politely to the woman, to address the same enquiry to her. She was in the very act of shaking her head when the child gave a sharp tug to her hand. The woman glanced down and then, presumably in response to some unspoken signal, bent down till her ear was beside the child's lips.

I saw her give a slightly perplexed frown, then she glanced up at me and said: 'My daughter tells me that she saw a man such as you have described—an old man with a white beard. She says he passed us by a short while ago. I must confess that I do not recall having seen him myself.'

I thanked them both warmly, assured them this was most certainly the man I sought and was just about to hurry on down the path in belated pursuit of my quarry when an even wilder thought flashed into my mind. Turning back to the woman I said: 'Madam, I beg you to excuse what must seem a rather curious enquiry, but would you mind telling me if your daughter attended the cathedral Service on New Year's Eve dressed in the costume of the White Bird of Kinship?'

The woman's eyes widened quite perceptibly—heaven knows what sort of a dangerous lunatic she thought I was!—and I saw her glance timidly past my shoulder as if seeking for an avenue of escape. I realized she was about to hurry her daughter away from me and in a sort of anguished desperation I turned to the child and said: 'Were *you* the one in Dean's Gate?'

The girl regarded me with wide brown eyes but said nothing at all.

With a muttered: 'I am sorry, sir. I cannot help you,' the woman tugged her daughter away from me, hurried her down the path and out of the West Gate. The last glimpse I had of them was of the child gazing back at me over her shoulder as her mother hustled her off into the throng of pedestrians in Broad Place.

The whole bizarre episode and my own irrational behaviour left me so inwardly shaken that I took refuge in the first tavern I could find and swallowed two large brandies one after the other.

March 12th

I have spent the better part of this evening reading through the record I have kept over the last six months. The contrast between the dull catalogue of diurnal trivia that made up the sum of my life until the first day of this year and the entries which succeed it strikes me as so wholly remarkable that if I did not know better I might well suppose the two parts to be the work of two quite different men. If I needed convincing that the events of New Year's Eve had affected my life, surely the evidence is here before me. But *what* has changed? Outwardly nothing. I have delivered my lectures, supervised my students, and carried out my academic duties exactly as I have done for the past four and a half years. And yet, suddenly, everything which heretofore has constituted the very fabric of my existence has, in the mere twinkling of an eye, become like the tissue of a dream, all insubstantial. It is almost as though I am trapped in the web of some extraordinary obsession from which I cannot break free. My behaviour yesterday in the Precinct was not the behaviour of a normal man and yet, within the context of the dream, it *was* normal. If the child was telling the truth then the old man *does* exist. But why should I ever doubt it? Have I not seen him with my own eyes in Dean's Gate, and on three other separate occasions?

At that point I turned back the pages and read again my accounts of sighting him. It had occurred to me that he appears before me whenever the reality of my experience on New Year's Eve is beginning to grow ever so slight hazier in my recollection. But examination proves this not to be so. Two of the sightings prior to yesterday's happened within the space of seven days; there is an interval of nine days between the initial Dean's Gate sighting and the next: and a whole month passed between that and the sighting in Prospect Place. Yet had I not pursued him yesterday I would never have spoken with the child and her mother. The thing spins round in my mind like a whirligig. I shall be heartily relieved to see the end of term.

March 16th

M. called round after lunch to return the Pardoe memoirs which I lent her last week. She informed me that she had now received confirmation from the hotel in Tallon and that two rooms have been reserved for us for the night of April 11th. She has also made a provisional reservation for the week commencing the 12th in a private guest house she knows of overlooking the river in New Exeter. 'The steamer sails from New Bristol at noon,' she said. 'It calls first at several places on the North Dorset coast and reaches Tallon at about five o'clock. We shall be able to lunch on board. There, have I not been commendably efficient?'

'I am overwhelmed with admiration,' I said. 'All that remains for me to do is to get myself to New Bristol on time. I believe there is an early morning steam-coach from Aldershot to Newbury which connects with the Bristol express and—why, what on earth is the matter, Margaret?'

She had gone very pale and was staring past me towards my desk for all the world as if she had spied a ghost. I turned my head and discovered that her gaze was fixed as though in a trance upon the little wooden carving which Jennifer had given me and which I was now employing as a paperweight. 'Is it my otter?' I said. 'Have you not seen it before? My sister gave it to me for my last birthday.' I reached out, picked it up and handed it to her to examine.

She drew back and I now saw that she was trembling quite uncontrollably. 'Are you feeling unwell?' I said. 'Sit down, my dear. Let me get you something to drink.'

She gave one enormous shiver and then, suddenly appeared to be her old self again. She blinked at me and shook her head.

It occurred to me that she might be suffering from one of those periodic indispositions to which young women are unfortunately prone so I replaced the little carving on the desk, pulled a chair forward and urged her into it. Then I stepped across to the chiffonier, filled two glasses with sherry, and handed one of them to her.

'I'm so sorry, James,' she said. 'I believe I interrupted you.'

'Are you quite sure you are feeling all right?' I enquired solicitously. 'You went as pale as a sheet.'

She looked at me as though she had absolutely no idea of what I was talking about. It really was most odd. I almost began to wonder whether I had imagined it. I lifted my glass in a silent toast, sipped at my drink and then walked across to the desk and retrieved the carving. 'Tell me, do you not think he is rather splendid?' I said, and handed it to her for the second time.

She took it from me without demur and held it in her left hand. 'It is beautiful,' she said, 'truly beautiful. Where did you get it, James?'

I blinked in surprise. 'Jennifer, my sister, gave it to me for my birthday. She found it in a local curio shop in Aldershot.'

Margaret lifted the little statue and stroked it gently against her cheek. 'It is an old Kin thing,' she murmured. 'I am sure of it.'

'It is certainly old,' I said. 'Jennifer told me that an antiquarian friend of hers had dated it back to the 31st Century, but I cannot vouch for the accuracy of that.'

She closed her eyes, touched the otter's head with her lips, then smiled and handed it back to me. At that moment I had the oddest sensation that it was something of hers which *she* was entrusting into *my* care.

Thursday, March 20th
A note from Philby asking me to call in at the University Press which I did this afternoon. He presented me with three copies of *Piper* out of an advance batch of two dozen which had come in from the binders yesterday. Unquestionably it is a most handsome and generous production and my praise was unstinted. P. showed me the list which he has drawn up for possible notices and asked for my own suggestions. I was able to offer the names of Piers Sackville (*Historical Review*) and Dr. Emilia Johnson (*Ecclesiastical Examiner*). Publication date has been set for Monday April 21st.

March 24th
Attended Foundation Banquet with M. We found we had been placed opposite John McIntyre who, knowing my love

of music, was moved to speak at length (and most interestingly) on the subject of harmonic ratio, during the course of which he endeavoured to explain to us some theory he called "Kalowski's hypothesis". This, insofar as I was able to follow it, is an attempt to explain all natural phenomena in terms of the mathematical relationship of musical intervals and certain numerically specified ratios. M. made a brave attempt to relate this to the central place occupied by music in primitive Kinship. McIntyre was reluctant to be drawn into what he termed 'realms of magic and superstition' but was prepared to concede there might be something in it.

After the dinner I took the opportunity to present M. with the copy of *Piper* which I had inscribed to her. She read the inscription and then kissed me on the cheek! An altogether unexpected and enchanting response!

While escorting her back to Scrivener Street I was suddenly moved to tell her of my curious and disturbing experience in the cathedral Precinct a fortnight ago. She listened to me in silence and then said: 'Why have you not told me of this before, James?'

'Because I did not care to reflect upon it,' I replied. 'I consider my own behaviour to have been both arbitrary and foolish to a degree. I tremble to think what that poor woman might have supposed to be my motives.'

'And you have not seen the old man since?'

'No.'

She reached out for my hand and clasped it in her own. 'Do you know *why* he has taken such a hold upon your imagination?'

'I can only suppose it is because I have grown to associate him with what happened to us both on New Year's Eve.'

'You wish to question him about it?'

I gazed at her in perplexity. 'I had not thought about that,' I said. 'I believe my primary concern has been simply to convince myself that I had not imagined him.'

'And now that the child has confirmed his corporeal existence?'

'But how can I be sure that was the same man?'

'I am sorry,' she said. 'I had not realized that the matter was still in question. You did not believe her then?'

'The circumstances were altogether exceptional, Margaret,' I said. 'The truth is I can no longer be sure *what* I believed at that moment. My behaviour was highly irrational. I acted purely on impulse.'

'For my own part I wish you would do so rather more often, James,' she murmured.

We reached the steps of her lodgings as she said these words and I was at a loss to know how she expected me to respond to them. It seemed prudent to pretend I had not heard them. I wished her a heartfelt good night and made my own way home by way of Prospect Place.

Aldershot; April 2nd

Yesterday, having first extracted from her a solemn promise that she would not mention a word of it to another living soul, I told Jennifer the story of the events of last term. Undoubtedly I would never have done so had she not been standing beside me at the ferry station when I saw "Him" again. The encounter gave me such a violent shock that J. later confessed herself to have been thoroughly alarmed by the sudden alteration in my appearance.

We had driven down to Guildford in the pony-trap to collect my portmanteau which was being brought over on the three o'clock steamer from Wycombe, and we were ready and waiting on the quayside when the boat pulled in. As we were watching the gangway being run out I happened to glance towards the upper deck, and there, standing just by the stern of the aftermost of the two starboard life-boats, I beheld the old man of Dean's Gate! For a moment my glance locked with his and I am prepared to swear on oath that I saw him give a little nod of his head as though in acknowledgment or affirmation. My heart gave a most painful leap within my breast and I clutched J. by the arm. 'Quick!' I cried. 'Look there! Do you not see that old man on the upper deck?'

'What? Who?' she said vaguely. 'What is it, Jim?'

'There! There!' I cried, thrusting out my arm in his direction, and at that instant the boat's landing whistle screeched and a cloud of white steam shrouded the upper deck. When it had dispersed the old man was gone and J. was holding on to my arm and asking me whether I was feeling all right.

I told her that I had seen someone I recognized and I began to scan the faces of the alighting passengers, but as by then I half-expected, there was no sign of him anywhere. When the last passenger had stepped ashore I moved forward and enquired of the officer on duty if he could recall having seen the old man. He assured me that to the best of his knowledge no person answering to my description had been on board.

As soon as we had supervised the loading of my luggage into the trap we set out for Aldershot. During the course of the drive, and in response to some shrewd questioning by J., I told her the whole strange history, and I confess to feeling a genuine sense of relief once I had done so.

She was, I think, almost as mystified by the original "miracle" as I had been though she seemed prepared to accept the existence of the old man more or less at my own valuation, with the understandable proviso that I had been mistaken in supposing I had seen him aboard the ferry. She was extremely curious about M. and asked me a number of searching questions, most of which I was able to parry adroitly. My sister, in common with most of her sex, seems predisposed to view any relationship between a man and a woman of marriageable age as a potential romance, and having extracted from me the admission that M. is undeniably comely she proceeded to subject me to a thorough cross-examination of all her various attributes. When she had concluded her interrogation I could not resist slyly informing her that I had already made arrangements to spend a whole week of my vacation in the company of this female paragon, thus precipitating a veritable avalanche of further questions! By now my sister must be almost as fully informed of my recent past and probable future as I am myself.

Monday, April 7th

A charming letter from M. on Friday suggesting we rendezvous on board the steamer at New Bristol. She intends to spend the previous night with friends who live in the city. I have written back to say that this arrangement strikes me as admirable in every way and that I am looking forward to our holiday with eager anticipation. J. has been reading the copy of *Piper* which I presented jointly to herself, Mother and Father. This evening she asked me whether I did not think that the Old Tale Spinner bore a striking resemblance to the old man of Dean's Gate! I told her that she must have been reading more novels than were good for her and recommended a stiff dose of Pargeter's *Consolations of Philosophy* as an effective antidote.

Thursday, April 10th

While preparing my travelling-case against my early departure I came across the sheaf of notes which I had drawn up in January in response to M's suggestion, and I found myself recalling vividly how she had suggested that the answers to my questions might even then be lying in the library of New Exeter Castle. The likelihood seems so remote as to border upon the impossible. Yet the undisputed fact that the Western Kingdom was the first of the seven to embrace Kinship must surely imply the existence of some strong primal link with Corlay. And even as I write these words I am struck by the curious coincidence that the town where I shall sleep tomorrow night bears the same name as that elusive genius who bequeathed to the world *The Donation Quartet*, the *Songs of the Seasons* and the three great *Visionary* symphonies. Or is the truth of the matter simply that I too am becoming infected by my sister's fondness for fanciful romance?

The Harbour Hotel
Tallon.
April 11th

Despite the fact that I was on the road at half past six this morning and a comfortable bed now awaits me, I feel a strong urge to commit to paper some record of the day's events before retiring.

The early part of the journey can be swiftly disposed of. The coach trip to Newbury having passed without incident I boarded the Bristol express shortly after nine o'clock and was at the quayside in New Bristol by a quarter to twelve. M. who had arrived some fifteen minutes earlier, welcomed me aboard the *Cheltenham Castle* and we at once repaired to the dining saloon where we reserved a table for lunch at 1.30. We then climbed to the upper deck and passed the time most agreeably in surveying the busy life of a great sea-port. There was just enough of a breeze to set the flags fluttering, the April sun sparkled upon the distant waters of the Severn Reach, and M. assured me that the Captain had promised us a calm passage.

At twelve o'clock the departure whistle sounded, the gangways were withdrawn, a bell rang, and to a great shuddering and splashing the huge paddle-wheels began to revolve. Within a matter of minutes we had churned away from the quayside and were heading towards the open sea attended by a flock of screaming gulls. On our way out we were afforded a distant sighting of the noble sail-steamer *Patrician* homeward bound on the last leg of her long journey from New Concord on the eastern seaboard of America. During the course of the afternoon we put in at Axbridge, Castle Carey, Yeovil and Chardport, finally entering the harbour at Tallon slightly ahead of schedule at ten minutes to five.

Tallon is a picturesque and thriving little fishing port of great antiquity and undeniable charm, much favoured by marine artists of the popular school. As a direct consequence of the construction of the road bridge at Bicknoller in North Quantock it has grown remarkably over the past century and now houses some four thousand permanent residents—the population rising to almost double that number during the summer months. The oldest houses are those to be found in the immediate vicinity of the harbour and fronting upon the cobbled Main Street which rises up the steep hill behind. There are magnificent views out across the Somersea to North Dorset and Blackdown Island. The church of St. Thomas which overlooks the town is unfortunately of no great antiquity or architectural merit. Our hotel (once the Customs House) occupies a fine site overlooking the harbour basin. Facing it is the Town Hall and ranged alongside are the Civil Guard station, the Post Office, and the New Customs House. There are numerous quaint little shops supplying the needs of the local populace, and a wealth of tea-houses, bazaars and the like, catering for the summer trade.

Following upon an excellent dinner I strolled with M. along the sea-front path as far as Tolland Point where we watched the sun setting magnificently over Exmoor. M. a thought pensive and subdued. When I taxed her gently with it she smiled and said she supposed it was the burden of history pressing in upon her, but she would not be drawn to elaborate upon this somewhat gnomic observation.

At her suggestion we have arranged for our luggage to be forwarded to the Old Ferry Inn at Bicknoller tomorrow morning. We shall walk the five miles to Aisholt, travel from A. to Bicknoller by the mid-day coach and there repossess our baggage and proceed onwards to New Exeter. It all seems extremely hazardous to me but the Hotel Clerk has assured us that we need have no cause to fear for the safety of our property. Let us hope he is right.

Towpath Lodge House
New Exeter.
April 12th

In a day which has contained so much to wonder at it is difficult to decide how best to describe it. If I tell myself to begin at the beginning I find I am in a quandary occasioned by my own inability to decide just where the beginning really is. Is it back in Oxford in January? Or two years ago when I first conceived the notion of producing an entirely new version of those early legends of the Boy? Or does it, as Margaret has suggested, lie somewhere so far in the past that I can have no conscious memory of it at all? I cast about for some firm ground upon which to take my stand and find that all has become as shifting sand, unreal, insubstantial.

We were awakened early to find that the day had dawned bright and clear. By half past seven we had breakfasted. At eight, having made the final disposition of our luggage, we set off up the hill away from the harbour with the morning sun striking warm upon our backs. We had climbed to the point where the houses of the old town begin to give way to more modern villas when M. paused at the entrance to a narrow alley winding between two high stone walls and I saw that she was examining a faded finger-board which bore the message: 'To the Old Pottery Tea Rooms. Visitors welcome.' Since we had plenty of time in hand and she was clearly disposed to visit to place I smiled and turned after her into the alley. No sooner had I set foot upon the paving stones than I experienced a most curious and unpleasant sensation which manifested itself as a profound reluctance to proceed. I felt the skin at the back of my neck tighten and a chill like a frost settle in the region of my stomach. The sensation lasted for perhaps ten seconds, just long enough for M. who was some paces ahead of me, to disappear around the corner. In an instant anxiety for her safety had banished my own trepidation. I ran forward calling her by name and as I turned the corner I saw her glance back at me over her shoulder. At the same instant, half concealed in the swathe of shadow cast by the wall of the ancient building directly ahead of her, I beheld that very same figure who has by now become almost as familiar to me as my own image in my shaving mirror. But this time I kept my gaze firmly fixed upon him and hurrying past Margaret I advanced into the open, paved area beyond. As I closed upon the old man I saw his hooded shape seemingly dissolve and reconstitute itself into the form of a large folded garden umbrella of dark blue canvas which I now perceived to be standing propped against the shadowed wall and creating a deceptive and freakish pattern of reflections in the glass of the nearby window.

I was still standing there staring at it in utter consternation when I felt M's hand upon my arm and heard her asking what it was that had so startled me. I turned to her. 'Nothing more than the illusion of my own familiar,' I said, and laughed, but my laugh was singularly devoid of humour.

'This place is full of shadows,' she replied. 'I can feel them everywhere about us.' She walked across to what had doubtless once been the pottery and peered in through the window. I saw her reflection gazing out at me pensively from among the dim spectres of tables and chairs still shrouded beneath their winter dust-sheets.

While we were peering in a woman called out to us from an upper window of a nearby house that the tea room was closed for the winter and would not be open until the end of May. We thanked her, took a last look around and proceeded on our way.

The sombre mood which my experience had engendered in me soon evaporated under the benign influence of warm sunshine, blue, lark-filled skies and Margaret's delightful company. We wandered through winding country lanes, leant over ancient gates to watch young lambs skipping in the lush Quantock pastures, and finally descended upon Aisholt just as the church clock was chiming ten.

It is a pretty village with a green at its centre and a circular pond upon which some snow-white ducks were disporting themselves. Unlike Tallon it appears to have remained much as it must have been when the Reverend William Cuthbertson was its incumbent. We entered the church to find that it had been brightly decked out with hundreds of spring flowers and that the April sunshine was flinging down a veritable rainbow of colour from the cornucopia of the chancel window. Above the altar hung a gilded rood to which was affixed a small but superbly carved wooden effigy of the Bird. I guessed at once that this must be that very treasure of which Dean Pardoe had spoken and which Cuthbertson had ascribed to the hand of the Master of Corlay.

I was on the point of drawing Margaret's attention to it when I saw that she was already gazing up at it with that same totally rapt expression that I recalled so vividly from her last visit to my rooms in Oxford. I watched her covertly and perceived that her eyes were glittering with unshed tears. The picture of her sweet, upturned face touched by the unearthly colours streaming down upon it from the high window is one that I shall carry with me to my grave. The scales fell from my eyes: I beheld in her a radiance almost frightening in its intensity: and I sank beneath its spell. Moved by some power wholly beyond my own volition I stole my arm about her shoulders, and turning her face to mine, kissed her full upon the lips.

At this point I feel sorely tempted to close up this journal and fling it out of the window into the river! It has more than served its purpose. But long habit dies hard and an intimate association of more than ten years' standing is not so easily severed. I had not thought ever to fall in love and now that I have done so I am as much astonished by my own presumption as by the discovery that my feelings for Margaret are reciprocated. What can I have done to merit such fortune? Truly I feel like the man who slept for twenty years and awoke to find himself in fairyland! Would that I had obeyed my impulse of Thursday evening and had slipped my beloved flute into my case. At this moment my trembling heart cries out to rejoice itself in music.

Enough. I hear the Minster clock striking twelve. Tomorrow with all its mystery and wonder lies in wait for us both.

Aldershot
Sunday, April 20th

I am astonished to see that *eight whole days* have elapsed since my last entry—positive proof, if such were needed, that keeping journals is the consolation of the lonely! Rather than contemplate the gloomy prospect of two long weeks bereft of the enchantment of Margaret's companionship I pick up my pen and command the recent bygone days to pass in review before me.

Sunday 13th: We attended morning service at the Minster and in the afternoon walked along the river bank out beyond Edgecott to Stickleford, returning via Hartcombe Woods and the Castle where we introduced ourselves to Mr. and Mrs. Talbot (Lady Harcourt's seneschals-in-residence) and were introduced by them to Mr. Digby the Librarian, with whom we arranged an appointment for 10 a.m. the following day. Passed a delightful evening t-à-t with Margaret.

Monday 14th: We presented ourselves punctually at the Castle to find that the admirable Mr. D. had been as good as his word and had laid out the manuscript for our inspection in the library. It consists of some eighty-odd pages of bound-up long-folio vellum closely written in a cursive script. The first thing I noted was that its title is not *The Witch's Tale* as Pardoe claimed but *Witchet's Tale*. However, as Digby pointed out, this is unquestionably an addition in a later hand and was probably interpolated when the sheets were bound together in the 33rd C. (?). From my very first glance at the text I was inclined to agree with M. that it was not a forgery but was almost certainly a transcript made from an original draft. Digby could give us little concrete information on its history but is inclined to the belief that it entered the Castle collection through an acquisition or deed of gift from the Winchester archive in 3210 where it is possibly featured in the Royal Catalogue under the title of *The Romance of the Singer and the Song* (noted as having been commissioned by Lady Alice of Petersfield *sub Pat. De man. auct.*). Since Lady Alice was the daughter of Robert, Earl of Exeter, such a provenance seems plausible—perhaps almost *too* plausible. I settled down to work, soon familiarized myself with the fist, and by tea time had deciphered the first fifty pages. M. was on tenterhooks to hear my verdict but at that point, though profoundly intrigued, I was not yet willing to commit myself.

Tuesday 15th: We returned to the Castle and I concluded my preliminary examination. On reaching the final page I daresay I was in a mental state somewhere between profound psychological shock and incipient euphoria. I remember raising my head (I was alone in the library at the time) and gazing blankly at the window in front of me. I must have been staring out blindly for the better part of a minute before I became aware that a figure which I at first took to be that of a gardener was peering in at me from the other side of the glass. No sooner had his presence registered upon me than he vanished. *And I did not even get up from my chair to investigate!* When M. returned a few minutes later I had regained sufficient control of myself to be able to inform her, almost casually, that I had been honoured by another visit from 'my familiar'. She asked me to describe him in detail but apart from the fact that on this occasion he had been carrying a staff of some kind (at first glance I had taken it to be a garden implement) I could tell her no more than that he looked just as he always looks. Reflecting now upon my own reaction I am astonished. Is familiarity breeding contempt?

Wednesday 16th: M. spent the whole day studying the manuscript. We had agreed not to discuss it until she had done so. Digby meanwhile showed me a number of fascinating documents relating to the early history of Kinship which he had extracted from the archive. Notable among them was a truly extraordinary holograph by a certain 'Master Surgeon Brynlas' purporting to be an eye-witness description of some mysterious supernatural orgy in which a 'Piper Thomas' had played a leading role. This had apparently taken place within the Castle itself in the year 3038 and (according to the Surgeon) had been directly responsible for the abdication of Lord Arthur—elder brother of the aforementioned Lady Alice—who was then ruler of the First Kingdom. The temptation to identify the Surgeon's 'Piper Thomas' with the protagonist of *Witchet's Tale* is strong indeed, and on that account must certainly be resisted.

Thursday 17th: Having spend the whole of Wednesday evening discussing the manuscript we now spent the whole of Thursday tramping over the moors still discussing it! We are both agreed in accepting its authenticity though whether as 'history', 'pseudo-history' or plain 'story' is not easy to say. M. inclined more to the history, I to the story. Probably the truth lies somewhere betwixt the two. We are both agreed that it must be published and we both marvelled at the strange coincidence of Witchet's little wooden carving of the otter (her 'spirit otter') which from its description could well have been the twin of the one Jennifer gave me for my birthday. Following on from this M. drew my attention to the parallels between my 'old man of Dean's Gate' and Tom's 'Morfedd', thereby constraining me to admit that the similarity had not escaped me. The urge to believe that destiny was calling the tune to which we were both dancing was all but irresistible and I knew that she was at least as sensible of it as I was when, standing at her side on the summit of Dunkery Beacon, I dared to ask her if she would consent to become my wife. She listened to my halting proposal with a kind of sweet and gentle gravity and has promised me that she will give me her answer when she returns to Oxford.

Friday 18th: We paid our final visit to the castle and had a long talk with Digby about the possibility of publication. D. was extremely enthusiastic and has volunteered to make a copy of the manuscript for us if we will obtain Lady Harcourt's permission. M. and I have agreed to write a joint letter of request to this effect when we return to Oxford. I have promised to send D. an inscribed copy of *Piper at the Gates of Dawn.*

Saturday 19th: Returned (via Porlock) to New Bristol where I took a fond farewell of Margaret and boarded the late train for Newbury, arriving home shortly before nine o'clock.

How dull and prosaic it all sounds in retrospect, yet in truth this past week has been far and away the most delightful and exciting period of my whole life. How many times have I not found myself returning in memory to that magical moment in Aisholt Church when, under the very wings of the Divine Bird, I first took Margaret into my arms! I drink from it as from some heavenly chalice and feel at once renewed in spirit as though by some potent elixir.

April 23rd

I broke off at that point and wrote a long letter to Margaret instead. Today I received one from her which had crossed with mine. So we must each have been inspired to write at the same moment! Happy thought. She returned to a point she had made during our first heady discussion of the manuscript, namely that the account of Tom's final meeting with Brother Francis must have a direct bearing upon the passage in the *Revelations* where Francis speaks of his 'failing in faith'. "If we may suppose," she writes, "that 'the Maid', 'the Bride of Time', and 'Jane' are all one and the same person, then she did not perish in the sack of Corlay but survived to give birth to this same Tom, who, we are both agreed, is none other than Thomas of Tallon, composer of the *Jubilate*, etc., etc. By lending Thomas the Boy's pipes Francis was tacitly acknowledging his prior claim to them, a claim which Thomas himself now recognizes. All of which brings me to that final section of the m.s. which I still refuse to believe was written by a different hand. Indeed I have become completely convinced that the symbolic 'burying of the pipes' *is the record of an historical fact*. I believe that Thomas, totally disillusioned in Francis' Kinship, made a pilgrimage to the childhood home of the Boy to offer back to Morfedd's shade the pipes which the Wizard of Bowness had fashioned for the Boy together with the transcript of that 'Song of Songs' which Francis had so coldly rejected. The place he chose was, I believe, that very same 'Wizard's Oak' (reputedly the tree under which Morfedd first heard Tom playing) which is specifically mentioned both in *The Book of Morfedd* and (very briefly) in the Carlisle m.s. If I am correct then the final conclusive proof of the authenticity of *Witchet's Tale* is in all likelihood still lying buried somewhere on a hillside above Bowness at a place from which the peaks of Scafell are visible between a cleft in the hills! Just imagine it, James! The pipes and 'The Song of Songs' waiting to be rediscovered after eight centuries! Could ever a better way have been devised to exorcise old Morfedd's restless ghost?"

Dear, incorrigible Margaret!

April 26th

In spite of myself I find that Margaret's suggestion, which at first I discounted as nothing more than a delightful romantic fancy, has taken such a firm hold upon my imagination that it has now begun to invade my very dreams! Last night I awoke in a terrible fright convinced that Dean Pardoe (no less) was standing before me wringing his hands and beseeching me with tears in his eyes to forgive him his sins and release him from the torments of his conscience! I am still at a loss to account for the fact that I was able to recognize him since to the best of my recollection he did not once introduce himself. I was in the very act of assuring him that I would do everything in my power to help when he pointed a trembling finger at my face and advanced upon me crying in the most awful voice: 'I charge you, James Cartwright! I charge you in the Name of the Holy Bird!' At which point I awoke in a cold sweat and it must have been all of an hour before I dared to close my eyes again.

Oxford; May 3rd

Margaret returned from York today. As we had arranged I went to meet her at the railway station. Almost the first words she addressed to me on alighting from the train were: 'My dear, I have such news for you! I too have been visited by your familiar spirit!'

As we were making our way to Scrivener Street she told me how, yesterday afternoon, she had taken her young nephew and niece for a walk beside the river Ure which flows through Boroughbridge. She had, she said, 'been thinking of nothing at all unless it was the joyful prospect of being back in Oxford with you again,' when her attention had been drawn to someone who was standing in the centre of one of the bridges which spanned the river and was looking down at her. She maintains that she knew at once who it was—'there was never the slightest doubt in my mind'—nor did she feel alarmed—'excited, curious, in a strange way *flattered,* but never fearful. I knew that he intended me no harm.' She gazed back up at him for what seemed to be several minutes but could in reality have been only seconds, then the sun had emerged from behind a cloud and struck straight into her eyes, dazzling her. When she could see clearly again her visitant had vanished and the bridge was deserted.

'And what makes you so sure that you did not simply imagine him?' I asked.

'Did *you* imagine him, James?'

'The earth hath bubbles as the water has,' I quoted. 'And he is of them. I am like Thomas of Tallon, Margaret. I find I no longer know what the word "real" means. I understand none of it.'

She smiled and laid her gloved hand upon my arm. 'Then how will you understand if I say to you now: "James Cartwright, I will marry you"?'

I stopped dead in my tracks. *'Is that true, Margaret?'*

'It is true, my dear. But there is one condition.'

'And what is that?'

'We spend part of our honeymoon in Bowness.'

'Such a condition merely gilds the lily,' I laughed. 'My dear, dear Margaret. You have made me the happiest man in all Oxford.'

And never did I speak a truer word.

(Editor's Postscript)

To the best of my knowledge the entry dated May 3rd, 3799 is the last my father ever made in his Journal. He and Margaret Coley were married on July 26th and they left for Cumberland the same day. The following account of the events which took place during their honeymoon was written by my mother many years later in response to a request from the editors of the Ecclesiastical Examiner *who were planning a memorial number in honour of my father. I am indebted to the present Editor for permission to reprint it here.*

T.R.C.

A Key to Unlock the World

Is there any more daunting intellectual challenge than to be asked to step backwards in time and attempt to recreate in one's own memory the shape, the feel, the essential presence of things as they appeared a quarter of a century ago? The problem is always the same. How is it possible to achieve the vital spiritual identification with that former "me"? It is as if a butterfly were seeking to become its own chrysalis and re-enter the constricting prison-house of the old self from which it escaped to freedom. It is in the truest sense of the word "unnatural"—a willed act of evolutionary regression.

And to say: 'I shall do my best simply to describe things as they were,' still begs the question, for I can do no more than attempt to describe things as they *seemed* to me then—or as *I now think* they seemed to me. Today, from the vantage point of hindsight, it is quite obvious that what I saw at that time, what then seemed to me so clear, was really nothing more than a dim, blurred travesty of the truth. I am reminded of those ancient explorers who discovered to their astonishment that their ships were invisible to the natives they encountered because the very size of the vessels placed them beyond the limits of an aboriginal's perception. So what follows must be seen as an attempt to re-create the events of the past as they appeared to that aboriginal "me" during one week in July, 3799, twenty-five years ago.

James and I were married in the church of St. Anthony in Boroughbridge at eleven o'clock in the morning on Saturday July 26th. The wedding was in no sense an elaborate affair. It was attended by members of our families and a few close friends. The reception was held at my parents' house. At two o'clock in the afternoon James and I said our farewells and were driven by my brother in a gig to Ripon where we boarded the train for Cumberland. It was a slow journey and entailed several changes, but we were so delighted to be together, able at last to draw breath after all the alarums and excursions attendant upon the ceremony, that the four hours seemed more like one.

James had brought with him the copy of the New Exeter manuscript which Mr. Digby had made for us. He told me he had received it just as he was on the point of leaving Oxford for his home in Aldershot—a happy accident which I chose to regard as auspicious. Mr. Digby had given his copy the title *The Singer and the Song* which, he believed, was the name it featured under in the Winchester Catalogue. I was rather glad that he had done so but James preferred his own choice, *Thomas of Tallon's Tale*. I thought this was too heavily alliterative.

We arrived at the Beck Hotel in Bowness shortly before seven o'clock. I had chosen it on my sister's recommendation and had been a little apprehensive as to what we might find, but in the event it suited us to perfection. It was picturesque, small, and friendly, and our bedroom had a marvellous panoramic view right out across the Windersea to Furness Fells, with the western tip of the Isle of Cartmel just visible far away to the south. So we had come to the true cradle of the Old Kinship. Eight hundred years ago Tom and Morfedd had walked and talked upon these very hills; Old Peter and Falcon Gyre had trodden these same roads; Brother Francis the Advocate Sceptic had once come here, a diligent ferret about his master's business. And then the centre had shifted to Corlay as once, long ago, the centre of the Old Faith had shifted from Jerusalem to Rome. And just as it had then, something had been changed in the process. Thomas of Tallon was right—the wings of the Bird *had* been clipped. Saint Francis had worked his miracle, but it was the wrong miracle.

Hanging upon the wall in the entrance hall of the hotel was a large framed map of the surrounding district. That evening after dinner I stood at James' side and studied it carefully. All we had to guide us was that single paragraph at the end of the manuscript and, for all we knew, there might be a hundred different sites which would fit that description of 'a place from which the peaks of Scafell were visible in the far distance between a cleft in the western hills.' With my fingertip I circled an area to the east which was marked 'Borwick Fold'. 'It's there,' I said. 'I'm sure of it.'

James drew his finger along a line from Scafell until it met mine. 'Yes, it's possible,' he agreed. 'Let us make that our first expedition tomorrow.'

'Why not now?' I said. 'It won't be dark for hours yet.'

'Thomas has waited for nearly eight centuries,' he replied. 'One more night won't make much difference to him. But it certainly will to *me*, Mrs. Cartwright!'

We set out straight after breakfast the next morning and began climbing the steep track through the woods above Bowness. As we emerged on to the more open hillside the church bells of Windermere began to ring out calling the faithful to worship. I stood at James' side and gazed out across a wilderness of bracken and foxgloves seeking for a glimpse of the far-off peaks of Scafell and I felt my heart sink. I suppose I had assumed that the place would be instantly identifiable, that I would somehow recognize it instinctively—perhaps *feel* it as a water-diviner feels the presence of a hidden spring. In fact I felt nothing at all, and the morning haze effectively constricted the western horizon to the hills of Hawkshead on the far shores of the Windersea.

James had had the foresight to jot down as many points of reference as he could extract from the manuscript. He now consulted his notebook and observed that the description stipulated an eastern flank to the hill, for it was down there that Thomas's young guide was said to have vanished. So we turned our faces eastward and began forging our way though the dewy bracken in the general direction of Kendal.

In about twenty minutes we rounded a shoulder of the hill and saw that the slope was indeed dipping away from us. James pointed down to the distant trees and then swung his arm round to the north. 'It cannot very well be below this crest,' he said, 'for that blocks off any view to the north-west. We'll climb up and take another look from higher up the slope.'

As we plodded up along the shoulder, James drew my attention to the numerous stumps of felled trees which were poking up among the bracken. 'Fifty years ago this must all have been forest,' he said. 'Finding one old tree stump here will be roughly equal to finding a numbered pebble on the beach.'

We reached an outcrop of rock and I sat down and looked out to the west. As the sun warmed the hillsides the misty haze began to disperse and the distant peaks seemed to creep in upon us as though curious to observe what we were about. We spread out our map and set about identifying the various landmarks. It soon became apparent that we had overshot our mark and we retraced our steps until, suddenly, we found ourselves standing at the precise point from which the twin peaks of Scafell and Scafell Pike were visible. The area was surprisingly small—scarcely more than twenty paces. Outside those limits either one or other of the two peaks was hidden. At once I felt all my early excitement re-kindle. I was convinced that it would be merely a matter of minutes before we alighted upon the exact site of Wizard's Oak and I set off up the slope hunting for some trace of the ancient tree.

For hours we paced up and down and back and forth across the hillside. We found tree stumps in plenty but not one of them was of sufficient stature or antiquity to suggest that we had discovered what we were looking for. In the end, weary, hot, hungry and dispirited we abandoned the search and made our way back to Bowness.

That evening we were engaged in conversation by Mr. and Mrs. Plaskett, the proprietors of the hotel. I asked them if they happened to know of any local legends concerning the Wizard of Bowness. They were not themselves natives of the district but they told us that the person we ought to consult was Mr. Hargreaves, a local antiquarian and the curator of the little museum in the neighbouring town of Windermere.

Next morning we walked along the coast road to Windermere and paid a visit to the museum. Mr. Hargreaves was out when we arrived but we were told that he was expected back shortly and we occupied ourselves by wandering round and examining the exhibition of antiquities on permanent display. In one of the glass cabinets I happened upon a collection of little models of people and animals crudely fashioned in baked clay. I drew James' attention to them and asked him if he did not think they fitted the description of the charms which were mentioned in the manuscript as hanging on the inside of the hollow tree. While he was quite prepared to agree that they did he also pointed out that such things could be found by the score in any folk museum throughout the United Kingdoms.

When Mr. Hargreaves appeared we introduced ourselves and asked him if he would help us locate the site of the so-called 'Wizard's Oak'. He told us that he had never even heard a mention of it but that there were a number of places on the Isle of Cartmel which local legend associated with the Wizard of Bowness and no doubt that was among them. We were on the point of leaving when some impulse prompted me to enquire as to the provenance of the little clay figures. 'Oh those,' he said. 'They were found seven or eight years ago up above Bowness in a place called Borwick Fold.'

I looked at James and James looked at me. 'Borwick Fold,' I murmured. 'You don't happen to know the whereabouts exactly?'

The curator shook his head. 'I believe they were brought in by a woodcutter,' he said. 'It's possible we have a record somewhere. Would you like me to take a look?'

He vanished into his office and returned bearing a ledger. I watched anxiously as he leafed back through the pages and finally saw him lay his finger upon an entry. 'Here we are,' he said. 'On March 3rd '92 we purchased seven small figures from a Mr. Timothy Arden for the sum of fourteen shillings.'

'Mr. Arden is the woodcutter?' I asked.

'No, Mrs. Cartwright. Tim Arden is the landlord of the Sailors' Rest in Bowness. But I remember his telling me he had acquired the figures from a woodcutter who had found them up on Borwick Fold. I daresay he might still remember who the man was.'

We thanked him for all his help, hurried back to Bowness and presented ourselves at the Sailors' Rest where we found that Mr. Arden was prepared to be every bit as helpful as the curator himself. That same afternoon saw us climbing back up the track to Borwick Fold, but this time, following Mr. Arden's detailed directions, we continued on along the forest track towards Kendal. About a mile and a half beyond the point where we had struck off across the Fold we came upon a cottage tucked away among the trees. We walked up the stone-flagged path and knocked on the door.

It was opened by a friendly-faced woman of middle age to whom I explained why we were there. 'My husband's away felling above Staveley,' she replied, 'but p'raps our Joanie can help ye.' She turned away and called out: 'Joanie! Do you come here a minute, lass.'

A dark-haired blue-eyed girl of about thirteen or fourteen emerged from the back of the cottage and stood regarding us wonderingly as her mother explained what we had come about. 'Aye,' she said, 'I do remember the dolls, for it was I as found 'em.'

'Yes, that's true,' said the mother. 'She was always the one for playing around her dad when she was a mite.'

'And do you remember *where* you found them, Joan?' I asked, scarcely daring to breathe while I hung upon her answer.

'Reckon I do,' she said slowly. 'I couldn't be right sure, mind.'

'Would you be prepared to take us there?'

As the girl glanced doubtfully at her mother, James said: 'We shall of course reimburse you for your time and trouble.'

'Oh, she'll go wi' you, sir,' said the woman briskly.

'There's no cause to fret about the bake, Joanie. I'll look to that.'

The girl stepped out into the sunshine. 'It's up the fell a way, sir,' she said with a shy smile. 'Close agin where I seen you and your lady a-walkin' yesterday.'

She led us out through the trees on to the open hillside and then along a narrow sheep track which climbed the shoulder of the hill towards the outcrop of bare rock on which we had rested while we consulted our map. But before we reached it she turned off to the right and took us round in a loop which brought us out on to a sort of small grassy plateau above the outcrop. Then she paused and looked about her. ' 'Twas somewhere hereabouts,' she said. 'Up a bit I think.'

She began pacing slowly across the gently sloping grass which sheep and rabbits had cropped down to a close, velvety sward, and then she suddenly pointed to a faint saucer-shaped declivity, pocked with rabbit holes, some twenty paces above the point where she was standing. ' 'Tis there,' she said. 'Next they coney burrers. That's where I found 'em.'

We hurried forward and gazed down at the spot, scarcely able to believe that this was what we had come to find. We might have walked back and forth for ever across the hillside and never even suspected its existence. 'Have you a name for this place?' I asked her.

She shook her head. 'Only for the stone yonder,' she said. 'They call him Piper's Rock.'

James left me sitting on the hillside while he went back to the cottage with the girl. He returned half an hour later carrying a garden spade and a trowel and together we set about lifting the turf. Soon we had uncovered most of the ancient skeleton of the tree base and had turned up two more of the clay manikins together with a silver 30th Century quarter, some rusty scraps of iron, and a bronze ring. So acute was my excitement that twice I had to stop digging and sit down with my head between my knees and my eyes closed while I drew in deep gasping breaths.

After we had been at work for about an hour James said: 'Lend me your trowel a minute, Margaret.'

'Have you found something?'

His expression was abstracted—almost as if he were striving to hear through his fingertips as he poked around with the trowel blade in among the long-dead tree roots. The iron blade struck against something hard and we both heard the sound at the same instant. It was quite unlike the noise of metal striking stone. *It rang!* Our eyes met. He tapped downwards again. Again we heard that mysterious, marvellous ringing note. Next moment, wild with excitement we were both scrabbling in the soil with our bare hands like a pair of demented puppies.

Within a minute we had exposed part of the black circular end of a glazed earthenware cylinder. I reached down, touched it with my fingertips, and suddenly, quite unable to prevent myself, I burst into hysterical sobbing.

James flung his arms around me and kissed me. I was laughing and crying at the same time. Then, when I had recovered somewhat, we levered the cylinder slowly up out of the soil in which it had slept for almost eight long centuries and laid it gently down upon the grass.

We brushed off the cold earth and James attempted to remove the cap from the cylinder but it was stuck fast and we both agreed we would have to carry it back with us to the hotel and work on it there. Before we left the site we carefully filled in our excavation and replaced the turfs.

We returned the tools we had borrowed and gave the silver coin and the trinket we had unearthed to Joan. Since James had already rewarded her with a gold crown she was quite overwhelmed by her unexpected good fortune. Then we washed our hands and faces at the cottage sink, said goodbye to the girl and her mother and made our way back down the forest track to Bowness as though we were floating through a dream.

The seal on the cylinder proved to be some sort of tarry substance which gradually yielded to the stream from a kettle in the hotel kitchen. James slowly eased off the cap, tilted the container, and out on to the kitchen table slid the Boy's pipes and the scrolled sheets of vellum in which they had been wrapped. So perfectly were they preserved that they might have been interred yesterday.

With trembling fingers James carefully unrolled the parchment. And there before our wondering eyes, just as it had been recorded in pale, sepia ink by Tom's own hand eight centuries ago lay *The Song of Songs*. In four closely penned sheets on the double stave lines of the old Vertical Notation was the master key which was to unlock the whole world. *And we did not know it!*

I have often been asked when it was that I first became aware of the truth. In one sense the answer is plain enough—at six o'clock in the evening on the 21st of August 3799 when Kinsman Piper Julian D'Arcy first played through the complete *Song* to James and myself and we perceived that *No man is an island entire of itself; every man is a piece of the continent, a part of the main.* That was the instant when the shutters of my soul were unlocked and thrown back, the window flung open, and through the inflooding brilliance I beheld the transcendental reality of the universe in which I lived and moved and had my corporeal being. Such for me was the death of Death; the flight of the White Bird; the living dream of Kinship and the freedom of the immortal spirit. And that surely was the moment when the truth dawned upon my conscious mind.

But I believe there is another answer to the question. I believe that the miracle which had first drawn James and me together—our shared moment of revelation on New Year's Eve—that was when I first became aware *that the truth existed to be discovered,* when I became in the ulti-mate sense, *committed to it.* So today, from the vantage point of acquired wisdom, it is quite clear to me that it was I who was the principal creator of James' 'familiar spirit'. Viewing the world through the lens of his 'apparition' he was forced to question the truth of his own sensual percep-tion, to allow his mind access to the possibility that there might exist a higher order of reality which transcended that of mere common sense. Yet even to speak in such terms, to use 'he' and 'I' in the context of the eternal verity is all but meaningless: it requires a feat of the human historical imagination tantamount to believing that the world is flat and the universe finite. Such concepts belong to some ear-lier evolutionary epoch, the chrysalis stage, another time.

Yet, that having been said, one image from the past has never ceased to haunt me. It is a phrase chosen either by Thomas of Tallon himself or by the unknown author of the New Exeter manuscript. Speaking of *The Song of Songs* he says: 'If pure crystals of sound could ever be imagined, then such most surely were what the Star Born quarried from within himself.' I sometimes like to fancy that those pure, perfect crystals of Kinship were what James and I were destined to rediscover and then let loose into the hu-man spirit, which, having once heard them, would never be the same again.

The Finest Fantasy Writers Come From Pocket Books

Marion Zimmer Bradley

___THE COLORS OF SPACE   44877/$2.95

Robin McKinley

___BEAUTY   60434/$2.95

Nancy Springer

___THE BLACK BEAST   61829/$2.95
___THE GOLDEN SWAN   62063/$2.95
___THE SILVER SUN   61117/$3.50
___SABLE MOON   44378/$2.95
___THE WHITE HART   60683/$3.50

Gene Wolfe

___THE CITADEL OF THE AUTARCH
49666/$3.50
___THE CLAW OF THE CONCILIATOR
47425/$2.95
___THE SHADOW OF THE TORTURER
54066/$3.50